LAND OF LAST CHANCES

LAND OF LAST CHANCES

A NOVEL

JOAN COHEN

SHE WRITES PRESS

Published August 2019
Printed in the United States of America
Print ISBN: 978-1-63152-600-8
E-ISBN: 978-1-63152-601-5
Library of Congress Control Number: 2019937406

For information, address:
She Writes Press
1569 Solano Ave #546
Berkeley, CA 94707

Interior design by Tabitha Lahr

She Writes Press is a division of SparkPoint Studio, LLC.

For Bruce

“The dangers of life are infinite, and among them is safety.”

—Goethe

CHAPTER 1

When a gynecologist wears cowboy boots with his suit pants and white coat, who knows what's going through his mind as he guides women's heels into his exam table's stirrups? Jeanne had been Dr. O'Rourke's patient for twenty years, long enough to find his sense of humor questionable, but this joke was over the line: "Jeanne, forget menopause. Think pregnancy."

She'd been wondering for the last couple of years if he was still with it. The guy had to be what?—eighty?—well past retirement age. She decided to indulge him. "Good one, Doctor."

He rubbed his hands together in delight, his white brush mustache following the curve of his smile. "Joke about pregnancy? Never. A change-of-life baby—I know a lot of women who'd be thrilled to conceive at forty-eight. They take hormones, use IVF. Spend a fortune."

Did they still call them "change-of-life" babies? The man was truly a Victorian. Jeanne's eyes swept the examining room with its all-white counters, window trim, and blinds, looking for someplace to focus besides O'Rourke's face, lit by an equally white, toothy grin. They settled on the ultrasound machine his smiling assistant wheeled out from the corner. Why was everyone so damn happy?

O'Rourke held the handle of what appeared to be a jump rope in his hand, only he called it a vaginal probe. "Just need to see your sonogram on the monitor." He urged Jeanne to relax as he indicated a pulsing spot in the middle of the screen. Relax! Her heart was jumping out of her chest, keeping time with the *phoom, phoom, phoom* the doctor described as a nice strong fetal heartbeat. "About twelve weeks along, I would say. Why don't you get dressed and come into my office so we can discuss next steps?"

She buttoned her silk blouse, pulled on her wool pantsuit, and stepped into her heels. The paper gown she discharged into the trash bin as though she bore it ill will. Her mother's voice seemed to come through the paging system: "Whatever you do, don't get pregnant. A baby will change your life."

Her mother had made it clear Jeanne's birth had changed hers, and not for the better, but she never seemed to think about the effect those words might have had on her daughter. To Mother's credit, she always added, "Reach for the stars." She made it clear reaching and having kids were mutually exclusive, so Jeanne reached and stayed single—single, but hardly celibate. What dismayed Jeanne was how hard it was to exorcise parental messages that had become internalized. By the time she'd realized her mother's advice was bullshit, the only men she met were flawed marriage prospects. She tried not to ask herself if she'd simply gotten into the habit of writing them off.

The doctor was at his computer when Jeanne entered his office. She slipped into the leather chair in front of his desk and took a couple of deep breaths. "I gather from your reaction, Jeanne, this pregnancy was unplanned."

She felt her face growing warm with embarrassment. "So many months had passed without my having a period—could have sworn it was a year—I stopped taking my birth control pills. I didn't stop because I wanted a baby."

"In that case, having an abortion could be a reasonable choice. You should consider, however, that a decision to terminate is likely irrevocable. At your age, I doubt you could conceive again, except perhaps with fertility treatments, and even then, the odds are low. Take some time to think about it. Would you consider discussing it with the father?"

"No point in letting the father know." She tried and failed to imagine Vince cradling a baby—a 2005 Cabernet maybe, but not a baby.

"On the other hand, you should consider that after thirty-five, the risk of birth defects is greater than for younger women. Amniocentesis in your fifth month would be definitive, but my observation is"—he looked down at the sonogram on his desk—"your fetus may well be free of Down syndrome. I'm going by the size of the neck and the distance between the eyes, very preliminary, of course. Lucky for you, given your age. Your copy," he said, extending his hand across the desk. Jeanne discovered her own hands were clenched around the armrests and unwound her fingers to accept the photo. She laid the picture of the smudgy white alien face down on her lap.

The doctor scribbled something on his prescription pad and tore off the top sheet. "These are the prenatal vitamins you should start. If you decide to continue with the pregnancy, and assuming you're on good terms with the father, I'd suggest finding out about heritable diseases in his family."

At her age, pregnancy was automatically categorized as high risk. Everyone over thirty-five was referred for genetic counseling to the Maternal Fetal Medicine Unit at Newford Wellman Hospital. She and the father would be advised which tests to undergo, including amniocentesis for her.

"We can talk about the sequence of visits when you make your decision. In the meantime, avoid these foods." Reluctantly, she accepted the list, although she'd known enough pregnant women to anticipate the forbidden items. Raw fish was out (giving up sushi was a heartbreaker). Alcohol was a no-no, of course. Skip sitting with Vince at the bar at Legal Seafood, feasting on oysters and beer.

"I know this seems like a lot to take in at once," O'Rourke said, "but you can call with questions." He rose and helped her gather her instruction sheets. April 18 was her due date.

"Due date," she repeated in a daze, not the due date for paying her credit card bill, not a project's required completion date. She'd had deadlines for three decades, but a baby wasn't a product intro that could be slipped a month. This entry in her spreadsheet couldn't be shifted by an Excel keystroke. Unplanned events were an anathema, and motherhood was nowhere on Jeanne's planning horizon. She fought to maintain control, though her chest felt like an overcharged electrical panel.

O'Rourke's waiting room was furnished with plump upholstered chairs occupied by even plumper pregnant women who radiated the serenity Jeanne lacked. As she hurried toward the exit, they seemed to regard her with faint knowing smiles, confirming she was part of their sisterhood. Had the medical building been on fire, she couldn't have fled faster, but there was no leaving behind the doctor's news.

When Jeanne pushed open the double doors of the medical building, the cold gust hitting her face felt like the snap of a hypnotist's fingers. Unfortunately, this was one trance from which she would not awaken. *What a fucking mess.* If she could just get back to her office, the world would be normal again. At the office, she knew who she was, a person who saw menopause as anything *but* a change of life, just a temporary set of nuisance symptoms to be handled like some disruption in the business cycle or an increase in the cost of capital. Adding the word "baby" to "change of life" was like tacking on "holocaust" to "nuclear."

Jeanne placed her hand over her heart as though that physical act could calm its agitated beat. Maybe she wasn't ready to face everyone at the office as though nothing had changed. As she drove, the phrase "change-of-life baby" repeated in her mind until it seemed to be coming from her GPS, which took it upon itself unbidden to deliver her to her mother's house.

When she visited this Newford Tudor, the home she'd been visiting nearly every weekend since her mother's death in May, she took bittersweet pleasure in returning to an earlier time. Not so today. Her footfalls reverberated off the plaster, wood, and glass of the vacant house, but the doctor's words followed her through the hollow gloom.

Jeanne's mother had favored ponderous furnishings, a Jacobean dining room set and maroon-and-navy-upholstered pieces for the living room. She seemed to need reassurance they wouldn't be swept away by an errant gust blowing past the draperies. In the end, they were swept away by an estate sale.

All that remained was the contents of the attic, where the daunting August heat had made expending effort unappealing. Now it was autumn, a season on a tight schedule. Foliage turned, peaked, fell, and blew down the streets as though hastily clearing a path for winter. Even daylight retreated. The season suited Jeanne. Thanks to Dr. O'Rourke, she understood why she'd felt so tired the last couple of months. No more. With purposeful steps, she ascended two flights of stairs to the unfinished space filled with her mother's forgotten possessions.

The top flaps of each carton were interwoven. She shook the dust off a discarded lawn chair before sitting and frowned as her eyes fell on a dark corner where the roof met the beams supporting the attic floor. Tufts of insulation protruded from the space where the floor boards ended, perhaps deposited by nesting mice.

Jeanne shuddered. It was embarrassing to remain fearful of rodents. As a child, she'd been afraid bats inhabited those corners, even had nightmares where she found herself trapped in the attic with screaming, winged creatures, unable to reach the stairs. Mother had assured her nothing hung in wait in those corners. Now the attic held the only thing her mother had feared—a pregnant daughter.

Jeanne pulled her tablet out of her bag. In moments, the screen displayed a spreadsheet, its rows and columns the tidy reduction of all that had filled the house. No evidence of sentimentality resided at the end of those rows, where each item was relegated to trash or Goodwill. She exhaled. Spreadsheets calmed her. She could almost hear Vince laughing. "Only you, Jeanne, could find comfort in a bunch of numbers printed in little white spaces."

What of it? The hairiest, most amorphous problem could be tamed by a spreadsheet. With the help of a few formulas, the numbers propagated themselves. The attic would yield to the same efficient approach, and the only thing left to shed would be the house itself. She sighed—and the baby. Apparently, propagation couldn't always be controlled.

The cleaning-out process had dragged on longer than the time she'd allocated, an excess she would never have permitted herself at work. Business risks proliferated when projects ran late. There were financial consequences to holding on to the house—continuing expenses and delayed income—but the house had some kind of hold on her.

She descended to the second floor, where her bedroom door stood opposite or in opposition to her mother's. The door wobbled a bit on its hinges, not surprising, given how often

Jeanne had slammed it shut. Her childhood still existed within those rooms in another dimension. Scents from the past lingered in the corners, and the echoes of conversations seemed audible still.

When Jeanne was seventeen and excited about leaving for Cornell, her mother had stood in this doorway, actually leaned against the doorframe in a pose more casual than was her custom. "I've heard the rigorous academics at Cornell are accompanied by a pretty active social scene." Jeanne wondered why she would make such an obvious observation, especially since Jeanne had never let social life get in the way of her studies. She braced herself for some pithy saying or piece of advice sure to deflate her. "There are actually people—gifted students, career-minded young women, even social butterflies—who have their tubes tied to eliminate all risk of pregnancy and avoid the bother of birth control."

Jeanne stared. "At seventeen?"

"Uh huh . . . just think about it."

~

She pulled her bedroom door shut. It had been a mistake going back there today. The house—the attic—needed her full attention, but her pregnancy was all-consuming. She couldn't stay.

~

Jeanne reached the Grand Grille that evening before Vince and asked the hostess to seat them in a booth, where she hoped they'd have a modicum of privacy. She'd deliberately come early so she could think about how to break the news to him. She slid into the booth and settled herself next to the wall, a position which felt secure from doctors dropping bombshells. Maybe she shouldn't drop one on Vince. She was going to have an abortion anyway, and he'd be shocked, maybe even pissed. There was no upside.

In spite of their seeing each other for a year, longer than she'd expected, the ground rules were clear. Neither of them was in the marriage market. Vince wanted to live together, but Jeanne didn't want anyone to know that she, a vice president, was sleeping with a key investor in her company—too cozy, too risky. Yet sleeping in Vince's arms was too cozy to give up.

That was the conundrum, like the pregnancy. She had no interest in becoming a mother, but she didn't like the idea that she would never again have the opportunity. Dr. O'Rourke had made it clear she was in the land of last chances.

She wanted to make her dilemma Vince's fault, wanted to be angry at him, felt the summoned anger rising from her chest, curling her fists, though she knew better than to target him. She was in no mood for fairness. *Use your head, Jeanne. Only unsullied logic yields good decisions.*

The waitress approached and asked if she'd care for a cocktail while she waited. "Yes," she said eagerly, uncurling her fists. "I'll have a glass of your driest white." She tried to settle her nerves by smoothing her napkin across her navy slacks. The napkin left lint on her pants, so she focused on brushing it away. The wine appeared, but still no Vince. She pulled the glass toward her and pushed away her momentary guilt. Alcohol would be bad for the baby. *Baby! Jeanne, what are you thinking? It's not a baby. It's a bunch of cells dividing, no different than a cancer.*

She lowered her head, ashamed, even though she hadn't spoken the words aloud. *Okay, it's an unwanted complication in my life, and it will soon be gone. The kid will be lucky, to boot. Who'd want to be born to me? My most successful long-*

term relationship is with my dog. She put down her glass. Didn't really want a drink, anyway.

Vince strode down the aisle. He was a couple of years older than Jeanne but could have passed for five years younger. She loved his perpetually tan complexion and the cleft in his chin and noted how sharp he looked in his dark gray suit, light gray shirt, and black jacquard tie. This was the other Vince, the astute assessor of business opportunities. If Jeanne hadn't seen him in a red gingham apron, there would be no way to conjure that picture from her imagination. He bought his clothes at the elegant Mr. Fred's in Newford, so he was careful to shield them from cooking spatter.

Not only did Vince love to cook, he'd happily wipe down refrigerator shelves when Jeanne hadn't noticed their opacity or climb on a chair to dust the brass dome of her kitchen light fixture. You had to love a guy like that. At the moment, though, Jeanne was not in a loving mood. She wanted to rail at the gods and seek retribution for her predicament. The gods, however, were unavailable. Only Vince was within range.

"Another exciting day?" He leaned in for a mini-kiss and slid along the bench opposite her.

"You have no idea," she responded with a wry twist to her mouth. Laughing, he beckoned the waitress. First things first: a Chivas straight up. His bright mood felt like an affront to Jeanne, and she had trouble keeping the acid out of her voice. "Must you be so cheerful?" She was slipping into bitch mode. A small voice in her head warned her not to pick a fight.

He observed her for a moment. "I know that look. What's eating you? Did I forget your birthday or something?"

She decided she would need the wine after all and took a good-sized swallow while the waitress centered Vince's scotch on a cocktail napkin. He thanked her by name after glancing at her ID tag. Ever the charmer, Jeanne thought, and debated waiting until they had ordered to deliver her news. The words had a momentum all their own. "I'm pregnant."

He stared for several seconds and then smiled in his quirky asymmetrical way, revealing more of his perfect teeth on one side than the other. Jeanne wondered if the baby would have teeth like that or her own orthodontist's dream of an overbite. "Right," he said. "That's a good one." She sat mute, and his smile faded. "Okay, that's not funny."

Why did he have such a confused expression? She wasn't his knocked-up teenage girlfriend with Daddy holding a shotgun. "Don't panic, Vince. I've only known for a few hours. I'm planning to terminate the pregnancy."

"Wait a minute. Give me a chance to absorb this." He took a sip of his drink. The furrows between his brows relaxed as his face took on a benevolent expression. "Why the hasty decision?" He put his hand over hers. "I think you should have it. In fact, I think it's great."

She withdrew her hand. "A minute ago, you looked like you were eying the fire exit."

"Not true—I was just surprised. When are you planning to abort?"

She had a vision of frantic mission-control engineers, alarms blaring in the background, exhorting astronauts to abort. The waitress returned to their table, ordering pad in hand, but he waved her away. Jeanne ignored his question. "You know, you could have asked how I'm feeling." She bit her lip in frustration. She knew she needed to stop.

At first, Vince looked wounded, but he quickly seized the offensive. "I'm sorry, but that wasn't the first thought that came to mind. I thought you were past menopause. Now you're pregnant. How did that happen?" His voice rose, and the couple across the aisle looked up from their soup and stared.

"How did that happen, Romeo?" she hissed. "Need me to draw you a picture?" She pushed away a momentary pang of guilt. Was she sure the baby was Vince's? The odds he wasn't the father were infinitesimal.

Vince recoiled. "You know what I meant, Jeanne. Weren't you the one who said you didn't need to bother with contraception anymore?" She hated him for speaking the truth. She was the idiot. Less than twelve months of missed periods did not a menopause make. "Whatever the reason, here you are—pregnant and planning to ab—terminate. I think having a baby is a good thing. You don't. I get it. Maybe you're right. You're married to your job and always have been. You might have trouble with the whole divided loyalties thing."

Jeanne choked with anger. Never mind that she'd thought only moments before that no one would want to be born to her; do men who have children get questioned about divided loyalties? The clink of silver seemed a din, the glare of track lights dizzying. Her hands twitched in her lap as she fought down the urge to scratch his eyes out. "How the fuck would you know?"

Vince leaned in. "I know you, Jeanne. You said yourself you don't want the baby." She looked away. The couple next to them was openly listening, making no pretext of eating. Vince sat back against the red leather.

Jeanne's guts twisted. He had her completely turned around, arguing both sides. How furious she was with herself, a professional who managed business risk but had proven she couldn't manage personal risk worth a damn. It was too much to bear, too much for her not to direct her ire at Vince.

She briefly hovered between collapsing in tears and lashing out. "On second thought, I don't want to dine with a *fucking asshole*. Do you think I got pregnant to entrap you? You're a three-time loser at marriage. Who would want you?" She grabbed her bag and slid out of the booth. “Go ahead and eat without me. I hear the *baby* lamb is tender.”

He followed her into the parking lot, calling her name. When she hesitated, he grabbed her arm. “I’m sorry—really—I wasn’t accusing you of getting pregnant on purpose.” She allowed him to guide her out of the roadway and onto a grassy berm, where he held her hands in his. “Please,” he implored. “Don’t leave.”

Jeanne never cried, at least not in public. That was strict policy. Tears she had willed to stay in place rolled down her cheeks and salted the corners of her mouth. How humiliating to play their B-movie scene in the Grand Grille parking lot. Home was where she needed to be, burying her face in Bricklin’s fur.

He waited for her to dig a tissue out of her purse, blot her eyes, and blow her nose. When she looked up at him, he dabbed at a spot on his cheek and pointed to hers. “Mascara.” She handed him a clean tissue, and he gently wiped away the streak. After a final shuddering breath, her shoulders relaxed. “Jeanne, I know how you feel about marriage. You’d never try to trap a ‘three-time loser’ like me.” He grinned. “The last words I ever expected to come out of your mouth, though, were ‘I’m pregnant.’ You didn’t give me a minute to catch my breath.”

“You can’t take back what you said. You think I couldn’t handle motherhood.”

“No, *you* think that, or at least you act like you do. Why did you get so angry if you were planning to get an abortion? Maybe there’s a part of you that wants a baby. God knows, you treat that dog of yours like Baby Jesus.”

“You mean he isn’t?” She managed a weak smile. He laughed and put his arm around her, and she allowed him to guide her back into the restaurant. “I’m sorry for attacking you. The pregnancy is my own fault, and I’m upset at myself.”

There was nothing wrong with Vince’s appetite. Jeanne

wondered if he were the one eating for two. Halfway through his porterhouse, he put down his fork, cocked his head, and observed her. "What," she asked, her fingers reaching for her face, "more streaks?"

"No, I take back what I said. I *can* see you as a mother and role model. You should reconsider. Have the baby, Jeanne. You could use a counterweight in your life. Financially, you can handle it, and I'm willing to do my share . . . on the money side, for sure."

His share was money? Vince wanted no part of the parenting he was urging on her. "Sleep on it," he said, placing his hand over hers. "Don't schedule an abortion without telling me."

As soon as Jeanne turned into her driveway and saw Bricklin, she exhaled away her tension. The honey-colored golden retriever was sprawled on the broad sill of the bay window like a cat. He abandoned his watch and was waiting at the door when Jeanne entered her condo from the garage. The dog's hindquarters wiggled from side to side, propelled by vigorous tail waving.

She knelt and hugged him. "If you were human, you could get a couple of hundred bucks an hour for this brand of therapy." She could have let him out back but instead removed his leash from its hook. "Can I persuade you to accept some biscuits and a walk in lieu of cash? I may need the walk more than you." Bricklin's tail provided the answer, and Jeanne kissed him on his soft muzzle. "Have I ever told you how much I value your predictability?" The dog tilted his head as though he had an issue with the question. "Okay, so I value predictability in everything. Doesn't mean I don't hold you in especially high regard."

The road through Jeanne's condo complex had no sidewalks, but the two of them were safe in the middle of the road, given how few cars drove into the cul-de-sac. The field beyond the last unit was Jeanne's favorite evening destination, because she and Bricklin were usually alone there. She could let him have as much freedom as his adjustable leash would allow. Street lights illuminated the field enough for her to make her way with a little help from her cell phone flashlight.

She would have been embarrassed to have anyone see how often she conversed with her dog. His face had such an empathetic expression when he looked up at her, she didn't consider these talks one-sided. After all, the moment she spoke, he cocked his head to show she had his full attention.

"When I left the house this morning, I had no idea how remarkable today would be. Bricklin, I'm pregnant. If I don't do something about it, my life will be irreversibly altered. I'm so used to the way things are, I can't imagine such a radical change." Nose to the ground, the dog seemed no longer engaged. "Your life is all about habits too, a daily routine, although, now that I think about it, you're a prisoner. Why don't you run away from me when you're off leash at the park?" Bricklin looked up at Jeanne with a quizzical expression. She stopped. "Is it possible? I suppose it is. Perhaps I'm a prisoner too." Bricklin's eyes were thoughtful, but he kept his counsel.

CHAPTER 2

Jeanne pulled into a parking space opposite her office building, turned off the motor, and peered at her face in the rearview mirror. It was irrational to think her pregnancy could show in her eyes, although the purple shadows beneath them testified to her poor night's sleep. Other than those, the usual Jeanne looked back at her. She would be at her desk soon, immersing herself in her work and grateful to be dealing with quandaries strictly business related.

Suddenly, face out of focus, her eyes sought the reflected action in the background. "No!" she yelled, whipping her head around, but her voice had no effect on the blue Toyota Camry smashing through the lobby entrance. The thunderous crash shattered plate glass and bent steel. She raced for the door that was no longer there.

The car had made it almost to the reception desk and was surrounded by giant shards. The white-haired driver in the front seat didn't move, and she imagined his face mirroring the front of the building, which looked like a gaping mouth with its teeth punched in. She steadied herself against the brick exterior and reached for her cell to call 911. Eduardo, the jockey-tiny Cuban who manned their reception desk, had flattened himself against the lobby's rear wall. He genuflected and slid down to the floor. From behind the couch, CEO Jake Tyler rose, wild-eyed and ashen as the rising plaster dust.

Jamming the phone into her pocket, Jeanne rushed in, ignoring the glass crunching beneath her feet, and yanked open the car door. Others spilled into the lobby from their offices, but she was the first to reach the driver, whom she judged to be in his eighties. Although his face, or what showed of it behind his airbag, appeared unharmed, the crosshatch of wrinkles around his eyes mapped his confusion. He peered at Jeanne. "I braked. Why did it keep going?"

The EMTs arrived quickly and herded everyone away from the car. Jeanne turned her attention to Jake and pushed her way through to his side. As she searched his face for signs of injury, his dazed blue eyes met hers. "I'm okay. Where's Franklin?" Jeanne scanned the crowd and spotted their board member, Franklin Burrows, pacing in front of the building, phone clutched against his ear as he gestured in the air with his free arm.

Jake saw Franklin too, and the sight of his agitated investor seemed to snap him back to reality. He bolted from the couch, shouting directives. "Fall back, everyone. We need to clear the lobby for the medics." He pointed a shaking finger at Eduardo, who had slid back up the wall to his feet. "Call the managing agent and get a maintenance detail in here to clear this glass and board up the front of the building."

Jeanne's legs felt weak. The acrid smell of burnt rubber filled her nose, and the whining sirens reverberated in her ears. Retreating to the solitude of her office, she shut the door she seldom closed and leaned against it. The air here was clear of plaster dust. Weary, she ignored the hanger behind her door and cast her coat over the hook, freeing a few slivers of glass. Although her desk chair was spare and ergonomically contoured, dropping into it felt like sinking into a down-filled sofa.

She ran her fingers through her hair and dropped her head back. She couldn't stop imagining what it had been like for Eduardo to see that car coming at him through the window, and Jake, vaulting the couch, must have been terrified. How close she had come to being in the lobby herself. If she had been killed, would she have counted as two victims, an autopsy revealing her pregnancy?

Emails rolled down her screen like credits after a movie. Vince, calling her cell, spared her from attacking the list. "Are you all right? I hear Jake freaked out."

"Franklin told you? I'm okay and Jake's pretty steady. He'll be fine."

"Maybe he will, but you definitely don't sound like yourself."

She didn't want to tell him she felt sickened and weak when she thought of the driver's face behind his airbag. How much of that was because she was pregnant? "The crash shook the building, and I was right there when it happened, so, yes, I was a bit shaky. I'm in my office now. I'm all right."

"That's my Jeanne, ever stalwart in the face of trouble. Unfortunately, I'm not sure I believe you—think I'll just check up on you later. Ciao." She leaned on her desk and covered her face with her hands. When she was a child, she had covered her face with her bedsheet because she believed the shadowy monsters on her wall would go away if they couldn't see her eyes. Surely, they'd be gone when she looked again. They were. She'd fallen asleep, and it was morning. If only she could do that with her pregnancy.

How could she have allowed her ovaries to betray her this way? Vince thought a baby was just what she needed, like a hobby, like taking up yoga. All she needed was a little more balance in her life. She needed to think, but the maintenance crew's hammer blows, rhythmic as her baby's heartbeat, distracted her.

Better to return to some normal activity like plowing through her email. Maggie, her buddy from Weight Watchers, had heard about the crash from a coworker. The story was already on local news channels. "No one hurt," Jeanne responded. "Fill you in at the meeting." Vince thought her participation in Weight Watchers was silly, but she had been an athlete as a kid and fifteen pounds thinner. She couldn't risk gaining any more. Because she believed in accountability at work, she favored the accountability of her weekly weigh-in rather than sporadic visits to her bathroom scale. Maybe pregnancy queasiness would help keep the pounds under control.

Two quick knocks on the door brought her back to the present. With reluctance, she gave permission to enter. Clara Nordell stood in the doorway looking down at her. Clara looked down at most people, since her height was somewhere north of six feet. She'd been the star center of the women's basketball team at Connecticut College, and she treated every challenge confronting the marketing department as an opportunity for a three-pointer.

Clara waved a paper at her. "Jake was supposed to okay his quote so we could get the press release out. When he didn't return my email, I took the hard copy down to his office. Jeanne," she said, lowering her voice, "he was catatonic—just sat there and ignored me—like he was watching an imaginary movie across the room."

"Leave the release with me." She took the paper from Clara's hand. "Jake was in the lobby when that car came barreling in. Of course, he's stunned. I'll bet Eduardo is too."

"Eduardo went home. Said he was having heart palpitations, and that poor old man . . ." She flattened her hand over her heart. "If anyone was going to have a heart attack, you'd think it would be him. I wonder if he hit the accelerator by accident, his being so old and all."

Jeanne listened to Clara's five-inch heels tapping their way back down the hall. She wondered if there was a man in Clara's life and, if so, how tall he was. Probably not five-eight like Vince, or she could eat apples off his head. Jeanne couldn't help smiling to think of her mother's favorite description of mismatched couples.

Had her parents looked well matched? Knowing so little about her father made him indistinct, the way people looked to her in the morning before she put on her glasses or inserted her contact lenses. Mother had told her he'd died young in an accident, and Jeanne had had to beg before she'd parse out additional information.

She did share that Jeanne had his wavy brown hair and brown eyes. Sparkling eyes, she'd said, that went with his sense of humor, but as a girl Jeanne could never catch sight of the sparkle, no matter how much she peered into her bedroom mirror in search of it.

Another sleepless night left Jeanne dragging and out of sorts. The front of her company's boarded-up building gave it the sad air of a bankrupt business. All that was missing was a sheriff's notice nailed to the door. When she reached her office, one glance at the number of messages in her inbox sent her fleeing to the kitchen, but she didn't get very far before she heard a familiar voice call her. Though she pretended not to hear, Parker Neal fell into step beside her. "Miss a deadline or something? You were sprinting."

"Busy, that's all. Just going for coffee."

"Maybe you should consider the decaf."

The thought of fencing with their CFO was less than appealing, but she was trapped. He stuck to her side the rest of the way. They passed through the lobby, which smelled of newly sawn wood, to the corridor beyond, where the engineering cubicles were clustered near the kitchen. Seeing how engrossed they were in their work gave Jeanne a pang of envy. She was too agitated to concentrate on anything but the miniscule embryo within her.

Parker offered to let her use the coffee brewer first, but she opted for chamomile tea. Getting wired seemed like a bad idea. Parker brewed his cup using an espresso blend and a limited amount of water. No surprise he needed a strong brew to grease his gears. Feigning youthfulness took a lot of his energy. The taut flesh tugging at the sides of his mouth were the legacy of a face lift, and his too-black hair had a life of its own—or more accurately, his toupee did.

Parker leaned against the cabinet and sipped his drink while she covered hers with a dome-topped lid. "What did you think of Jake's reaction yesterday?" he asked in a lowered voice. "I mean diving over the couch and all."

"'And all'? Should he have stood his ground and grabbed the front end of the car like Superman? I didn't think that was in the CEO's job description." Of course, Parker wasn't in good enough shape to clear the couch, but there was no profit in pointing that out.

Parker straightened up and patted his rug-covered pate. As Jeanne turned to leave, he gestured toward the engineering conference room. "Give me a minute, okay?"

Shit. "A minute is all I've got."

He closed the door behind them. After taking a seat at the head of the table, he reached out to swivel a side chair in her direction. She perched near the edge, poised for departure. "Jeanne, I've seen the look on your face in Jake's executive staff meetings, and I can tell what you're thinking. Tell me I'm wrong, but I think we all know the company's growth has taxed Jake's ability to manage. Isn't it time to replace him?"

Jeanne squinted into the morning sun spilling through the slats in the conference room blinds, prompting Parker to jump up and jerk on the cord. He was impatient for her response, but she was unprepared to give one. "You really want to talk about this in the office?"

He was right. She had unspoken frustrations with Jake's operational weakness, but she was disturbed she'd let her feelings show. Parker's statement was based on more than the nonsense about Jake's couch vault. Jake was the classic engineering founder—brilliant at creating technology but challenged when it came to managing growth. "I understand your hesitation," Parker continued. "I like Jake too, but I'm looking at what's best for Salientific."

Jeanne understood there was a case to be made for replacing Jake, at least at some point, but had no doubt Parker's reasons had more to do with his own ambitions and sense of urgency than concern for the company. She shifted in her seat and looked down at her hands. Parker was an over-the-hill wannabe CEO, actually over several hills. He didn't have the leadership skills for the job, the reason he'd been passed over so often. It didn't help his cause that he cut a ridiculous figure. No matter, he'd compete hard and doubtless saw her as a rival. Jeanne tightened her grip around her cup. "At the rate we're growing, Parker, we may, at some point, need a CEO with a different skill set, but I don't think we're there yet."

"Believe me, we are. Why are you defending him?" She averted her eyes and took a sip of her tea, wondering why, indeed, and noting how inadequate chamomile was for this exchange. Parker swiveled his chair back and forth. "What do you think about going to the board—all of us?"

His words took a moment to register. "Mutiny?"

"I didn't say that."

Her cheeks grew warm. "What you're suggesting amounts to the same thing, and there's little, if any, justification. It's absolutely nuts and would certainly backfire. The board still has confidence in Jake."

He stopped his chair. "I suspected you'd say that, given your special relationship with Jake." Parker's smile was unpleasant. "I've already talked with Franklin Burrows, and, though it may surprise you, he was receptive to my concerns. He wants to know if the rest of executive management has the same issues."

"And you think we do? I don't believe the whole executive staff would threaten to quit, even if they shared your opinion."

"If you don't want to go to the entire board, you might feel out a certain investor." Parker's sideways glance was sly. "I believe you have some influence. . . ."

So, he knew about her and Vince. "I don't," she snapped. "I respect Jake for the job he's done at Salientific. Give him a chance to grow with the company before you give up on him." She'd leave it at that. It was bad enough Parker knew about her social life, but if anyone suspected she and Jake . . . She grasped her cup and rose to leave. "The company's doing too well for the board to take action against Jake. It's not like he's some kind of ax murderer."

Parker scowled, and when he stood, black coffee sloshed on the table. "Well, I'm on record. I'd rather work this through the board, but if you won't help . . ." His eyes narrowed. "Does your venture capitalist boyfriend know you're the apple of Jake's eye? You think what happens at an office party stays there?" Jeanne's face colored. "Maybe you ought to consider the risk to yourself if you're the only holdout." How good it would feel, she thought, to yank that toupee off his head and stuff it in his mouth.

He rearranged his features into a more benign expression. "I'd rather work with you, Jeanne, than against you. Let's not be adversaries when it serves both our interests for Salientific to win big."

She bolted for the door, ignoring his belated altruism and pausing just long enough to point at him. "Don't try to manipulate me." Her temples pulsing, she slipped out the door.

Placing Bertucci's and Weight Watchers next to each other had to be the work of the devil. Stepping from her car at six o'clock, Jeanne was all but sucked into the restaurant's doorway, so tantalizing were the aromas. Instead, she stiffened her spine and marched to her weekly showdown with the scale.

Perhaps tonight's meeting would be her last. Although the program was billed as a lifestyle change rather than a diet, she didn't want to watch the scale register her escalating pregnancy weight—if, that is, she stayed pregnant. She could see from the lines at the three stations in the entrance area that she hadn't arrived early enough. Not only did the receptionists need to weigh each client and inscribe in their booklet the week's gain or loss, they had to answer questions from the evening's new enrollees. Jeanne skipped the weigh-in and went straight into the meeting.

Maggie was sitting in her usual spot—right side, third row, first seat off the center aisle. Her hand was on the metal folding chair next to her, and she patted the seat as she caught sight of Jeanne. Since Jeanne always occupied the seat next to

Maggie's, the gesture was superfluous, but that was Maggie, ever welcoming.

Maggie was a permanent fixture at Weight Watchers and had lost over a hundred pounds while Jeanne had been wrestling with her recalcitrant fifteen. In spite of the difference in objectives, the two had bonded. Maggie was a good ten years younger than Jeanne, but she possessed a steadiness that made her seem older, a trait Jeanne attributed to her work as a nurse.

Work commitments and business travel had made Jeanne a perennial quitter and re-joiner who joked she'd still be at Weight Watchers wrestling with her fifteen after Maggie became a sylph, but Maggie encouraged her as though their tasks were equal. Maggie had gone from chunky child to plump adolescent to ever enlarging adult. Jeanne refrained from mentioning her own athletic youth, during which her mother had insisted she learn to compete and win. "That's what you'll need," she'd said. "No matter what the feminists say, the truth is it's a man's world." Jeanne's work schedule left scant time for exercise, and with so many restaurant meals over the years, the pounds had crept on.

Maggie eyed Jeanne's cashmere sweater and tailored gray skirt. "So, bet you wish you could wear scrub pants and smock tops like me. Shame you're stuck with those smart-looking duds."

Maggie's scrubs suited her. In Jeanne's mind, Maggie was the epitome of the helping professional. "You're the most glamorous nurse I know," Jeanne teased. Maggie's sculpted brows and long-lashed blue eyes used to be lost in her fleshy face, but her striking features had become more prominent as her face had narrowed.

"I'm the *only* nurse you know," Maggie whispered, as the room grew quiet. They turned their attention to the front where their leader, Lucy, was positioning her flip charts in front of the group and greeting the assembled. Good turnout, Jeanne thought, looking around the room. No shortage of overweight people to fill in the seats. In the back row sat a young woman nursing an infant. Her breast was draped with a flannel baby blanket. Jeanne swallowed hard.

Lucy, who wore a sweater and pencil skirt with chunky turquoise jewelry, was always turned out in clothes that were not only trendy but dripping with colors overweight women avoided. She never failed to make motivational reference to her own seventy-pound weight loss. When Lucy came to the part of the meeting when she asked who was celebrating a weight-related accomplishment, she seemed truly invested in that person's success, probably the reason her groups did so well.

At the end of the meeting, Jeanne joined the weigh-in line, while Maggie perused the newest cookbooks. A two-pound weight gain for Jeanne, but at least she wasn't showing yet. She looked around for Maggie, who had moved to the snack display and was comparing the labels of the miniscule Weight Watchers Chocolate Caramel Mini Bars and the Chocolate Pretzel Blast snacks. "Why are you bothering? You know you're addicted to Mint Cookie Crisps."

"I know." She sighed. "Everything I buy is the same. Everything I do is the same. It's sad to bore yourself." She replaced both boxes in the display rack and grabbed two handfuls of her favorite treat.

"You don't talk to me about technology, which automatically makes you less boring than the rest of my associates."

"Great. I'm interesting because of what I don't talk about. Isn't that called 'damning with faint praise'?"

Jeanne batted her with her weigh-in card. "You know what I meant." Not much did change week to week, she thought, while Maggie paid for her Mint Cookie Crisps. In spite of Maggie's impression that Jeanne's life was full of corporate excitement, her routine consisted of long, pressure-filled hours at work, sex with Vince or those who had preceded him, and walks with Bricklin. She was counting out her life in rows, columns, and dog biscuits. Measurable progress, not the unexpected, had been her comfort zone.

"So how are you doing? Good week?"

"I'm pregnant."

Maggie looked as shocked as Vince had after Jeanne had turned loose those words. "Congratulations—I think." She looked as though she wanted to hug Jeanne, but the look on Jeanne's face held her back.

"I—uh—I'm not sure I'm having it."

"I get that."

"I guess I just had to tell someone besides Vince. No one at work knows."

"I don't want to be presumptuous, but do you want to talk about it?"

Jeanne, who was unaccustomed to seeking personal advice, hesitated. "I guess maybe I do, but . . ." She looked at the wall clock. Bricklin would be waiting by the window. "Do you have time to meet for lunch Saturday?"

"Maybe an hour—I'm working this Saturday." They agreed on a Salad City that would be convenient for Maggie. "Courage," Maggie said, patting Jeanne's arm as they stepped out into the night.

CHAPTER 3

Jeanne was getting used to the idea that she was pregnant. She knew she had wasted days she could have used to schedule an abortion, but making such a consequential decision required the calm, logical reasoning she used when she was in her normal state of mind. The same applied to seriously engaging in the business tasks she'd been putting off, so she was engrossed in an upside-versus-downside analysis for Jake when a knock on her door was followed by Bart Connelly's face peering in at her. He dropped into the armchair opposite her and smiled as though he'd received a warm welcome.

Bart's specialty was endless demands, all of which were urgent. She was glad she had this legitimate business-related reason for disliking him, because she had a bunch of bad reasons, and without a substantive complaint, she'd have to admit they were petty. Those who hated him called him arrogant, while others defended him as merely cocky, common enough in a sales VP. If Jeanne had met him in another context, she would have considered him an asshole, but in business, many a talented, hardworking asshole was counted as an asset.

Bart's smile was often smug, and he had a thick head of black hair and a compact, muscular body. If you didn't know him, Jeanne thought, you'd find him attractive. She sat upright and pulled her chair closer into her desk. With Bart, the best strategy was to get right down to his issue, so you could get rid of him quickly.

He crossed his legs, which drew Jeanne's attention to his pants. Bart's chinos annoyed her because they were pressed like a uniform. She could imagine getting a paper cut—a khaki cut?—if she touched the crease, although this was rarely possible with Alberta's thigh so close to his during executive staff meetings. Jeanne could only imagine where Alberta's hand was when the two had privacy.

Since Alberta was their human resources VP, "inappropriate" didn't begin to cover her behavior. Bart was on the road most of the time. What happened on the road stayed out of Alberta's sight, not to mention Bart's wife's, but Jeanne had heard it involved lap dances—probably why Bart's pants needed aggressive pressing.

Bart held a printout in his hands, and Jeanne could see the crossed-out entries and notes in the margins from across her desk. "The leads from the Chicago seminar sucked. Not a genuine sales prospect among them." Bart thrust his head forward, and several strands of dark hair shook loose from his perfect wave. She watched him reunite the stragglers with the rest of his coif.

Jeanne's staff had organized a set of seminars across the country to help generate sales opportunities for Bart's reps. Her staff had performed well on the front-end work that was marketing's responsibility: obtaining lists of technology decision makers, arranging the venue, sending out invites, and arranging for speakers. "There were plenty of attendees," she said. "Maybe the problem was in the follow-up by telesales. Those folks report to you, no? You've got enough deadwood there for a marshmallow roast." Bart wouldn't fire his telesales reps. He'd hired foxes, and whenever he was in town, he spent considerable time leaning over their shoulders as they sat at their computers. He called it mentoring. Jeanne called it cleavage assessment.

Bart leaned back in his seat. She'd noticed that his strategy for dealing with her was to change the subject when she scored any points off him. "I want to brief you on the annual sales kickoff. I've got a great idea for a theme. Actually, Parker made me think of it." Jeanne had mixed feelings about kickoffs, since they were expensive annual parties for sales reps. Marketing, engineering, accounting, and services had nothing comparable. She had to admit they were motivational, though. The sales force was pumped afterward.

The last kickoff had been at the Seaport Marriott. Though many of the sessions over the course of three days were educational, there was entertainment, and there were fun team-building activities like a chili cook-off contest. Senior management made presentations about Salientific's goals for the new year and accomplishments during the fiscal year just ended. Jeanne spoke about marketing's plans. Sales wanted to hear that advertising, public relations, and trade shows would support their selling effort, but beyond giving those assurances, Jeanne would need to make her talk entertaining. She hoped Bart's theme would stoke the flame of her creativity.

"Do you own a flak jacket?" he asked.

"All VPs of marketing own flak jackets. We get fired more than the VPs of any other discipline."

"More than sales? I doubt it, but you know that's not what I meant. How do you feel about presenting in camouflage? The theme is 'Year of the High-Value Target.'" Bart smiled and nodded at Jeanne. "Great, huh?"

Jeanne sat back in her chair and regarded Bart. She did not think a military theme was great. In fact, she thought it sucked. Not only were military metaphors business clichés, a military theme was in excruciatingly bad taste. The pullout from Afghanistan was still incomplete, and no one would forget how many soldiers had died there and in Iraq. As for 'high-value targets'—weren't they terrorists? "Bart, to say I have reservations would be an understatement."

"But it fits. Really, it does." He became earnest in a boyish way, and Jeanne reminded herself she had more than ten years on him. "I found out there's a Department of Defense term, Quick Response Force—QRF—that's a perfect description of what the whole company needs to be."

"Catchy." He ignored her sarcasm.

"It also fits what I want my sales reps to do: target the biggest revenue opportunities, the high-value targets; don't chase pocket-change deals." He leaned forward like an imploring child, eyes wide, lips parted. Jeanne looked out at the sky, hoping to find some celestial inspiration that would help her manage Bart.

"I do understand—really—and QRF is a good way of describing how everyone in the company should be ready to back up sales. It's just, you know, the country's war-weary."

Bart pressed his case. "Remember that old Mel Brooks musical, *The Producers*? It was about Hitler, only tongue in cheek. Mine's tongue in cheek too. People will get it. And think what a great resource we have in Jake. He's a veteran."

Jeanne had more confidence in Mel Brooks's sense of humor than in Bart's, but she could see he was emotionally invested in his military theme. She couldn't imagine Jake as Bart's creative muse for the sales meeting, but she'd wait to see if Bart could pull it off. "Let me know what Jake says before I rush out to buy camo."

After checking the thermometer outside her kitchen window, Jeanne hunted for a warm jacket for her Saturday morning hike with Bricklin. She stuffed her pockets with the necessities—plastic bags for scooping poop, a couple of dog biscuits, and a water bottle. She draped the leash around her neck.

Bricklin stood, tennis ball in mouth, as close as he could to the door leading to the garage. He was taking no chance that Jeanne might squeeze by without him. "Do you think I'd leave you, boy? Not a chance." As soon as she opened the car door, he bounded into the back seat, launching puffs of fur into the air. Jeanne eyed her car vacuum in the corner of the garage and turned her back on it. Keeping up with a shedding golden was a Sisyphean task.

Ten minutes later they arrived at the Weston Reservoir. They both loved the trail encircling it and the scenic paths leading away. In the autumn, the woods were so full of fallen leaves that the trails were all but obscured. Obscure paths, she thought, that seems like the order of the day.

Although Bricklin stayed on leash to cross the road, once Jeanne set him free, he became a honey-colored streak through the woods, tearing around in big loops. She smiled at the simple joy of it. "We're a family, Bricklin. Why should I have a baby when I don't want anything to change?"

Bricklin showed no interest in Jeanne's musings. This was his time, and he intended to wear himself out running, playing, and sniffing. She wondered what it would be like to have no need to pace oneself. Bricklin was ten, as old as a human in his seventies. He'd slowed down some but was every bit the puppy when he had a ball in his mouth. She couldn't bear to think about life without him.

She tried to focus on the beauty of the leaves floating in the wind, the iridescent reds her favorite, but her mind refused to enter anything resembling a meditative state, wandering instead from one source of consternation to another: her improbable pregnancy, Parker's impractical mutiny, her childhood—all about achieving rather than experiencing. She felt alone, alone except for Bricklin.

She whistled for him, and dutifully he appeared, tennis ball clenched between his teeth. He trotted toward her, limping. "Bricklin, what happened?" He wagged his tail as she crouched in front of him and peered at his paw. "That's no answer. Help me out here."

As soon as they returned home, Jeanne had Bricklin sit on the kitchen floor so she could lift his paw. She examined the pads underneath closely and ran her hand up his leg, squeezing and pressing gently, but he showed no evidence of pain. "It's okay, boy. I know you're supposed to conceal injuries from predators, but everyone in this condo complex is domesticated. It's safe to let me know where it hurts."

When she reached his shoulder, he flinched slightly. "I know you don't want to hear this, but we need to see the vet." She sat back on her heels, frowning, as he limped over to his window, assessed the required jump, and instead lay down on the carpet.

Just before noon, Jeanne arrived at Salad City and took a table with a clear view of the door. Since Maggie was late, she alternated between checking email on her iPhone and watching the entrance. Arriving diners were mostly older shoppers with Walmart and Target bags. Four young women commanded everyone's attention when they made a noisy entrance in tight jeans and strappy high heels. Tell me those shoes don't belong in bondage porn, Jeanne thought. Either that or I'm getting really old.

Maggie came in right behind the girls, an incongruous presence beside their stick figures. She was out of breath and impatiently brushed her hair from her eyes. "Jeanne, I'm so sorry. We're short-staffed today. Would you mind terribly if we got our salads to go and ate at Dawning Day? I know that's not what you had in mind as a place to talk, but . . ."

Jeanne glanced around the restaurant, where harsh light from the storefront reflected off metal tables—not an intimate setting either. She threw on her coat. "Your home should be quieter anyway."

Three women ahead of them at the counter were debating the merits of wraps versus sandwiches. Maggie turned to Jeanne. "We're an assisted living facility, not a nursing home, remember? Our residents are wonderful, at least most of them. They've led fascinating lives and have tales to tell."

"I don't doubt it," said Jeanne without conviction. To her, old people were incomprehensible. They obstructed the passing lane on the highway and left their turn signals on for hours. They braked for yellow lights. They left their shopping carts in the middle of supermarket aisles while they scrutinized the per-ounce prices on the shelf labels. Didn't they get it? Time is money.

A young girl in a white uniform and a ponytail poking through the back of her baseball cap stood poised behind the counter, plastic bowl in hand, waiting to take their order. They chose ingredients for their custom-made salads, and as they neared the register, Maggie reached for her wallet.

"Not today." Jeanne put her hand on Maggie's arm. "Think of this as your consulting fee."

Dawning Day resembled a Victorian castle on the outside, not Jeanne's idea of homey, although the interior was inviting.

The Queen Anne style furniture was upholstered in deep jewel tones. A sweeping staircase led to the second floor, although Jeanne suspected the elevator got more use. Her nose guided her eyes to the left, where the dining room was full of talkative residents eating what smelled like boiled chicken. "We're going to the Alzheimer's wing," Maggie said, pulling Jeanne toward a door off the reception area. She punched a code into a keypad on the wall and recited it for Jeanne to remember. "It's a locked wing. You'll need the code to exit."

Locked wing? This was going to be depressing. "Maggie, maybe we should have our talk some other time."

"Oh, c'mon. They don't bite. In fact, most of them can't." She laughed and tugged on Jeanne's sleeve. The Alzheimer's wing consisted of a large country kitchen open to a spacious common area. There were no hallways leading to rooms. Instead, the residents' doors opened onto the lounge. Music from a Fred Astaire and Ginger Rogers movie played softly in the background. Jeanne tried to place it. "A Fine Romance?" She wondered if the residents were trying to place it too.

"Let's eat in the office," Maggie said, leading the way into a staff room with a couple of empty desks. "Everyone's with the residents right now." She pulled the swivel chair from one desk over to the other. They opened their salads, and Maggie attacked hers, while Jeanne pushed her greens around in the vinaigrette as though ensuring each lettuce leaf was coated was a task of great significance. She debated how to start.

Maggie broke the silence. "So, how'd you get pregnant? Not on purpose, I assume."

"Hardly." Jeanne's smile was halfhearted. She recounted her initial visit to Dr. O'Rourke's office. "Seriously, I can't believe I made such a bonehead miscalculation."

"You're entitled to an occasional mistake, although I'll

admit, this was kind of a big one. Have you been in the corporate world so long, you've forgotten you're human? Never mind. I know you have. What are you going to do, or is that my consulting assignment?"

It wasn't Maggie's fault she didn't understand how simplistic her view of business was. Jeanne looked around the office as though there were guidance to be found on the staffing schedules or emergency procedures tacked to the bulletin boards. Her forte was decisiveness; her competence, crisp articulation. Surely, she could distill her "what now" dilemma for Maggie and avoid melodrama. "At first, I was certain I didn't want a baby. Never wanted one—still didn't. Then I wavered. Now I'm wondering whether my original decision was the right one."

Maggie waited, fork in the air. "That's all?"

"That's the executive summary."

Maggie's mouth bent into a wry smile. "I think I need to read the whole report."

Jeanne wondered how far back she should go. Mother's admonitions about childrearing were as relentless as rain. She opened her mouth to speak but shook her head instead. "I've never been so confused in my life."

"Your work life," Maggie said.

Jeanne forced a smile. "Is there any other kind?" What was she expecting from Maggie anyway, advice or unleavened sympathy? She didn't need a lecture about how hard she worked. Jeanne thought for a moment of the old friends she'd lost track of and how she'd neglected those relationships. She didn't want that to happen with Maggie, but work had to come before everything else. The pressure was inexorable.

She picked up the plastic cover for her salad. "I shouldn't be dragging you into this. I have to assess my options on my own, and there's no reason to take up your time when you're needed here."

"It sounds like you've been assessing around in a circle. You can't do a cost-benefit analysis on whether to have a baby. You don't need advice from me. You need to consult your feelings."

An aide with an African head wrap appeared in the doorway, and Maggie raised her palm. "I'm coming, Amala." She sighed and covered her salad. "Guess this is going into the refrigerator." She stood and looked down at Jeanne. "I'm so sorry our conversation is getting short-circuited. I thought we'd have more time. You don't have to leave, though. Eat your salad." When she bent down to kiss Jeanne on the cheek, they exchanged awkward hugs.

"I'm going too," Jeanne said and tossed the rest of her salad in the trash. She pulled on her jacket and followed Maggie, who was accosted outside the office by two elderly women. One had hanging pillows of loose flesh beneath her arms and breasts that sagged to her waist, while her companion was waiflike and less than five feet tall. The waif had hooked her arm around her friend's. "We're going out to the barn," she said. "Have to put away the horses."

Maggie smiled. "Good idea. Thanks."

Jeanne shook her head as the women wandered away. "Don't they know there is no 'out' and no 'barn'?"

"We give them pleasant days. Why yank them back to a reality they won't remember five minutes from now?" Maggie turned toward the kitchen. Jeanne wished she could forget the reality of her pregnancy.

A voice nearby caught her attention. "Mom, look at Jennifer's sweet baby. He's named after Dad." An attractive brunette, in her fifties, with long hair brushing the tops of her shoulders, leaned in and made earnest entreaties. She laid her manicured hand on her mother's arm, the magenta polish vivid against the crepe-like skin. "Mom." She shook her mother's arm.

The old woman's face was crowded with wrinkles, but she

had a beautiful brow and thin braids of gray hair across the top of her head like a milkmaid's. Her sad mouth was pinched, and there were sparse hairs growing on her upper lip and chin. A woolen cardigan enveloped her as though she'd shrunk several sizes. Hands in her lap, she rocked herself and muttered, "Mama, Mama, Mama." The young girl tried to get her grandmother's attention, but the old woman's eyes remained downcast. "Mama, Mama, Mama."

On impulse, Jennifer leaned over her grandmother and pressed her son against the flaccid arms. Without hesitation, the old woman clasped the child to her bosom. When she cradled him and kissed his forehead, humming a barely discernible tune, her daughter's expression changed from apprehension to surprise to joy. Jennifer spoke softly and placed her hand on her grandmother's bowed shoulder. "Yes, Grandma. That's just what he likes."

Jeanne couldn't watch. She turned away, her eyes moist. Hurrying through the lobby and out to the parking lot, she ignored the receptionist's cheery goodbye and avoided meeting anyone's gaze. Golden leaves, propelled by a cold wind, rained down on the pavement. Shivering, she turned up her collar and wiped her eyes with her coat sleeve.

How? Why? Questions crowded into her mind. The tools of rationality were the rock she clung to, but they couldn't explain what she'd seen.

Did there have to be a reason? Maggie was right about Jeanne's instincts—to find a cause, to intellectualize the moment, to analyze. Perhaps enlightenment lay elsewhere. Looking back at Dawning Day as she climbed into her car, Jeanne wondered at the formidable physical and emotional power possessed by that tiny baby. A woman wandering lost in her own mind knew, from the moment his skin touched hers, there was a connection between them.

Had Jeanne's mother felt the power of that connection? If so, she'd succeeded in concealing it from her daughter. It was a perversion of maternal feelings to love Jeanne's future more than she loved Jeanne. Companionship, romance, sex—Jeanne was taught she could have them all without the burdens of motherhood. Without the burdens, but without the joys either. She turned on the ignition. As the engine came to life, she moved her hands from the steering wheel to her abdomen and intertwined her fingers.

Mother's house was cold as a mausoleum. Jeanne had turned the heat down to fifty degrees, a sensible temperature for an unoccupied home, but the chill penetrated her coat. She hadn't planned to work in the attic today, but searching her mind for moments of connection with her mother had jogged loose a memory. Climbing the stairs to the attic, she felt the warmth of risen heat and a sense of anticipation.

Her cell phone flashlight reflected off a taped carton under the eaves. *It was still there.* Elated, she dragged it out and tried to pry the flaps apart. The box defied opening, so mummified was it with tape. The label read: "Time Capsule: to be opened in 2029."

Jeanne ran her fingers across the words. She remembered the conversation, how excited she'd been after learning about time capsules at school. It was Mother who'd suggested they each create their own, to be preserved together in a single carton.

"When can we open it, Mom? In five years?"

"Has to be at least fifty." Jeanne was aghast. Why, she'd be sixty-two, and Mother would be . . . "Don't worry. I'll still be alive and kicking. Besides, putting off present pleasure for future gain is the mark of maturity." Mother was full of these life lessons, but to young Jeanne, she was a born killjoy. "You'll thank me someday for teaching you the importance of strong character." Thirty-six years had passed, yet Jeanne could still remember her disappointment. Right or wrong, she'd never tendered her thanks, depriving her mother of that satisfaction before she went to her grave.

Jeanne fished out her house key and drew it swiftly across the carton seam, which, though rutted, resisted penetration. Surveying the attic, she saw nothing that would cut through its multiple layers. Downstairs, not a knife or pair of scissors remained in the kitchen she had cleaned out so thoroughly even the crumbs in the crevices of the drawers were gone. The box wasn't heavy, in spite of its awkward size and unbalanced weight. She worked it down the stairs and maneuvered it into her trunk.

After hauling the box into her condo and depositing it on her carpeted living room floor, she attacked the tape with a serrated kitchen knife. Bricklin sat down beside her, cocking his head in puzzlement. She stopped to stroke him, and as she buried her hand in his neck fur, his eyes closed in pleasure. "Did Mother really think I was going to open it early?" Bricklin opened one eye to acknowledge the question and check that it was rhetorical. "No adult would be deterred for long by packing tape, only a child." Truth was, were it not for Mother's death, the box would still be tucked away under the attic eaves.

Jeanne's hands became quiet, prompting Bricklin to push his wet nose into the crook of her arm. "Sorry, boy. I need both hands for this." He withdrew to a respectable distance and continued to gaze at her as she pulled back the flaps and reached in. The two boxes lay next to each other, and, mercifully, Mother hadn't taped them closed. Jeanne pulled out the smaller one, her own time capsule, which bore her name and the date printed in her twelve-year-old hand. She'd included her middle name, Hayley, to make her sound more grown up.

Jeanne remembered parting with her Little League team hat so it could emerge in fifty years—they'd won the city championship that spring—but she was hazy on what else she'd put in. Certificates lay on the bottom with two trophies and three medals on top. Medals from Camp Wampanoag, of course, in swimming, tennis, and lacrosse—Jeanne had often been told she had awesome athletic potential. She pinched her love handles with a sigh. Hard to tell today.

The trophies were from gymnastics and soccer. She fished out the yellowed certificates underneath and leafed through: first prize in the sixth-grade spelling competition, first prize for her essay on the UN. She let her hands drop and the papers slip to the floor. What a letdown. The only storybook was *The Wizard of Oz*. She remembered her fascination with the movie. Life could change in magical ways with the right path to follow and a good witch for a mentor.

Sure, she had been a smart kid and an excellent athlete, Jeanne remembered that much, but what was important to her? What did she love? What did she dream about? The box provided no clue, only proof of her successes, proxies for what her mother valued in her, valued her for. Her mother's time capsule probably contained more of the same, since she considered achieving the highest form of good, her eleventh commandment, "Thou shalt excel." Dispirited at the evidence that Jeanne's twelve-year-old self had already bought in to her mother's philosophy, she pushed the box aside.

CHAPTER 4

How Bricklin sensed she was awakening, Jeanne never understood, yet she had only to open one eye to find him sitting at the foot of the bed, regarding her intently. His tail began its slow swish across the blanket as she swung her legs over the side. When she stuffed her feet into her fleece-lined slippers, he stood and wagged his tail fast enough to create a perceptible breeze. Anticipating her path, he trotted ahead toward the kitchen as Jeanne belted her robe.

"Still limping, puppy boy. You must have really wanted to be on my bed to jump up there. We're going to take it easy today, starting with coffee and the Sunday paper. This afternoon will be for work"—she glanced into the living room—"and the other half of that time capsule." Jeanne's agenda failed to excite Bricklin, and he pushed his nose into the crack of the back door. She opened it and linked his collar to the snap hook of his cable tie-out.

Annoyed by the inconvenient ringing coming from the bedroom, she debated ignoring her cell. It was not, however, in her DNA to avoid what might be a business call. She reached her phone by the sixth ring. Vince's number was displayed on her caller ID. "I thought you were out of town."

"Nice greeting. Try this. Good morning, Vince. I'm sooo happy to hear from you."

"I am happy to hear from you. Just haven't had my coffee yet." She cradled the phone in her neck so she could let Bricklin back into the kitchen.

"Lucky for you, you'll have a chance to atone for your grumpiness. I decided to drive back this morning instead of tonight. Need to get in a couple of hours at the office. Mind if I swing by? You've been on my mind all weekend." She agreed, though, in truth, she was not anxious to see him. Vince would want to know her decision. Some part of her wasn't sold on abortion. The scene she'd witnessed at Dawning Day had affected her more profoundly than she could explain. Maybe she just wanted to see if she could do a better job than her own mother had. Bricklin waited patiently at his food dish. Jeanne scooped out his kibble while serving up the bad news. "We're going to stick to leash walks until the vet tells us what's going on with that leg."

When Vince arrived, Jeanne was dressed in jeans, a red wool turtleneck, and leather boots. Outdoors seemed a better place to talk than on opposite sides of the kitchen table—more space to back away from each other if they disagreed. The issue was more complicated than whether she should have the baby. If she had it, what would Vince's role be? What should it be? Growing up without a father, Jeanne could only define fatherhood by its absence.

Vince was barely across the threshold before enveloping Jeanne in a bear hug. His stubbly cheek sandpapered hers, and she reached up to rub it. "How are you *feeling*?" he asked. "See, I remembered to ask that first. I'm coachable."

"And sweet, when you want to be." She kissed him and extricated herself from his arms. Reaching for her corduroy barn jacket draped over the newel post, she suggested he keep his jacket on. "Up for a walk? Should be peak color this weekend, and I want to catch the display before the wind blows the trees bare."

"Maybe, if you're nice to me, I'll whip up a little Sunday brunch for you after our walk. Let's see . . . Belgian waffles, eggs Benedict, croissants with farm-fresh butter—"

Jeanne groaned. "And you'll come with me to Weight Watchers to explain to Lucy why I gained five pounds this week. Let's go."

"To the reservoir?"

"Bricklin's limping. Thought we'd just go across the road and walk the trail through the conservation land."

Vince crouched and ruffled Bricklin's fur. "Hey, buddy, got a sports injury? Have to listen to the team trainer." They strolled down the center of Birch Brook's curving access road, admiring the chrysanthemums and pumpkins adorning the front porches. The crimson blossoms were the most striking, but Jeanne's porch was bare. She was too busy to commit to watering a pot of her own.

The wind whipped their clothes as they crossed Route 30, and Bricklin raised his wet nose into the air. Scents seemed to come to him from afar on windy days, bringing information from the wider world. How useful, Jeanne thought. How much more efficient a use of time than reading a newspaper. A hint of smoke from burning leaves reached her nostrils but nothing more. So rare that signature smell of autumn was, now that burning leaves was illegal without a special permit.

As she and Vince started down the trail into the woods, Bricklin tried to pull away. "Sorry, boy. Not today." They walked single file on the narrow path, giving him all the sniffing time he desired to compensate for his tethering. When the path widened,

Vince pulled even with Jeanne. He looked as though he were about to speak but thought better of it.

She was sure he wanted to know if she was keeping the baby, but for some reason he seemed as tethered as Bricklin. She thought about his reaction at the Grand Grille—first dismay and then what had seemed genuine pleasure. Was he dishonest or just ambivalent? If the latter, could she, in fairness, blame him?

They climbed the winding trail in silence until they reached its highest point, where the path looped around a craggy outcropping of rocks and led back toward the park entrance. Vince surveyed the woods below. "Wind's out of the northwest. If we get a storm, that color won't last. Looks like a lot of the leaves are down already."

The spectacular but ephemeral New England autumn—it was autumn for Jeanne too, her last-chance season. She found a rock flat enough for sitting and stretched out her legs, providing a leafy bed between her feet, where Bricklin promptly settled. Vince turned from the woods and, crouching as close to her as he could with Bricklin in the way, took her hands in his. "Have you made a decision?"

"I'm leaning toward having the baby." She winced at the tentativeness of her own words.

He frowned. "Leaning?"

"What do you want to hear? If I tell you I'm having the baby, it may only be the decision du jour."

She'd been afraid he would take her words as a verbal commitment, contract to follow. He did, yet she could have sworn she saw an instant of panic, a momentary widening of his eyes, a twitch of the lips, eclipsed in a flash by a radiant smile. "I'll settle for 'leaning.' That's awesome." He pulled her up into a hug, which included Bricklin positioned between them. "I was afraid to say anything more than I did in the restaurant, but

I'm really glad." He released her but held on to her hand as they circled back toward the entrance.

He was full of questions about her pregnancy and plans, each one prefaced by "assuming you go forward" or "if you have it." He even asked which room in the condo would be a nursery. He sounded like a father, even a husband. For a moment, she thought he was leading up to a proposal and felt a pang of panic. They had an understanding, never articulated, that theirs was a relationship with no project milestones, no engagements, no rings. Steady state. He flambéed in the kitchen, and she kindled a flame in the bedroom.

When the path narrowed, the questions ceased. Vince grew thoughtful and began to trail her. "I'll have my lawyer draw up a legal agreement covering our respective parental rights and responsibilities."

"What?" She stopped and looked back at him. She'd heard him perfectly, but if Vince weren't suddenly backing away, why couldn't he meet her gaze? In spite of his smiles, he wasn't ready to be a father. Did she want him orbiting her and the baby like a planet, never approaching, never departing?

"My lawyer—"

The leash jerked in Jeanne's hand as Bricklin took off after a squirrel. "Bricklin, no," she yelled. "Come." The squirrel scrambled to safety high on the trunk of an oak, and the dog limped back, his leash trailing. "Son of a bitch, look at his leg. Now he's worse." She pulled off the leaves stuck to the leash and held it tight in her hand. Though her impulse was to hasten home, there was no quickening the pace. Bricklin couldn't keep up.

The sky seemed grayer to Jeanne, as though Vince's declaration on contractual obligations had altered the light. If he was going to focus on the pragmatic, she would too. Did he think he was the only one with practical issues? "I need to consider how my pregnancy will affect my position at Salientific. A couple of people are already aware we're seeing each other, so I'm thinking I'd be better off keeping your fatherhood quiet. I don't want people gossiping about how I'm wired to our investors."

He stiffened. "Seriously? Executives are always wired to their companies' investors, even the very investors who sit on their boards' compensation committees. When you've been in the industry as long as you have, competing loyalties are inevitable." He kicked a stone down the path, and only Jeanne's grip on the leash kept Bricklin from pursuing it.

"Okay, so maybe conflicts of interest abound, but I'm not sure that for me, at this time, at this company . . . Look, let's not argue right now. I'm worried about Bricklin's leg. See how he keeps stopping and holding his paw in the air?"

When they returned to Birch Brook, Vince didn't go in with them, much less repeat his offer of brunch. "Got to get to the office," he mumbled and took off. Jeanne wondered if he felt as drained as she did.

After giving Bricklin a biscuit, she instructed him to rest. "Follow my lead, pup." She pulled off her boots and stretched out full length on the sofa. When Bricklin curled up on the rug beside her, she reached down to scratch behind his ears. Eyes closed, he made the snoring-purring sound that goldens make to show pleasure. So easy to please, she thought. Vince should take a note.

With her head cushioned by a throw pillow and another folded within her arms, she curled into the sofa back, waiting for sleep that didn't come. Instead the memory she'd banished from her thoughts pushed its way to the foreground—the summer morning she'd found not Vince or Bricklin, but Jake in her bed.

Though Jeanne was as well acquainted with lust in the evening and regret in the morning as with the wine and food pairings at her favorite French restaurant, her night with Jake had inspired exponential remorse. On awakening, he'd looked over at her and said simply, "Uh-oh." A smile, surrounded by morning stubble, creased his gaunt face.

"Oh my God. Not funny, Mr. CEO. I'm not supposed to be under you anywhere but on the org chart." Dismayed, she clutched her sheet to her chest and slipped out of bed, exposing Jake in all his hirsute splendor. She groaned and backed out of the room, retrieving her clothes along the way.

"I'll be in the powder room till you're dressed," she called out, catching sight of the empty bottles in the kitchen as she passed. All that open champagne from the party—she and Jake hadn't let it go to waste. Had she poured it out, they would have made short work of the cleanup, and Jake would have left soon after the rest of their colleagues. Elation, libation, libido—a troublesome trio.

When Jake knocked on the bathroom door on his way out, he tried to ease her mind. "As far as I'm concerned, it never happened. A pact of silence—deal?"

She had agreed, but silencing her inner voice had been more difficult than keeping up appearances at work. Guilty feelings had lodged in her psyche, ever expanding until she'd pushed them down, down, down. What was the big deal about a one-night stand at her age?

Jeanne's hand rose to her cheek as though it still stung from her mother's hard slap. A one-night stand had been a monumental deal to Mother, who'd assumed Jeanne was being deflowered by eighteen-year-old Roy Sax when she came upon the two of them in Jeanne's bed. Roy, who instantly lost his condomless erection, grabbed his clothes and fled. Jeanne, mortified and furious, was hauled off to her mother's gynecologist for a birth control pill prescription.

Jeanne's mental hand-wringing was interrupted by Bricklin's paw. She turned to face him. "What if Jake is the father, Bricklin? I can't even imagine telling Dr. O'Rourke I need a paternity test, much less telling Vince this isn't his baby."

Jeanne was sure she saw empathy in the depth of Bricklin's eyes. She'd learned to read his desires from his eyes, their expression changing when he wanted to eat (pretty much all the time) or when he heard terrifying thunder. When he chewed a greasy napkin he found under the table, his eyes betrayed his guilt. He'd taught her the power of nonverbal communication. His sweet temperament more than made up for his lack of intellectual discourse. Canine wisdom had its limits, though. What she really needed at that moment was advice.

Maybe she should talk out her problem with a shrink, clergyman, or friend, but Jeanne had neither of the first two and few of the third. Pathetic, she thought, my best friend is Google. Her study was in the loft, where her desk sat in front of windows overlooking wooded wetlands. Bookcases filled with hardcover nonfiction, mostly on business subjects, lined the wall beside her desk. She flipped open her laptop and searched for "paternity test while pregnant."

She'd first thought she'd have to wait for amniocentesis. At her age, the procedure was recommended anyway, to test for Down syndrome and spina bifida, among other genetic conditions. A paternity test could be done at the same time. Some commercial laboratories seemed to be advertising a way to find out sooner through a blood test, but she didn't quite understand it. Dr. O'Rourke had instructed her to see a genetics counselor. She hadn't even told the doctor yet whether she was keeping the baby, much less pursued genetic analysis.

Jeanne closed her browser. Reading about the incidence of birth defects made her stomach tighten. She didn't need to see the statistics to know the risks were greater for change-of-life babies. Having the baby would be irresponsible. On the other hand, how great was the probability of a defect?

If she were doing a business analysis, would she consider the risk to be in the acceptable range? She wasn't sure. Her assessment of acceptable risk, in the instances when she'd been proven wrong, had only erred on the side of excessive caution. She feared the unpredictable future with its power to prove her choices and business decisions imprudent, and she was anything but philosophical about the consequences of being proven wrong.

The smart business choice, at this point in her life, would be to pursue her goal of becoming a CEO. Maybe as a young woman, she could have figured out how to combine a career with motherhood, but it was too late, unless . . . unless Maggie was right. Jeanne didn't need to do a cost-benefit analysis. She needed to consult her feelings, a skill she had never cultivated.

Bricklin was chewing the corner of the time capsule, so Jeanne shooed him away and moved the carton back into the center of the living room. Opening the flaps of her mother's box revealed contents that rocked Jeanne back on her heels. Her favorite stuffed animals were on top: a dusty Steiff tiger with green eyes and a Winnie-the-Pooh holding a honeypot. She held the bear to her cheek and sneezed.

At least forty years had passed since she'd cuddled these animals and sought their comfort, hiding her tearful face in their softness. Had she outgrown that need? Was she exploiting Bricklin for his fur? Feeling guilty, she glanced over at him. He regarded her with the same trusting eyes as always, with no sign of resentment.

Jeanne and her mother, her mother and Jeanne—there had been no one else in the house, no second parent to mediate disputes, no other shoulder to cry on, no pet. The tiger's fur was off-putting in its synthetic shade of tangerine, yet its ears were so soft, they had been more comforting to her childhood sensibilities than a tissue.

Beneath the stuffed animals were clothes. Jeanne fingered a pink tulle tutu. Could she really have worn this? She could scarcely remember herself as a girly girl, but, yes, she had convinced Mother to let her take ballet lessons. Curious how Mother had saved that tutu as well as special occasion outfits: Jeanne's ruffled pinafore from the first day of kindergarten and the red velvet Christmas dress she had worn when she was ten.

She crossed her legs on the floor. Her task was discarding the last of Mother's possessions and finishing her spreadsheet, but she couldn't get herself to stop running her fingers across the netted surface of her tutu. Psychics' visions were inspired by touching people's belongings. Perhaps that wasn't bullshit after all. Jeanne was there—performing in a dance recital. Mother, her blond hair pulled back in a severe knot, her expression anything but severe, sat beaming in the front row. How had that slipped Jeanne's mind?

Crafts projects were stashed beneath the clothes: a potholder woven with cotton bands, a crude clay dog sculpture, and the wooden word "Mom" Jeanne had carved in shop class. Near the bottom, her childhood books lay nestled together: *The Lit-*

tle Engine That Could, Mike Mulligan's Steam Shovel, and *Where the Wild Things Are* among them. She flipped through the pages, releasing the musky smell of mildew, and ran her fingers over the covers and down the spines, handling each book as though it were a rediscovered old master. How she had loved them.

The Runaway Bunny, so often retrieved and revisited, was the most dog-eared, and Jeanne carried it to the couch, where she curled up against the pillows the way she'd curled up in her mother's lap. Opening the cover released an envelope. She slit the flap and peered inside. "No way." A lock of baby hair and a baby tooth lay in the bottom. Sentimentality had been all but a sin to Fay Bridgeton, and Jeanne couldn't summon an image of her young mother tucking away such mementos in a book.

She read slowly, savoring each word and illustration, although she could have recited the story from memory. The resourceful bunny challenges his mother and threatens to run away, but no matter how many identities he plans to assume—a fish, a rock on a mountain, a bird, a sailboat—she insists she will follow, as a fisherman, a mountain climber, and even as the wind. She will catch him in her arms, hug him, and bring him home. Did he hope to hear anything else? Of course he will stay and be her little bunny. Jeanne closed the book and clasped it to her heart.

This box could not have been packed by the brainy, laconic woman who'd raised her. It shouldn't even exist. Mother's mouth might as well have been taped for her habitual reticence, yet she must have required a physical space, a repository for her keepsakes. She needed to know they existed in a place outside her memory, even if that was the attic's deepest shadows, where her daughter feared imaginary bats.

She had to have known the adult Jeanne would not be deterred by tape and cardboard. She had meant for Jeanne to know but not until now, not until Jeanne had stayed her little bunny, grown up, become successful, and remained childless.

Jeanne felt the heat of her rage rising in her chest before it exploded. She hurled the book across the room. Bricklin jumped to his feet, eyes wide with alarm. "She lied, Bricklin! She lied!" As tears burned her eyelids, Jeanne covered her face with her hands. Bricklin tried to nuzzle in behind them, and she threw her arms around his neck. "Why couldn't I have known she'd loved bringing up a child? Was my success so important to her, was she that selfish, she couldn't risk my becoming merely a mother?" Bricklin pushed in closer to Jeanne, offering what comfort he could, but it wasn't enough.

CHAPTER 5

Bricklin trembled at Jeanne's feet as they waited for the vet to come into the examining room. She stroked his head, patted his side, and assured him everything would be fine, and they'd soon be on their way. Bricklin, she knew, wasn't buying it. He'd spent enough time at the Wayland VetStop to know his visit would be longer than a stop. If he could have protested the false marketing, he would have.

These appointments were never like pulling up at a 7-Eleven to grab a quart of milk. Even when the vet tech took him in the back for a quick vaccination, something untoward happened, like having his blood drawn or his nails clipped. He always returned to Jeanne with reproachful eyes.

At that moment, her concern was more his worsening limp than his anxiety. Dr. Chu, a lean, round-shouldered man in scrubs and a white coat, opened the door and removed the medical chart from its plastic sleeve. When he crouched and reached out to Bricklin, the dog went to him with a tucked-under tail that twitched at its end, as though, under the right circumstances, it might wag. "What did you do to your leg, Bricklin?"

The vet's deft fingers worked themselves into Bricklin's fur and traveled the length of his leg and through his shoulder region. His frown alarmed Jeanne, who asked if the shoulder was dislocated. "It just happened this weekend, but maybe I should have had him seen sooner at an emergency facility. I'm sorry."

"Don't apologize. Screening symptoms is tricky. I'm going to sedate Bricklin and X-ray his shoulder. You can sit in the waiting room till I come get you." He picked up Bricklin's leash and led him through the rear door of the examining room. Bricklin looked over his shoulder at Jeanne as he limped dutifully at the vet's heel.

Since there were several vets in Dr. Chu's practice, the waiting room was packed. Jeanne squeezed in between a woman whose enormous cat was too big for its carrier and a teenaged boy whose Jack Russell terrier paced nervously at the end of his leash. Mounted in front of her was a rack of pamphlets on health issues, sure to push an anxious owner over the edge: fleas and ticks, obesity, diabetes, heartworm, periodontal disease . . . She looked up at the wall clock instead. Its second hand annoyed her with its metronome-like jerks, exacerbating her own jumpiness. Why couldn't it sweep the clock smoothly? She pulled out her phone and began perusing emails, but concentrating was difficult.

After both the king-sized cat and the Jack Russell had departed, Dr. Chu emerged from the back and asked Jeanne to join him in one of the examining rooms. "I'm afraid I don't have good news for you, Ms. Bridgeton. Bricklin has what appears to be an aggressive tumor in his shoulder."

"Cancer?"

"Usually this kind of tumor originates in the lung, which we X-rayed as well. There's no sign of a growth there, but sometimes a spot can be too small to detect."

"What next? Surgery? Chemo? Radiation?"

"Unfortunately, the tumor has done considerable damage to the joint. We need to do a biopsy to determine what type of cancer we're dealing with. Amputation is one alternative, although Bricklin is a larger breed than optimal for managing on three legs. Ms. Bridgeton . . ." His voice softened. "Your dog is ten years old. It may not be wise to put him through that." Jeanne slumped in her seat. "Since he's still feeling the effects of the sedation, I'd like to keep him overnight. You can call me tomorrow morning."

Jeanne was overwhelmed with a sense of helplessness. After starting the ignition, she sat with her hands pressed against the steering wheel. Harder and harder she pushed until her arms were straight out in front of her and her back pushed deep into the leather seat. "*No, no, please no.*" She banged the back of her head against the headrest as she beseeched unknown gods. A courtesy beep startled her. A van had pulled close, awaiting her space. Embarrassed, Jeanne nodded and pulled out.

Owners had a responsibility to make difficult end-of-life decisions for their pets, but was she a hypocrite if she refused to put Bricklin down? She had all the data, thanks to Dr. Chu, but he didn't know Bricklin the way she did. Her dog had so much spirit, she was certain he could fight his way back from an amputation.

She remembered Maggie at Dawning Day telling her the staff tried to give the residents pleasant days. Couldn't Jeanne ensure Bricklin had good quality of life? Would that be shirking her responsibility? For a moment, the thought of his attempting to walk with only three legs roiled her stomach. She tried instead to imagine what Bricklin would want if she could ask him. He would sit in front of her, put his paw in her lap, and look up at her with eyes filled with trust. Maybe she was being selfish, but he had to go on living. Her baby would live, and so would Bricklin.

By the time Jeanne arrived at work, she was calm. She hadn't arranged a meeting with Jake, but they needed to catch up. She found him intent on his monitor and was relieved to see his relaxed posture. He seemed fully recovered from the crash. When he saw her, he flashed a broad smile. "Just thinking about you. Have you seen your email?" She shook her head. "Bart's been brainstorming for the sales kickoff. He wants a live bugler playing call to colors, and he plans to have the regional managers dressed as drill sergeants."

Rising from his chair, he unfolded his tall, lean physique. He gestured toward his conference table, but before joining him there, Jeanne closed the door behind her. "Seriously," she said. "Are you sure you're comfortable with this military theme of Bart's? I still have some issues I've shared with him. You of all people . . . it doesn't offend you?"

"Don't worry, Jeanne. I'll make sure he keeps it light and uses only the positive messages—discipline, persistence—that kind of thing. And where else can I be a general? It's a big jump in rank."

Behind Jake's desk hung a painting of a soccer game. Jeanne had heard he'd been an All-American in college. On the side wall, over his bookcase, he'd displayed framed advertisements for Salientific. She nodded toward the pictures. "I'll start working on recruiting posters to replace those. 'Wanted: a few good men and women.' We can use Bart as a model Marine."

Jake laughed. "Bart's not a model anything, but he sure knows how to close business."

Jake looked at her expectantly, ready for her next agenda item. What to say? She rubbed her forefinger over a smudge on the table till it was eradicated and took a deep breath. "Do you mind if we discuss something else first, a personal issue? What I need to tell you is—this is going to be kind of a curveball—I'm pregnant." Jake's blue eyes widened, stared. When he finally spoke, Jeanne sensed what was coming. She couldn't risk his asking about the night they'd spent together. She rushed to add, "I'm not leaving the company."

"I'm not questioning your commitment, Jeanne. I'm just surprised. Never thought motherhood was on your radar."

"It wasn't." She hesitated. How much to tell? "It's hard to explain, but I've had a change of heart."

"Jeanne, you don't owe anyone an explanation for why you want a child."

"I know I don't *owe*, but people gossip. I'd rather put it out there and be done with it. I was thinking maybe at this afternoon's staff meeting, if that's okay with you."

"Whatever works for you."

"I'm at an age . . . well, frankly, this was my last chance, so I decided to use a sperm donor." The lie was easier to tell than she expected. Vince would be furious, though. They hadn't settled the issue of a cover story. Letting him claim the baby as his own, moving in together—how could she do that if she didn't know whose . . . ? Though Jake's eyes probed hers, she couldn't hold his gaze. He suspected.

"Becoming a single mother will be challenging," she rushed to add, "but I've always embraced challenge." Yes, these were words she was comfortable with, the language of business: challenge, opportunity, strategic change. Maggie's face flashed before her. If she knew Jeanne thought of motherhood as strategic change . . .

"I'm sure you'll do fine. I loved having kids, although my son and daughter now live with my ex-wife. We divorced not long after I returned from Afghanistan. Cause and effect, I'm afraid. Some experiences, some memories . . ." He shook his head. "They can be more vivid than the present."

She swallowed hard and pulled her sweater tighter around her as though that might ward off any memories he was considering sharing or somehow protect her baby from them. "I'll . . . uh . . . touch base with Alberta about maternity leave and the like." She felt guilty for avoiding the subject of his service. What right did she have to avoid the horrors of a war for which they all bore responsibility?

Jake seemed deflated. She looked at the soccer painting behind him. He'd probably considered the game fiercely competitive in his youth, but compared with fighting to the death in Afghanistan . . . How that must have dwarfed everything in his life that had gone before. No wonder he was divorced.

As Jeanne stepped into the hallway, a distant siren drew closer. She winced as the driver delivered a powerful horn blast at the intersection. The siren wailed first on one side of their building, then the other. Whether the emergency vehicle was an ambulance or fire truck, it was headed elsewhere in the office park.

An ominous thump behind her made her turn. Jake was neither in his chair nor at his conference table. She re-entered and closed the door. Walking behind his desk, she found him crouching, pale as paper and shaking. He clambered out, collapsed into his chair, and covered his face with his hands.

"You have post-traumatic stress disorder, don't you?"

"I hate that term." He jumped up. "*Disorder*—a euphemism for the aftermath of experiencing the terrors of hell." He walked to the window, where he looked out between the slats of his vertical blinds and then parted them, resting his hands against the metal window frame. "I thought I was past it." He turned to her. "The crash—that car coming at me through the window . . . They're back, the flashbacks and tremors."

"Jake, you don't have to—"

"I want you to know what happened." He took a deep breath. "I had worked with and trusted a Taliban translator. Turned out to be a suicide bomber. His truck was coming right at us without slowing, so one of my men started shooting. The spray of bullets penetrated his windshield, and wounded, he looked straight at me. At the last moment, he turned his wheel. Probably thought he was doing me a favor, sparing me, but I lost half a dozen men—boys." His voice broke. "One kept calling for his mother." At that, Jake's tears began again. "The injuries . . ." He pounded his forehead with his palms. "I should have died."

"Oh my God, Jake." Jeanne felt hollowed out. There were no words of consolation equal to the task. Calling his reaction survivor's guilt would be minimizing it with a label, as she'd done with PTSD. Jake sank into his chair, so she moved closer and rubbed his arm. "I have no standing here, but look at the value you've created since then for everyone around you, the technology, the company." Even as she spoke, the words sounded like self-help pabulum.

What was business compared to war? Yet war was business, often motivated by economic desires parading as causes. The country fought for a future its soldiers might never see. They could live only in the present, moment to moment, and when they were finished fighting, their future became hostage to their past.

"I shouldn't have put this weight on you, especially now when you should feel . . ." He struggled for the right words, his language processor making a clumsy switch from the vocabulary of war to that of greeting cards. "Joyful anticipation." He forced a smile. "I'm fine, Jeanne, really fine. I beat this thing before. The lobby crash was a blip on the radar."

He didn't look fine with his flushed face and red eyes, and Jeanne was reluctant to leave him, but he stood, signaling she was to go. She closed his door behind her and saw Parker coming down the hall. "Jake on the phone?" he asked.

"A personal call and, from the sound of it, he's going to be a while. I'd come back in half an hour."

"Shit." He turned on his heel.

As much as Jeanne yearned to talk with someone about Jake's condition, she had few options. Parker was watching Jake for missteps. Alberta had the HR experience, but not the judgment or maturity. Vince was on the board, so informing him of Jake's instability could jeopardize Jake's position as CEO. Bart was . . . well, Bart. Perhaps Lou, if she could catch him after the staff meeting. Jeanne walked toward HR, half hoping Alberta's office would be empty. She tried to put Jake out of her mind and focus on spinning the news of her pregnancy. If she could think of it as just another press release . . .

Alberta's eyes lit up when Jeanne told her she was pregnant. "Have to say, I'm a little envious. Waiting around for that special someone really sucks, if you know what I mean." Jeanne read this as a reference to Bart. Alberta must actually believe Bart was going to divorce his wife and marry her. "I respect you for going it alone, Jeanne." As little regard as Jeanne had for her, she couldn't help but feel pity. Love may be blind, but Alberta's love had eclipsed all five senses.

Alberta had a face that was, at best, pleasant looking. Her pasty complexion was not improved by the foundation she slathered on, nor were her eyes enhanced by the heavy black eyeliner that turned upward to create the effect of cats' eyes. What she did have was long blond hair and the kind of curves no man could ignore, and Bart was not one to admire from afar.

Jeanne was eager to change the subject from Alberta's allusion to "going it alone." Although she had checked the web for local sperm banks in case anyone probed her lie, her technical knowledge of the artificial insemination process was at the turkey-baster level. "About maternity leave—I'm due April eighteenth and expect to work right up to the end."

Alberta swiveled around in her chair and opened a file drawer in the cabinet behind her. She pulled out a folder and opened it to show Jeanne the necessary forms to fill out. "I can email copies to you if you'd prefer, and you can fill them out online." Jeanne thanked her as she stood up.

Bart would undoubtedly hear the news from his indiscreet paramour, but at the staff meeting, he'd feign surprise. One advantage of Jeanne's sperm donor tale was that Parker would think her relationship with Vince had ended. Perhaps that would stop his requests to leverage her connection to BTF Venture Capital in the service of his mutiny against Jake.

As two o'clock approached, Jeanne felt anxiety roiling her stomach like a piece of bad shellfish. Jake's revelation had upset her homeostasis, and announcing her pregnancy was hardly the usual update from marketing. Teasing would likely come her way along with the congratulations. At least that would ensure a convivial staff meeting and take some pressure off Jake.

She was the first to arrive in the conference room. She helped herself to a cup of decaf from the thermal carafe on the side table. Jake and Lou showed up at the door together, but Jake allowed Lou to precede him into the room. Lou took up the entire doorway. Jeanne imagined how daunting it must have been for opponents to face him on the college football field.

For years, Lou had tackled nothing beefier than a Big Mac and an engineering schedule, but woe to anyone impeding his project plan. When his engineers fell behind, he'd threaten the laggards with a trip to the hood where his homies were waiting to teach them a lesson about commitment. Never mind that Lou had grown up in affluent Lexington and studied at MIT. If he had homies, they weren't hanging around the streets.

Jake took his seat and slammed his notebook down on the polished walnut table. "Goddamn crash—*Globe* reporter won't quit calling me for a follow-up." A deep crease formed between his sandy brows. Jeanne berated herself. She should have insisted he go home earlier, when his instability was obvious. Jake peered into each face in turn and gripped the edge of the table. "Louis," he barked, "let's talk about product development. What's the latest on Version Two? Will it go into testing first quarter?" The late afternoon sun filtering through the blinds made Jake look as though he were wearing war paint. He walked to the window and jerked the blinds shut.

Lou leaned in to rest his powerful forearms on the oak table. "There's a piece of functionality we're having trouble with. I'd hoped this wouldn't happen, but I did warn you. The schedule's going to slip. It's unavoidable."

When Lou said something was unavoidable, Jeanne believed him. She squirmed with discomfort as Jake exposed his weakness. Though a technological visionary, Jake was out of touch with the engineering effort required to produce a piece of software. His idea of long-term planning was flossing. Lou had been the perfect hire to turn Jake's ideas into products, and until this moment, Jake had accepted Lou's recommendations.

"Maybe we should talk about recalibrating our product intro plans," Jeanne offered.

Jake smacked his cell phone on the table. "No! I'm not changing anything I've told our investors. This whole cybersecurity market is going to go the way of buggy whips if we don't get Version Two on the street."

Alberta's hands were clasped in her own lap. She was a model of good posture, and Bart's face lacked its customary smirk. While Jake and Lou continued their testy debate, the rest of the team remained mute. Parker rolled back from the table and stretched out in his seat, content to observe Jake's implosion. She bit her lip, wishing she could make him stop. A slip in the schedule was regrettable, but they were doing fine. Only three months ago they'd been celebrating the company's performance.

Lou made the necessary commitments to wrap up their discussion, but Jeanne suspected his objective was simply to defuse Jake's anger. Lou turned to Bart. "Don't worry about your sales meeting. Everything will be on schedule by then. Last thing my team needs is a bunch of suits storming engineering."

Bart laughed. "I want my guys psyched up for a fight but not an internal one."

Jeanne gave Bart credit for breaking the tension, although in the past he had waged war, and surely would again, against other departments. Jake looked as though he had just awakened and found himself in the conference room. He smiled and looked over at her. "Jeanne, want to share your news?"

"Um . . . telling you all together seemed like a good idea. . . ." She looked around the table. "Efficient use of time and all that, but now I'm not so sure." Alberta glanced at Bart, who ignored her. "I'm pregnant." Jeanne went on to deliver her sperm donor story, taking note of Lou's wide-eyed reaction and Parker's single raised eyebrow. She didn't owe them an explanation but thought it best to head off speculation on the father. "So, the next time you come to my office, you'll see a new project on the marketing whiteboard with a due date of April eighteenth."

Talking about her personal life this way was just too weird. She eyed the door with longing, but Jake had several more agenda items to cover. When he finished, she bolted.

Parker was close behind Jeanne as she headed for marketing, but he was not, as she feared, pursuing her with questions. His purposeful gait had some other objective, one she suspected would be of no help to Jake.

When Jeanne arrived at Birch Brook, she swung by the bank of mailboxes and collected a heavier batch than usual. "Junk," she grumbled. "More food for the recycling bin." Opening the kitchen door from the garage, Jeanne half expected to see her tail-wagging official greeter. No human would show such excitement at her return or welcome her with an offering, which, in Bricklin's case, was a squeaky dog toy.

After tossing the mail on her kitchen table, she hung up her coat and collapsed on the couch. It really wasn't fair. She'd decided to have a baby, and her reward was yet another life-and-death choice. She stared at the empty window, sill feeling hollowed out. No matter what she did, Bricklin would never jump onto it again.

Her limbs felt heavy, but she forced herself to return to her kitchen table. Starting with the letter on top of the pile, a credit card offer, she dealt unopened envelopes into a trash pile. Her mother's mail had diminished in volume but continued to arrive. Never mind that Jeanne had closed all her mother's accounts, even the dead were credit worthy.

An envelope from the estate lawyer for Fay Bridgeton stood out by the quality of the ivory paper even before Jean saw the return address. Another copy of documents, she thought, setting it aside while sorting the rest of the mail. *Cybersecurity News* and a couple of other industry magazines joined a pile of periodicals Jeanne had neither the desire nor focus to read.

She looked at her watch. No call from Vince, who was probably still pissed at her. Cooking was unappealing, given how she was feeling, so she opened a can of chicken noodle soup and ladled some into a bowl. If only she liked to cook as much as she liked to eat. After surrendering the bowl to the capable ministrations of her microwave, Jeanne slit open her attorney's envelope.

The lawyer apologized for his belated discovery that Jeanne's mother had rented an additional safe deposit box to the one Jeanne knew about at Sovereign Bank. It was at the Bank of America and had only come to light recently. He would provide Jeanne with the contents as soon as he had filed the necessary paperwork and could gain entry to the box. Jeanne shook her head. No one could beat Fay Bridgeton at locking away the past. The microwave signaled the end of its heating and beeped several more times before Jeanne rose from her chair and rescued the soup.

CHAPTER 6

Dr. Chu's office opened at eight, and Jeanne made sure she was the first phone call of the day. When she told the vet she was going to take her chances with the amputation, there was silence at the other end. She was afraid he would challenge her decision, but instead he offered to try to set up an appointment for that day at Angell Memorial Animal Hospital. Jeanne could have the necessary prep work done and get Bricklin's surgery on the calendar.

Between the lengthy visit to Angell Memorial and an update to Scott, the dog walker, Jeanne didn't get to her office till afternoon. With Bricklin's surgery scheduled for the following Monday, she needed to change a few appointments, but instead of sending out emails, she became distracted by pop-up messages, not on her screen, but in her mind. How could she be doing this to Bricklin? How could she not? What were the odds she'd regret her decision, a decision Bricklin would be the one to live with?

She was surprised to see Vince's name on her caller ID, the ring interrupting her self-torment. She wanted to ask if he was still annoyed with her, but the anguish caused by Bricklin's illness spilled out instead, along with her feelings about the best of bad alternatives she'd chosen. "Aren't you the person who doesn't believe in second-guessing yourself?" he asked.

"That was before I was faced with such a complicated decision. How many variables does it take before an equation becomes unsolvable?"

"In cases where there are too many unknowns, I recommend taking the complaint up with the big guy in the sky."

That would be helpful, Jeanne thought, if she were a believer. "At least I'll know where to call if I decide to lodge a complaint with customer service." She wondered if Vince would be offended if she told him she didn't think humans were created in the image of God or that human life was any more sacred than other forms of life. In fact, she believed dogs were the most highly evolved creatures on the planet. Humans, she was sure, were over-evolved and destined to kill themselves off along with the rest of the animate world.

If Mariana Hidalgo hadn't cleared her throat, Jeanne wouldn't have noticed her in the doorway. Not that Mariana was easy to miss, her red hair and green sweater dress a veritable traffic signal, but Jeanne's phone was still in hand and her thoughts on Bricklin. "Do you have a moment, Jeanne?" Mariana was a favorite of Jeanne's for her sense of humor and organizational skills, both of which were required for a marketing events manager, the former for working with the sales organization, the latter for planning trade show participation. "I met with Bart this morning on the sales conference."

Jeanne responded with mock seriousness as she gestured toward her table and chairs. "Don't tell me you're not a fan of his military theme?"

Mariana set her folder on the table and aligned the bottom with the edge of the surface. "Umm—not so much. I don't know if you've heard the details, but Bart wants to open the meeting dressed in combat fatigues with martial music playing."

"Oh, I can just imagine."

"He'll explain the theme to his reps—the way it ties in with our approach to the sales process in the coming fiscal year, kind of a take-no-prisoners approach." Jeanne nodded. "He wants Jake to go next and tell the sales reps how the whole company is ready to support them as they march into combat." Mariana paused and seesawed her pen on her pad. "Am I the only one who thinks it's a little creepy to have Jake wearing his real combat fatigues from Afghanistan?"

"Jake told me he was okay with the theme, but I thought he was supposed to dress up like a general."

Mariana shook her head. "Not enough of a battlefield quality. Bart wants everyone to feel we're in this together." She squirmed in her seat. "You too."

Jeanne leaned back and hooted. "Maternity camouflage?"

"I wanted to congratulate you straight off, but I wasn't sure if we were all supposed to know yet."

"Oh, I'm guessing the whole company knows by now."

"Word spread fast, because everyone was so surprised. . . ." Mariana's hands began to flutter. "I'm sorry. I didn't mean it to come out that way."

A wry smile stretched one corner of Jeanne's mouth. "No worries. I know what you meant." Jeanne was okay with the idea she was no one's image of a glowing young mother-to-be, but an uncomfortable feeling in her stomach testified to her concern she might be the butt of humor—not the teasing that comes with a big belly, but behind-her-back ridicule. Too late now.

Mariana grasped her folder. "I can email you when the rest of the agenda is worked out, and I know Bart wants to talk to you about what he'd like you to stress in your presentation. There's one problem I need your help with, though. I asked Jake if I could meet with him, because Bart needs him more than once during the event. When I got to his office and started talking about supporting the troops, he turned toward the window. I thought he was listening, but then . . . it was creepy . . . he seemed to forget I was there. I didn't know what to do, so I just left." She pushed the folder over to Jeanne. "Can you talk to him about his role? These are my notes."

"Probably a momentary lapse, given all that's on his mind. I'll handle it." Mariana thanked her and made a speedy exit. Jeanne leaned back in her chair and groaned. "Jake," she whispered to herself, "help me out here." She opened the folder, skimmed its contents, and emailed Jake to set up a meeting. Good thing Bart was on the road, where Jeanne couldn't get her hands around his neck. Let's see how he likes it when his VP of marketing presents to the sales force with her belly bulging under a camouflage pup tent.

When Jeanne took off her coat at Weight Watchers, Maggie giggled. "What?" Jeanne asked.

"You're showing." She pointed to Jeanne's stomach. "And early."

Jeanne looked down. "It's just a bump, don't you think? Probably a good thing I told people at work."

"And you're just getting around to telling me?" Jeanne's face fell. "It's okay. I'm just happy you've decided to have it. After I heard your executive summary, I wasn't so sure." She leaned over and enveloped Jeanne in a hug. "I suppose Vince knows your decision."

"He's thrilled, but there's a complication." Maggie's eyebrows rose. Lucy began setting up her flip charts on the easel, and the room grew quiet. "Subject for another conversation," Jeanne whispered.

When the meeting was over, Jeanne weighed in—up two pounds. She groaned. "So, it begins."

"I don't want to hear it," Maggie protested as she walked Jeanne to her car. "This weight gain is legit. Want to borrow some scrubs to wear to work?"

"I am going to need maternity clothes, although I don't know when I'm going to find the time to shop. Can't close the buttons on my pants."

"Want some help? Shopping, that is, not closing buttons. I don't have to work a week from this Saturday. If you can pull yourself away from your computer, I'll go with you."

"Really? Why would you want—I mean, are you sure that's how you want to spend your Saturday afternoon?"

"It'll be fun, and that's the only way I'm going to hear about your *complication*. We can meet for lunch first. Make a list as best you can, and we'll figure out the rest at the store."

The next morning Jeanne called Dr. O'Rourke's office and begged his receptionist to get him to the phone. When he came on the line, Jeanne could hear the concern in his voice. "Is something wrong? Any staining?"

"I'm fine. Sorry to drag you away from your patients, but I didn't want to leave this in a message. I've decided to have the baby." After he congratulated her, she asked whom she should see at Newford Wellman for genetic counseling. He told her what to do and transferred her back to his assistant. Jeanne felt good, more like herself, being decisive. She'd already committed herself publicly, but there was something official about telling her doctor. Her heart was racing, but whether it was from excitement or fear, she hadn't a clue.

When the lawyer's manila envelope arrived, Jeanne opened it eagerly. She told herself the contents were most likely pedestrian—birth certificates, insurance policies, paid-off mortgage contracts. The first document she saw was a death certificate for Thomas Bridgeton. The date was February 28, 1965, and the cause of death was head trauma—no surprise there. Jeanne's mother had told her he'd died in an auto accident when he was fifty-one. Theirs had been a late-life romance by the standards of the day, and Jeanne was born when her father was forty-nine and ten years older than her mother.

She flipped over the certificate and laid it face down. The next page was a letter to Fay Bridgeton from a neurologist, Dr. Amos Kingman. Jeanne read it twice, the second time with hands turned cold and clammy. One passage leaped out:

Although I don't have the means to be certain, I believe your husband suffers from Alzheimer's disease. He is unusually young for such pronounced memory loss; however, cases like his do exist. They tend to be concentrated within certain families, many of whose members present with symptoms of the disease at an early age. The implication is that these early-onset cases have a hereditary component. You should take this into consideration if you are contemplating further pregnancies.

Jeanne shook her head slowly. Mother had told her Thomas Bridgeton was the smartest man she'd ever known. People like that just didn't get Alzheimer's at forty-nine or fifty, the doctor's letter notwithstanding. Scientists didn't know as much in 1965, undoubtedly the reason for what Jeanne was certain was a misdiagnosis.

Slapping the letter face down on the desk gave force to her denial, but there was no un-reading its message. If she accepted its premise, she'd have to accept that his disease was hereditary. The lights in the room seemed to dim as though there had been a brownout. She repeated "hereditary" to herself over and over until it lost its meaning.

A ragged-edged newspaper clipping poked out from the sheaf of unread pages. Her eyes widened as she read the headline, *Disoriented Man Dies on Local Highway.* Thomas Bridgeton, afflicted with Alzheimer's disease, had wandered from his home, where his wife had been distracted by a crying baby. When she realized he was gone, she'd called the police, but it was too late. He had walked up the ramp of the interstate and into the path of a tractor trailer.

"A crying baby." Jeanne was numb. I was the one who distracted Mother, and if I hadn't . . . Jeanne felt her temples beginning to pound. Did her mother blame herself or her infant daughter? Did she look at baby Jeanne and think *if only* . . . ? Maybe she was glad her husband was gone and felt guilty. Maybe, maybe . . .

Clipped to the article was a longer one, a feature story, sympathetic in tone. Fay Bridgeton, frazzled and exhausted, was caught between two dependents. Her husband suffered from Alzheimer's disease, and his needs were endless, his requests repetitive. A wailing baby kept her from giving him timely assistance.

Jeanne wanted to share the writer's empathy. The story was horrifying, revelatory. She wished her mother had ignored baby Jeanne's wails and saved her father instead. She was furious at her mother for letting her father wander off, yet at the same time, she was ashamed of herself for being furious.

If only that moment in time could be undone. If only Jeanne had stopped crying long enough for her mother to hear the door close. If only her father had wandered in a different direction. Jeanne blinked back tears. She tried to put herself in her mother's place, because Fay Bridgeton had surely felt the frustration of those *if onlys* more acutely than Jeanne decades later.

Jeanne could understand why a guilt-ridden widow would keep from her child the gruesome story of her father's death, but why keep it from her adult daughter? Did Fay Bridgeton, diligent accountant, think she could relegate material information about the past to some obscure bank vault as though she were hiding assets or losses in an offshore subsidiary?

Jeanne grimaced as she pushed away the remaining papers. Her mother was a clever woman. She knew that after her death, the contents of this safe deposit box would be given to Jeanne. She didn't care that her daughter would draw the only conclusion possible—her mother had been too much of a coward to tell her the truth.

~

The next morning, Jeanne was in no mood to shop. As soon as she was dressed, she would call Maggie to cancel. Dressing, however, was problematic, since none of Jeanne's pants would close. Shopping would now be like work—she would have to do it whether she was in the mood or not.

Maggie had chosen the Cheesecake Parlor for lunch because of its diverse menu. In spite of the restaurant's name, it offered healthier choices than cheesecake, and "Let's face it," Maggie had said, "pretty much everything is healthier than cheesecake." Jeanne slid into a leather banquette across from Maggie, who wore a blue fleece top that matched her eyes. "See, I'm not always in scrubs. I couldn't wait to wear these jeans, one size smaller than my last ones."

Jeanne smiled. "I'm happy for you, although I'm headed in the opposite direction. Only thing holding my pants closed is the rubber band stretched between the button and buttonhole."

They perused the limitless menu for several minutes until Maggie sighed and laid hers down. "Virtue is such a burden. I'm having the 'heart healthy' burger." Jeanne didn't feel virtuous and decided on a personal pizza.

The tea Jeanne ordered came right away, and she tipped the diminutive silver teapot and watched the steam rise from her cup and grow diffuse. Although the restaurant was noisy, the background buzz created a welcome illusion of privacy. When Jeanne raised her eyes, she found Maggie looking at her expectantly. "Remember? 'It's complicated,' you told me at Weight Watchers. The *it* has to do with Vince, doesn't it?"

Jeanne's devastating discovery, courtesy of the estate lawyer, had overshadowed her previous concerns, and she'd forgotten her commitment to explain those complications to Maggie. She swished the teabag, debating how to begin. If she gave Maggie an executive summary, she'd be called on it, but it was hard to break the habit of netting things out.

Maggie rested her cheek on her hand and sighed. "Okay, I've got time."

"I'm not certain Vince is the father of my baby." Maggie's eyes appeared as round and blue as the Wedgewood in Fay Bridgeton's hutch. "It's really only a tiny chance." Jeanne related the story of Salientific's summertime party and the champagne headache she and Jake had slept off together.

"Does Jake suspect? Does Vince?"

"Everyone at work thinks I used a sperm donor, although I'm not positive Jake bought it. When Vince finds out I used that as my cover story, if he hasn't already, he'll be furious. I mean, we're not married. I don't understand why he's got this pride of authorship thing going. He wants me to have the baby, because he thinks motherhood would be good for me, or, at least, he doesn't want to be the one to deprive me of it. He doesn't seem ready to embrace fatherhood, though, just the legal and financial obligations."

The food arrived, but Jeanne found she couldn't eat with her usual relish. Maggie chewed thoughtfully. "Will you tell your 'sperm donor,' once you know?"

"What's the upside? I don't know what Vince's reaction will be if he's not the father, but, for sure, he'll be pissed I slept with someone else, especially a guy I report to directly. An angry, disappointed Vince would not only be a problem for me personally but for my career. His firm's the primary investor in Salientific. If I tell Jake he's the father, who knows what he'll do. He's been . . . well . . . not himself lately—a PTSD relapse, I think. If word got out, I'd have to leave the company. The more I think about it, the more I think I don't want to know."

Maggie laid her fork on the table. "Jeanne, are you listening to yourself? Upside, downside, career consequences—do you realize most people don't make decisions that way about their personal lives? We're talking about the implications of paternity for your child, not your career. You know you don't have to wait for your amniocentesis to find out, don't you?"

Nonplussed, Jeanne drew back. "You just don't understand. Maybe it's because you're not part of a corporate hierarchy and don't have a career path in your kind of work." Jeanne covered her mouth with her hand, but Maggie's stricken expression was instantaneous. "I'm sorry. I shouldn't have said that."

Maggie's delicate complexion reddened. "No, Jeanne, you shouldn't have, because you don't know what you're talking about. There are innumerable nursing careers. Do you think I have no aspirations?"

How had she so miscalculated where Maggie was coming from? Jeanne twisted her fingers in her lap. Another friendship was about to slip away. What was wrong with her that she couldn't be a friend? If she cared about Maggie—and she did—why was she so thoughtless? "I'm so sorry. Sometimes, I don't seem to be on the same wavelength as other people. I don't know why."

Maggie didn't let up. "As for the paternity test, you don't have to take it. You can just go on letting Vince think he's the father and never tell him or your child you were too much of a coward to find out."

A coward who never tells her child. How those words stung. Was this the way Jeanne's mother had started? Jeanne would be perpetuating a wrongheaded family custom, aggregating secrets to keep from yet another generation. Ashamed and miserable, she offered to get the check and leave Maggie to finish her lunch in peace.

"Peace is what I get in my empty apartment. What I want is for you to wake up."

Jeanne rubbed her temples with her fingertips. "I'm not sure I can. I'm turning into her." She leaned back in her seat and closed her eyes.

"Turning into whom? Open your eyes, Jeanne, and get a grip."

"My mother. This is just history repeating."

While Jeanne detailed the letter from her father's neurologist, Maggie picked at her burger and nodded encouragement. At Jeanne's retelling of the newspaper stories, Maggie's hand flew to her chest. "What a shock you must have had. How old did you say he was?"

"Only fifty-one—not much older than I am now. Do you see any reason why my mother would keep the story from me as an adult? I mean, yes, it's disturbing, and she probably felt guilty, but I'm telling you, that woman was wired to keep secrets . . . and, apparently, so am I." Jeanne waited for Maggie to chastise her for blaming biology.

"Shouldn't you learn more about Alzheimer's disease? I hear you that your father died in 1965 when less was known, and maybe you're right that he was misdiagnosed, but it would be worthwhile to educate yourself. Maybe you'd understand your mother better too."

Though Jeanne's first instinct was to research Alzheimer's on Google, Maggie had in mind a more interactive setting. A professor from Fenway University School of Medicine was coming to Dawning Day the following Tuesday evening to give a talk on the differences between Alzheimer's and normal aging. The audience would be residents' families and some Dawning Day staff, but Jeanne was welcome.

"If I can escape from work at a reasonable hour Tuesday, I'll be there."

"Jeanne, do me a favor and make it a priority."

Jeanne shifted in her seat. "Ow." Her hand was on her waist, where the rubber band holding her pants closed had snapped.

"You have some big issues to think through, but, unfortunately, your big waistline has become a priority. Let's shop."

When they arrived at MomChic, Maggie suggested checking out jeans and tops first. She gestured toward a rack of casual clothes. Jeanne reached into her bag for the spreadsheet she'd created. "I jotted down a few things—just to ensure we made good use of the time."

"On a spreadsheet?"

"You said to make a list. How else do you keep track of things?"

Maggie rolled her eyes and beckoned a salesperson.

The perky young woman took the list from Jeanne's hands. "This will be quite helpful," she said with a dimpled smile. "Half my job is done."

"Be careful," Maggie warned. "She'll be running the business by the time we leave."

"Then I'll teach her what she needs to know." She held out her hand to Jeanne and Maggie in turn and introduced herself as Sara. "Do you have clothes at home from previous pregnancies?"

"Uh, no, this is my first."

Sara moved on quickly to cover her faux pas. "Great, then you'll need everything. May I suggest a few modifications to your list?" Jeanne nodded, suddenly noticing how much younger the other shoppers appeared. Glancing into a mirror, she peered at her face. There was no denying the lines around her mouth and across her forehead and the shadows under her eyes. Worn, more than old, was how she looked. But wasn't that the same?

Feeling as out of place as the only overripe banana in the bunch, she was happy to let Sara do the browsing for her. "I can't do the T-shirt stretched over the big belly look. I don't have that kind of job."

"I never would have guessed that." Sara winked at Maggie. The next two hours were more pleasant than Jeanne had expected as she modeled for Maggie and Sara tailored slacks with expandable panels and coordinating tops. Maggie started hunting for a few things Jeanne could use just to hang out in.

She handed Jeanne some stretchy jeans and a roomy sweater, then held up a T-shirt that said, "Does this baby make me look fat?"

"Great, I can wear it to Weight Watchers." She shook her head at the royal-blue winter coat Maggie brought to the fitting room, but Sara concurred. Jeanne would never be able to zip up her existing one when the winter blizzards arrived. By the time they got to underwear, Jeanne was too tired to stand and flopped down on an armchair near the register.

She had in no way considered if she was going to nurse her baby and, if so, for how long. Who knew there were so many choices for bras that would double for maternity and nursing?

"You're cooked," Maggie said. "I'll handle getting your stuff rung up." Jeanne wondered how anyone could be so solicitous, especially after Jeanne had insulted her. If this was how Maggie treated her patients, Jeanne was ready to move into Dawning Day.

Bricklin spent Saturday night curled up behind the bed in the upstairs guest bedroom, a place he never went. Sick and dying dogs hide, and it broke Jeanne's heart to find him there. Vince thought a quiet evening at home would help Jeanne cope, so he brought takeout Chinese, including General Tso's Chicken, her favorite. He even remembered to make sure it had no MSG.

Jeanne wondered how her stomach would react to the well-sauced Americanized version of Chinese cooking. "I guess this is when we find out if the baby likes Chinese food," she said, after raising her filled chopsticks to her lips.

"Kids come preprogrammed to like every kind of takeout. It's a modern mutation." After dinner, Vince popped *Ocean's Eleven* into Jeanne's DVD player. She'd never seen it, and he promised it would divert her. They cozied up together on her couch, and when the movie was over, he stretched his arms wide. "Ready to turn in?"

Jeanne sat up. "Can we talk for a minute?" Vince yawned an unidentifiable answer.

"I know I should have brought this up earlier, but the evening was so pleasant, it sort of slipped away. I'm showing a lot for how far along I am in my pregnancy. Water retention, they say." She laid her hand on her stomach.

"I noticed."

"So, I told everyone at work I was pregnant, and I—uh—told them I used a sperm donor. I know when we were in the park, you dismissed my concerns about the career implications of going public with our relationship." Vince jumped up and walked to the window. "I thought about it, really I did."

He ignored her and stood close enough to the window for Jeanne to see the fog his breath made on the glass. A full minute went by before he turned back to her and spoke. "Do we have a relationship? I mean, where do I come in the pecking order—after your pissant job and your aging dog? After the kid is born, are you going to tell him who his father is so long as he promises not to tell anyone in the industry?"

"Honestly, Vince, you're comparing yourself to my dog?"

"I don't know who to compare myself to when you make unilateral decisions that affect both of us, as well as our child. It's not as if we haven't been seen in public together. You think no one knows?" He strode across the living room and yanked his jacket off the banister. "Don't worry. I'll slip out the back door, so nobody sees me."

Jeanne jumped up from the couch. "Vince—" A cold blast swept into the room. The door Vince slammed was ajar, caught on the corner of the doormat. He didn't bother to stop, and she didn't go after him.

CHAPTER 7

A Monday morning nor'easter did nothing to relieve Jeanne's anxiety as she prepared to take Bricklin to Angell Memorial for his amputation. The word alone made her heart hammer like the rain striking her kitchen skylight. Bricklin came in from the yard with his coat soaked, but he was so unsteady that toweling him off was a delicate process. After drying his head and ears, she kissed his forehead. "I'm so sorry, sweet boy. If only there were another way." There was another way, the way Dr. Chu had suggested, but that was even harder to contemplate.

The lobby of Angell Memorial smelled of damp fur and wet boots. Handing Bricklin's leash to the vet tech, Jeanne had an urge to hang on. As the ridged nylon lead slipped from her hand, the young man spoke reassuring words, none of which Jeanne heard. She hurried from the lobby, hanging on to her composure.

Falling apart was not an option when the whole work day stretched before her. She managed to hold it together till she was inside her car, where she wept into her hands till tears ran down the insides of her cuffs.

By afternoon, the temperature had dropped enough for freezing rain to glaze the roads. Jeanne observed the gloomy scene from her office and ignored the calls that came to her cell until she saw Angell Memorial on her caller ID. She picked up before the first ring finished. "Bricklin came through the surgery just fine," said the impossibly young-sounding vet. "We removed the leg and entire shoulder joint to be sure we got the whole tumor. The margins were clean." Bricklin was still recovering from the anesthesia, but Jeanne could call the next day to see how he was doing. Bricklin—with no leg and shoulder—she closed her eyes to make the picture go away.

Tuesday morning, Jeanne emailed Maggie to confirm the time of the Alzheimer's presentation at Dawning Day. She still believed her father had been misdiagnosed, but even if that were true, her reading on the Internet was hardly comforting. If her father's dementia had a different cause, most of the alternative conditions would have been—and still were—as untreatable as Alzheimer's. She Googled the neurologist who had signed the letter to her mother, but all she found was his obituary.

Bart had set up a ten o'clock meeting with her to review plans for the sales conference. Jeanne wanted to include Mariana, but Bart said they didn't need her yet, and Jeanne found out why when Bart closed the door of his office. She had only to hear the words "Parker and I" to know the rest of Bart's sentence would disturb her. The words "had a drink together last night and talked about Jake" confirmed her intuition. "You know Parker wants to go to the board, don't you?"

"Yes," she replied, "and I've already told him I don't agree. I imagine he told you that, so why are we having this conversation?"

Bart leaned back and swiveled his chair from side to side. "I thought my persuasive charms might get you to change your mind. We sales types are optimists." He smiled, confident she would appreciate his attempt at humor.

"I'm not as easily mollified as Alberta, you know."

"Ouch! You have nails for breakfast? You can't honestly think Jake isn't in over his head, can you?" Jeanne was silent. "I have the best handle of anyone on the revenue we're likely to bring in over the next couple of years, and the good news is Jake would have to manage a growing operation. The bad is he's already maxed out. At least that's what Parker and I think."

"What happened to your enthusiasm for having our inspiring leader pump up your sales troops at the kickoff?"

Bart cracked his knuckles before replying. "We talk to the board now but keep Jake long enough to do his military thing. Parker hasn't met with Lou yet, but I'm sure he'll go along. You saw how Jake reamed him at the last staff meeting. Don't be the holdout, Jeanne. You don't want to be the one who spoils this for everyone else."

Jeanne felt her cheeks flush. "Is that a not-so-veiled threat?"

He put up both hands. "I wouldn't think of threatening you. I know how much Salientific means to you, but if you want the company to have a future, you'll do the right thing." Bart's manipulative appeal to her company loyalty was as irritating as Parker's had been. They were sharing the same playbook. There was no escaping the fact, though, that "the right thing" for Salientific might well be replacing Jake. She left Bart's office without committing to anything and resolved to speak with Lou as soon as possible.

That evening, she arrived at Dawning Day preoccupied with work and regretful she'd agreed to attend. Maggie didn't seem her cheerful self either, but she came out to meet Jeanne and showed her eagerly into the dining room, where the speaker was focusing a slide projected from his laptop onto a screen. He had wiry gray hair and a trim gray beard and mustache. Jeanne judged him to be close to seventy.

Several tables were already occupied by Dawning Day staff, and Jeanne guessed, from the jackets draped on the backs of chairs, the remaining attendees were residents' family members. Maggie ushered Jeanne up to the front of the room and introduced her to Lucas Menton. "I'm looking forward to your talk, Professor Menton."

"'Luke' is fine." He shook Jeanne's extended hand.

"Jeanne is the friend I mentioned to you," Maggie said, "the one with family history." She and Luke exchanged looks. Jeanne was puzzled, but there was no time to ask Maggie why she'd told Luke about her ahead of time. He withdrew a business card from his pocket and offered it to Jeanne, urging her to follow up with him if she had questions.

Luke was an excellent presenter, and Jeanne's standards for speakers were high. He made complex concepts understandable yet didn't talk down to his audience, most of whom had firsthand, if not scientific, knowledge about Alzheimer's.

Jeanne was surprised to learn that everything she thought she knew about Alzheimer's was wrong. Just because aging was a significant risk factor didn't mean Alzheimer's was normal. It was a disease, one that afflicted 44 percent of the population between seventy-five and eighty-four years of age. The ramp started earlier than she had realized too, because between sixty-five and seventy-four, about 16 percent had Alzheimer's. With fifty in Jeanne's line of sight, sixty seemed perilously close.

When Luke put up a slide listing Alzheimer's symptoms, many in the audience nodded and murmured their concurrence. Not just a cause of memory loss, the disease led to cognitive problems and could induce personality changes like hostility, depression, and paranoia.

He took pains to distinguish the changes of normal aging from dementia, the set of symptoms that usually signaled the presence of Alzheimer's. Many of the residents' family members around Jeanne sat forward in their seats so as not to miss a single word. Worried, she thought. They're afraid they're going to get it themselves. Will they? And if they will, could I be vulnerable?

Luke seemed to read her thoughts. She felt as though he were looking at her alone when he segued into known risk factors and their relative influence. Scientists had identified some of the predisposing genes, but those genes could tell one nothing for certain. Genes that actually predetermined, rather than predisposed, though rare, were sure-fire predictors of early-onset Alzheimer's, at forty, fifty, or sixty years of age. As horrifying as it was to consider, some victims were in their thirties. "Remember," Luke continued, "early-onset cases make up a very small percentage of the total. When the disease is caused by a predetermining gene, it will usually occur throughout a family."

Jeanne froze in her seat. If Thomas Bridgeton had Alzheimer's, he might have had the early-onset familial kind. He'd died at fifty-one. She told herself it couldn't happen to her. She was sharp—at the top of her game. Was it possible intellect didn't matter? Jeanne's mind raced forward in time. Alzheimer's meant no career. Forget becoming CEO of a startup, capitalizing on all her experience. Experience lived in memory, and without memory . . . Who would care for her child if she developed Alzheimer's? *What if her baby had already inherited the gene from her?*

The audience was applauding. "Are you okay?" Maggie asked. "You're pale. Don't you have questions?"

Jeanne wondered if Maggie's thoughts tracked her own. No, Maggie was way ahead of her. "You knew, didn't you?" Jeanne whispered. "About the chance I had one of the genes?"

"I'm no geneticist, just a worrier. I get paid to worry and anticipate."

A rueful smile flickered across Jeanne's face. "Yeah, me too, in a different way—whole lot it did for me."

Maggie pointed at the many hands in the air. "Luke will be leaving soon. You might want to jump in."

Jeanne looked around. So many people in their fifties and sixties with parents, she guessed, in their eighties. Suddenly she felt young, too young to ask questions about early-onset Alzheimer's without everyone knowing she was asking for herself. Couldn't they all see her pregnant belly under her forty-eight-year-old face? "I wouldn't know where to start—better to follow up with Luke offline."

She pulled on her coat and gave Maggie a hug and a whispered thank-you. As she passed through the lobby, she avoided looking at the door to the Alzheimer's wing. Living on the other side of it was unthinkable.

Walking across the parking lot, Jeanne groped for her phone. Once seated behind the wheel, she flipped on the overhead light and pulled out Luke's business card. His email address was listed, so her thumbs flew across the surface as she requested an appointment. It seemed a puny gesture against an incurable disease. Her mother hadn't settled for puny gestures. She'd made a career of preventing Jeanne from conceiving a child.

Bricklin was ready to leave Angell Memorial. Jeanne was ecstatic, or so she thought, until she approached the glass entrance doors, when her stomach did a flip-flop. She took a deep breath to steady herself and prepare—for what? The scary part was not knowing exactly what to expect or how much help she might need with Bricklin. She hated depending on anyone, but she would have felt better if Vince were with her. Vince's allegation that she cared less about him than Bricklin had precluded her calling.

The hospital lobby smelled antiseptic with none of the wet

dog smell of her previous visit. The desk clerk handed Jeanne the discharge instructions and pointed her toward the cashier's office. The charges were substantial, and Jeanne wondered how many people could afford to make the choice she had.

She tried not to think about Dr. Chu's advice to euthanize Bricklin. He hadn't used the word, but his meaning was clear. Jeanne's analytical skills usually insulated her against ambivalence about decisions, but she'd begun to doubt herself, and doubt spawned doubt.

The waiting room was packed with ailing pets and their owners, but the day she'd brought Bricklin in for his surgery, she'd paid little attention to them. Scanning the room, she was struck by the knit brows and drawn faces. She couldn't remember such collective angst in any human doctor's waiting area.

They're our children. She wondered if her attitude toward Bricklin would change after her baby was born. Were faces in pediatricians' waiting rooms as full of consternation? No, the comparable setting would be a children's hospital, where kids were being diagnosed with cancer. So much could happen to a child. A world of worry she'd never considered would soon be hers.

"Ms. Bridgeton?" Jeanne didn't see his face, only his heavy thighs struggling past each other as he walked, because her eyes were fixed at the level of Bricklin's. She gulped before answering. Sensing everyone's eyes on her, she went to him. "Let me help you out," the vet tech said, giving her no time to embrace Bricklin or even assimilate his altered appearance. Bricklin's head and chest rose and fell with each three-legged step. "Don't worry. He'll get used to it. He's weak and dealing with some strange sensations besides."

"Pain in a phantom limb? Dogs have that?" She didn't want to tell the vet tech she felt dizzy. When they reached her car, she leaned one hand against the cold metal before opening the back door.

"Easy boy." Bricklin eyed the seat, but the young man didn't give him time to put his single front paw up. He hefted the dog into the car, and Bricklin lay down, exhausted from the short walk. "You have someone to help you at the other end? Don't want him to tear his sutures."

"I'll take care of it," she replied, wondering how she would. After closing the door, she thanked the vet tech and settled into the driver's seat. A quick look back at Bricklin confirmed her first impression. He was withdrawn, his eyes expressionless. Periodically, she would check her rearview mirror to make sure he was okay, and she drove home so slowly she felt compelled to keep her flashers on.

Lionel Chambers, Jeanne's neighbor, was a retired professor and often home during the day. He was fond of Bricklin and, when he received Jeanne's call, readily agreed to help. Lionel was watching from his window when Jeanne pulled into her garage. Seeing familiar surroundings, Bricklin struggled to get up. "Stay down," she begged more than commanded.

When Lionel arrived at her side and saw Bricklin, he shook his head. "A grim sight, indeed." As soon as the two of them pulled Bricklin out and set him on the garage floor, the dog limped forward. Jeanne rushed ahead to get the door while Lionel called after her to get in touch if she needed more help.

Bricklin limped into the kitchen and lay down under the table. In an instant, he was asleep. Jeanne crouched and inspected him, the fingers of one hand pressed against her lips. The side of his body was shaved clean and horrifyingly concave where the shoulder had been excised. The area was bisected by a black-stitched red gash. Jeanne let her legs slip out from under her until she was sitting under the table with Bricklin. She wanted to cry, but her throat felt constricted, and no tears would come.

She had planned to spend the rest of the day working from home so she could help Bricklin in and out of the yard. Although she didn't need Scott, she'd asked him to come at his usual time so they could discuss Bricklin's current needs. At the sound of Scott's voice, Bricklin rose, tail wagging, and limped to the door. "Wow," Jeanne said to the stubble-chinned young man. "I didn't think he had the strength to greet anyone."

"It's not me. He's just feeling better. Aren't you, pal?" He scratched behind Bricklin's ears with his weathered fingers. "Bricklin's not the first amputee dog I've cared for. He'll adjust. Dogs don't moan and groan, 'Why me?'" He straightened up at the sound of barking from outside the condo. "Hear that, Bricklin? Your friends are in the van waiting for you to go with them for a run. Get better quick so you can join the party."

"Bricklin's not the only one that feels better. Thanks for helping me feel less like a mutilator."

"The way I see it, you gave him a shot at life. Not everyone would have done that." He scowled. "You wouldn't believe what I've seen owners do with their dogs."

He promised to look in on Bricklin a few times during the day and walk him in the yard. When he turned to leave, Jeanne had to hold the dog's collar to keep him from following. "That's a good sign," he said, giving Jeanne a thumbs-up.

Bricklin seemed to be mastering the three-legged walk, although Jeanne hated seeing him sink each time he needed to put down the fourth leg that wasn't there. Exhausted by Scott's visit, he returned to his spot under the kitchen table and fell asleep. Jeanne set up her laptop on the surface so she could keep watch.

By the next morning, Bricklin's energy level and Jeanne's spirits were improved. He was eating, a good sign, and managing his three-legged gait better. She hated to leave for the office but said a silent prayer of thanks to Scott and turned up the collar of her coat. While the calendar showed over a month until the official start of winter, the wind was brisk, the sky overcast, and the air smelled as if the promised rain might be snow.

The first email in Jeanne's inbox was a company-wide message from Alberta. She had decided Salientific needed a Christmas contest to celebrate the holiday and was urging everyone to provide a childhood photograph. The picture could be an individual portrait, a funny snapshot, or, at the very least, a team or class photo with the appropriate face indicated by an arrow on a Post-it note.

All employees were encouraged to submit a list of guesses as to the identity of the people in the numbered photos. The person with the most correct answers would receive a holiday turkey. Jeanne thoroughly approved of humor as a morale builder, only now it was her own morale that needed the uplift. She remembered seeing some loose childhood photos in Mother's time capsule. She'd look again.

Jake had agreed to a morning meeting on the kickoff, so Jeanne grabbed the folder Mariana had left, still parked on the exact corner of Jeanne's table, and detoured to get a cup of decaf before swinging past Jake's office. She wasn't sure which Jake she would find, the pre- or post-crash version, but perhaps enough time had passed for his PTSD relapse to have subsided.

He was at his desk looking serious but steady. He motioned her in and gestured toward his table and chairs before closing the door. Jeanne's antennae were up. There was a tension in Jake's body that worried her.

"Thank you," he began, "for helping me the day those disturbing sirens passed our building." Easier for him, she thought, to reference the external stimulus and not his cowering under his desk. "And thank you for your discretion."

"You're welcome," she said with a quick nod. She wanted

him to consider a leave of absence to get himself together but was afraid if he left, he would open the door wide for Parker. If he stayed, Parker's budding mutiny might succeed. Either way, he was screwed, and so was she, if she continued as his defender.

Habitual expressions etch lines in people's faces even before aging deepens those lines. Perhaps because Jake's face was so thin, his eyes stood out. His crow's feet and the furrow between his brows conveyed his earnestness, and Jeanne could always read the words he had yet to speak from the expression in those eyes. At that moment, his eyes foretold pleading. Jeanne's hands, folded on the table, felt clammy, and she unfolded them.

"I know we agreed not to discuss last summer, but . . ." Her heartbeat seemed audible as she bent the tab of Mariana's folder back and forth. He leaned forward and put his hand over hers. A tremor ran through her, part anxiety, part another kind of physical response altogether. Not again, she thought, this is no good, but she didn't pull her hand away. "Jeanne, I keep wondering, doing the math. Your baby, is it mine?"

She wanted to hold him, right then in his office, yet she didn't move. Did she want the baby to be his or Vince's? She reminded herself that at the moment there was no Vince. What to say? Could be yours, could be another guy's? No disputing how that would sound. She knew what she would do if she had a business problem and no good alternatives—cut her losses.

His fingers remained on hers as she disengaged until their tips grazed her nails. "I used a sperm donor." There, that extinguished the fire, for her anyway. It wasn't a lie, not exactly. She just didn't know which donor. Feminist guilt flooded her thoughts. Now who was an object? At that moment, she fervently wished never to know who the father was, but Maggie had called her a coward. Had Jeanne's mother felt the same agony over concealing the truth about her father?

Jake's face fell. "I understand." What did he understand? That she was telling the truth or that she wouldn't admit he'd fathered the baby. Maybe all he understood was that she wouldn't allow any further physical intimacy. He fell back in his seat, his torso drained of its energy, his face blank.

Jeanne looked down at the folder in her lap and wondered how to segue to the sales meeting. Jake spared her the awkwardness. He straightened up. "You came in to ask me about . . . ?" She pulled out Mariana's notes on his role in the sales conference agenda. It wasn't the agenda he'd hoped to discuss, but it was all she could offer.

Luke's calendar was packed, but he offered to meet Jeanne for breakfast two weeks after his presentation at Dawning Day. Morning traffic made Baker's Sweet Shop inconvenient for Jeanne, but she was too grateful for the chance to ask her questions to object. Parking in Newford Highlands was scarce, so she ended up several blocks away in front of one of the area's "painted lady" Victorians.

Tugging her maternity coat tighter across her swelling bump, she walked west into the raw wind. In her bag was a new spiral notebook, dedicated to her research into Alzheimer's. She didn't want the information on her laptop, her tablet, or her phone—paranoid perhaps, but she wanted no digital record of her concerns.

Luke had already secured a table in the bright, cheerful restaurant and had a large cup of coffee before him. He was texting when Jeanne walked in but looked up and smiled. "Hope you don't mind, I started without you." She eyed the line at the counter and sat down across from him.

"Think I'll wait. I don't have the same feeling of desperation as I used to before my first cup of coffee. My obstetrician threatened bodily harm if I didn't switch to decaf."

"You must be very excited. First pregnancy, right?" He put away his phone and sat back in his chair.

"I was, but now . . ." As she described the safety deposit box's contents, she withdrew from the front pocket of her notebook the letter from her father's neurologist to her mother and handed it to Luke. "How could that doctor know it was Alzheimer's? Was there even a way to diagnose it in the early sixties?"

"How old was your father?"

"Fifty-one at his death."

"The sixties were when scientists figured out that the disease-causing brain changes in the relatively young were the same Alzheimer's disease diagnosed in older people. They didn't know the genetic underpinnings, however, till the nineties. Your father's Dr. Kingman could have reasonably concluded, given your father's age, that the clinical symptoms indicated Alzheimer's."

Jeanne's mouth went dry. "Do you mind if I get that coffee after all?" She jumped up and hurried to the counter, where the line had diminished. It felt good to have something hot between her hands, and she started sipping even before she returned to her chair.

His voice softened. "It's frustrating to learn things about your parents after they're gone."

She looked into his kind eyes. She was used to frustration, even game changers. In a technology business, you had to expect them. "Since my mother's death, I've discovered my past, my future, even my attitudes were never my own. They were predetermined. I was engineered."

"I doubt that. You're too smart a woman. We do have a way of internalizing, though, allowing our parents' admonitions to haunt our thinking, even into adulthood. We don't even realize what we're doing in the absence of a good psychiatrist to point it out." Jeanne wondered if that was an oblique suggestion she needed a shrink.

"I imagine your mother thought she was doing you a favor, concealing your father's illness. She probably thought it was hereditary and found that a frightening prospect for you. She wouldn't have wanted you to worry about dying prematurely. Tell me about your father's family history. It's important to know if anyone else showed symptoms of dementia."

"My mother said he was an orphan, adopted by a childless older couple, the Bridgetons. Not terribly helpful, I know." Her hand fell heavily on the table. "There's got to be a way to find out if early-onset Alzheimer's ran in my father's family."

"Well, let's see. First, you'd have to track down the adoption records. If they're sealed, and your father's biological parents are deceased, you'd have to get them unsealed, a difficult, perhaps impossible, task." Jeanne took a quick swallow of her coffee and burned her tongue. "There are probably websites you could use, although I'm not familiar with them. I'm afraid by the time you got your answer, you'd be past your twenty-fourth week, with abortion no longer an option. Without a genetic analysis, we have no way of knowing if your father carried a mutation in the presenilin 1 or 2, or the amyloid precursor protein genes. If he did, you had a fifty-fifty chance to inherit the gene, assuming your mother was free of it."

Fifty-fifty—that's what it all boiled down to. A coin toss. Even money. "You need to understand," he continued, "those genes only account for a tiny percentage of cases, less than 5 percent. Maybe a few hundred families in the world have these genetic mutations. It's the e4 allele of APOE that raises the risk for late-onset Alzheimer's. Two copies of APOE-e4, rather than one, can raise that risk and increase the likelihood that late-onset

Alzheimer's will appear somewhat earlier. APOE-e4 is estimated to be the primary cause of 20 to 25 percent of the cases. There are a few other genes, like SORL1, that have mutations that also increase the risk for Alzheimer's."

"Isn't APOE-e4 the one you said was only a predisposing allele?"

"Everyone inherits a form of APOE from each parent. One can inherit the e4 version and not develop the disease. One can develop the disease and not have the e4. There may be other genes involved we haven't discovered yet."

She gazed longingly through the glass door to the street, wishing there were a physical exit out of her dilemma. "I get it. Even if my father did have early-onset Alzheimer's, he might not have had one of the rare predictive genes, just two copies of the bad susceptibility gene, or even a gene that scientists don't know about. The net of it is—no guarantees."

"I'm afraid so."

This was her worst nightmare—lack of clarity. The right thing was to have an abortion. She owed it to her unborn child to spare it the curse of inheriting early-onset Alzheimer's or enduring the heartache of growing up without a mother.

"I know your friend, Maggie, was concerned for you, but you need to realize it's extremely unlikely you have one of the genes that would ensure the early onset of Alzheimer's disease. Your father's dementia could have had a different cause. I would suggest you see a genetics counselor, and perhaps a therapist," he added gently.

Jeanne sat up straight in her chair. "A genetics counselor, yes, but I haven't got time for therapy."

"I understand, but given the impact the results can have, you might want to reconsider."

"Trust me, I can handle it." Even as she spoke the words,

she wondered if it was time to abandon her standard response to a challenge.

"What kind of support network do you have? Who can help you sort through the issues?"

Jeanne hesitated, hoping to appear less discomfited by his question than she was. "Friends, colleagues . . ." The baby's father was a conspicuous absence.

"Has your doctor recommended a genetics counselor? I imagine, given your age, you've seen one already."

Every conversation had "given your age" embedded in it somewhere. Pregnancy should make her feel fertile and youthful. Instead she felt like a brontosaurus preserved for the ages. "I've been meaning to make an appointment at the Maternal Fetal Medicine unit. Just so busy . . ."

"Newford Wellman?" She nodded. "I don't know if they handle genetic tests for Alzheimer's. They send some of their tests to us. If you need my help again, please let me know. Happy to put you in touch with a resource."

No need for now to ask the rest of her questions. She was already overwhelmed by the magnitude of the issues swirling around the miniscule being growing inside her. It was hard to imagine how her baby could float serenely in a sea of amniotic fluid when there was so much turmoil on deck.

That evening, Jeanne began refilling her mother's carton with the contents of her time capsule. She checked for photos that might have lodged between the pages of books. Bricklin, who was making steady progress, lay down on the living room floor beside her. Hard to believe she'd reverse engineered the entire contents of Mother's house, only to be stymied by a box of mementos. What to discard, what to keep, whether to chuck the whole thing or keep it as the physical embodiment of who her mother really was . . .

Jeanne stroked Bricklin's head. "I guess when people talk about the elephant in the living room, this is what they mean." Bricklin wagged his tail along the floor, agreeable, as always. Jeanne leaned over and rested her head on his. "I love you so much, boy, and I'm so proud of you. Don't leave me. Please don't leave me. You're my whole support network, although I couldn't tell that to Luke. You're enough." Bricklin lay quiet, unaware of the tears wetting his fur.

CHAPTER 8

Jeanne was useless at work. The technology acronyms that populated her incoming emails gained no purchase in her mind. Her thoughts were preoccupied with the ones Luke had talked about: PS1, PS2, APP, APOE-e2, e3 and e4. . . . She pushed her chair back in disgust. She needed something, anything, to divert her attention.

Where was that photograph? In a zippered pocket of her briefcase, she felt its glossy surface and pulled it out. Could she ever have been the girl gazing back at her? Some days it seemed she had sprung from the head of Zeus, fully formed and at work at her desk. Once her mother had weaned her from ballet, Jeanne had fallen in love with sports, and she'd excelled just like her father, a gifted athlete. That he played football was one of the few precious morsels her mother had shared with her.

Gazing at her photo aroused the same sense of wistfulness she'd felt going through her mother's box. She closed her eyes and tried to remember the day it had been taken. The grass on the ball field was intensely green, not yet trampled by daily games. The dirt the team kicked up was newly thawed and smelled rich and fertile. How warm the spring sun felt on her shoulders. If only she could relive that moment. She would know now to hang on to it. At least her mother had thought to preserve the image.

As Jeanne approached HR, she saw three people standing in the hall in front of the cork wall. She poked her head in Alberta's door. "Quite the attraction. What happened to all the stuff that's usually tacked up there?"

Alberta laughed and rose from her desk. "Let's hope the OSHA police don't come after me for moving those postings. The contest is getting a great response. Have you looked yet? Some of the pictures are amazing."

"Guess I'm a latecomer. I brought you mine, though."

"As soon as they leave, we'll add it. I just need to write your name on the back."

"No need. My mother was an efficient labeler." As soon as the three employees drifted away, Alberta took the photo from her.

"Wow! That's you?" She tacked it up in the corner and stood beside Jeanne, who was perusing the board. "Guess you were a jock, huh?" Jeanne, eight years of age, looked wiry holding her baseball bat as she waited for a pitch. Her prodigious curls sprang out from under a Red Sox cap. Over the years, the curls had relaxed, which was more than she could say for herself.

"A million years ago—that's when it was taken." A ringing phone pulled Alberta away. So many adorable babies. They were lined up on the bulletin board in rows reminiscent of a hospital nursery window. Her hand crept to her belly.

The images showed children of different ages, most appearing younger than ten. Here and there were professionally posed shots, school photos taken against blue backgrounds with painted clouds. Most were candids: kids on trikes, bikes, skateboards, and in groups of siblings or teammates. The group photos had tiny red arrows stuck on them pointing to the faces of Salientific's future employees. Amazing how easy it was to put names to some of the faces. The lucky ones now looked like older versions of themselves, while others were changed by age in significant and unattractive ways.

How much bias, though, did people bring to their perceptions? When people saw babies, they thought *baby*. They were first conscious of them as belonging to a category and only second as possessed of blond hair or turned-up noses. People perceived old people the same way, as belonging to a category. They saw the aged visage first and the features second. Only when people saw adults did appearance register before category. They didn't think, there goes an adult. Jeanne thought of the Dawning Day residents, the ones in the Alzheimer's wing, and felt a twinge of guilt. Objectifying them was so much easier than seeing human beings who had worked, laughed, fought, and made love.

Alberta had disqualified the executive staff from winning the prize turkey, but they were allowed to compete along with the rest of the company. Jeanne's phone was in her jacket pocket, and she drew it out to record her initial guesses. The group pictures required closer perusal, and she rested her forefinger on the board as she peered at them. The basketball team—oh, of course, it was Clara Nordell. Even seated, her head was a foot above those of the other girls. Too easy. Jeanne made note of the number of Clara's picture and moved down the row.

She stopped at a gymnastics group picture. Could that mop-haired kid be Parker Neal? So hard to tell without the toupee. Certainly, it was one of those faces rearranged by time or, in Parker's case, cosmetic surgery. No clue in the school name, but wait . . . Jeanne's eye was drawn to the coach in the back row. His features were familiar. She must have worked with him somewhere before. Jeanne gritted her teeth. That face was going to drive her crazy like a song she couldn't place.

She tried moving down the row, but she couldn't concentrate on identifying the others. She had to remember. *Is this how it starts*, she wondered? *The more you try to grasp memories, the more they elude you?* She shoved her phone back in her pocket and returned to her office.

Work would be the antidote for her frustration. A priority email from Lou asked if she was up for a walk at lunchtime. Odd he should suggest a walk rather than a lunch, but perhaps he was finally trying to burn off some calories. She looked out at the sunshine and checked the temperature on her phone. It was over sixty degrees out, unseasonably warm for November. That explained it. Everyone would be grabbing an hour of fresh air on one of the few mild days left before winter. She agreed to meet him in the lobby at noon.

Lou was chatting about football with Eduardo when Jeanne approached. She eyed his shirtsleeves and wondered if she'd be hot in her jacket. Tying the sleeves around her waist was no longer an option, but Lou ushered her out the front door before she could reconsider.

"You've got that pregnant glow people talk about."

"Thanks, but I think people just say that because most women's faces are green their whole first trimester. Glad to have that behind me."

Lou laughed and gestured toward the road leading away from their building. Jeanne noted his avoidance of the popular walking path around the property but let him lead the way and set their speed, one unlikely to qualify their stroll as cardio. The sun shone through the leafless trees, and, in spite of their leisurely pace, Lou began perspiring. She itched to do some Weight Watchers proselytizing but would never risk offending him, so she offered a tissue from her pocket and said nothing.

Lou cleared his throat as though he were beginning a presentation. "You know about Parker and the board?" He didn't wait for her response. "He isn't wrong, you know." She noted his circumlocution. Lou hated business politics, so she knew it must have cost him to broach this subject.

"I know Jake's having some problems right now," she replied. "I'm hoping they're temporary."

"Temporary or not, Jake's problems are mine, and he's in my face so often now, it's hard to get our product issues resolved."

"Literally in your face?"

"Hell, yeah. He keeps showing up in engineering like some old codger bellyaching that dinner's late."

A bus roared by, and Jeanne wrinkled her nose as the exhaust fumes reached her. "So, you agree with Parker and Bart."

"I didn't say that."

"But I thought—"

He stopped and sighed, as though he needed a moment to shore up his patience. "Jeanne, I like Jake as much as you do, as much as the board still does, but we both know the revenue projections. He's going to become increasingly inadequate until his limitations start bending that revenue curve downward. Parker wants to do what's best for the company." He began to walk again but stepped up his pace.

"You don't question Parker's motives?"

Lou was breathing hard. "Motives don't matter, only results. Do the right thing for the wrong reason, and I'm okay with it."

Jeanne was not okay with it. She was worried about unintended consequences, but this was no time for a philosophical debate. "So, you're lobbying me too?"

"I didn't say that. I'm not sure we've outgrown Jake's talents, though that time is coming. I'm surprised you don't see that."

"I've had reservations about every CEO I've worked for, but I'm not going to waste cycles contemplating a decision that doesn't need to be made yet, nor do I plan to approach the board. If and when Jake needs to go, they'll figure it out." In spite of her words, the burden of being Jake's sole defender felt oppressive. As they turned back toward the office, she wondered how she'd keep her marketing staff from noticing she was odd person out if the rest of the executive team seemed to shun her.

"Don't worry, Jeanne. I'm not going to the board either—for now."

How much time did she have to get Jake to shape up, and what were the odds she could even do it? If she told Jake about the risk he faced, it might feed his PTSD fears. She thanked Lou for sharing his thoughts with her and committed to weighing the issues carefully. What else could she say? She couldn't promise to return Jake to a steady state. Only Jake could do that.

Jeanne's heartbeat rose from her chest till it pulsed in her neck and behind her eyes. The fan-shaped picture was clearer this time. She couldn't take her eyes off it. When she finally turned away, she couldn't look back. Pulled and repelled, wanting her baby yet wanting to end its gestation, she closed her eyes.

How wrong the pro-lifers were to think the sight of a live fetus would reverse the decision of a woman contemplating abortion. What an outrageous oversimplification of human emotion and our capacity for gut-wrenching ambivalence. Jeanne forced herself to look at the screen. *To allow that thumping heart and half-formed body to develop would be the crueler alternative.* It would be selfish, irresponsible. Seeing it convinced her.

Perhaps her face betrayed her churning emotions, because Dr. O'Rourke felt the need to comfort her. "You're not unusual in finding this a moving experience. Everything looks fine, though. Normal pregnancy, normal fetal development. Get dressed and come into my office."

She hardly noticed what she was doing as she pulled on her clothes. When she leaned down to pick up her handbag, she saw her trouser socks lying on the floor. She'd put on her boots without them, and rather than remove them, she stuffed the socks in her purse. Her feet rubbed against the stitching inside her boots as she walked down the hall to O'Rourke's office. It was an easier pain to focus on than her feelings.

The doctor had entered another examining room while Jeanne was dressing, so she dropped into one of the leather chairs in front of his desk. She'd never paid much attention to the bulletin board on his wall with its collage of baby pictures and hand-scrawled notes thanking Dr. O'Rourke for all he had done. So many exclamation points. A happy business he was in, or was that just marketing? Why would he want to be reminded of anything else: the babies born with deformities, mental defects, congenital diseases, drug addictions? Did those mothers send thank-you notes too? Weren't there mothers who didn't want their babies because they didn't have the time, money, or inclination to nurture them?

By the time the doctor strode into his office, she was slumped in her chair, eyes downcast. "You're the most dejected patient I can remember, especially for one who's just seen her baby on a sonogram."

Jeanne leaned forward, twisting her hands in her lap. "There's a good chance, maybe even fifty-fifty, I'm carrying one of the genes that causes early-onset Alzheimer's." The doctor frowned and lowered his generous body into his chair. She told him what she'd learned about her father's condition and related Lucas Menton's observations. "I may have to abort my baby. . . ." Her voice broke.

"Let's not assume anything yet."

"But I have a responsibility. . . ."

"Not yet, you don't. Let's get things in the right order." He leafed through the folder in front of him. "You haven't seen the genetics counselor yet? I don't see a report from her. You understand, don't you, that your baby is at greater risk for conditions like Down syndrome than for Alzheimer's?"

She nodded. "I'll call. I promise. But even if the genetic test is negative, my father showed his dementia so young, how can I be sure there isn't something terribly wrong in my DNA?"

"It's only natural your mind is jumping from one bad alternative to another, but let's not make a decision before we have to."

Her very words to Lou, but this situation was different. She was in purgatory, and working in the unpredictable world of Jake's ups and downs felt in no way comparable. "Every day that passes tears me apart a little bit more. Will I or won't I have to terminate my pregnancy? It's getting harder to part with this baby." She pulled a tissue from the box on his desk. "I couldn't even part with my dog, for God's sake."

"I don't know how your dog is connected with this, but I do know you're going to have to live in limbo until your genetic results come in. In the meantime, you need to schedule your next monthly appointment. Did you find out the health history of the baby's father? Assuming you're free of the Alzheimer's gene, we have to plan for your amniocentesis next month."

Jeanne's guts twisted. "I don't know who the father is," she blurted out, flushed with embarrassment, "but there are only two possibilities." She felt like a teenager who'd spent time in the respective back seats of two boys' cars.

One of O'Rourke's eyebrows rose. "I assume you want to know. Why don't you take a paternity test? You can easily do that yourself."

Same question Maggie had asked. Of course, Jeanne wanted to know. Ignorance wasn't bliss. It was contemptible, at least she'd always thought so, yet if she never found out which of the two was her baby's father, would that be so terrible? The sperm donor story had its appeal. Her child, if she had it, would be all hers. She tried not to think about her own father and how much she'd longed to know him.

Each day, focus and concentration seemed more elusive than the day before, and Jeanne's command of details, a skill she took for granted, eroded. She defended herself against the assault on her self-confidence by blaming "pregnancy brain," though she didn't really believe it.

How could she possibly have misplaced her precious Alzheimer's notebook, the repository for all her information on the disease from Luke Menton and the Internet? She had used the folders in the notebook's divider pages to hold printouts from the websites of the Alzheimer's Association and several universities, including Fenway's School of Medicine.

She'd been keeping it in her briefcase. It was too large to fit in her pocketbook, since she deliberately carried a purse small enough to be stuffed into her briefcase. She hated showing up at business appointments with multiple shoulder straps like a photographer on a shoot.

Was this how it started? Short-term memory was the first to go. Had she put the notebook somewhere for safekeeping and failed to file the location in her brain? If she sat quietly and mentally retraced her steps, she'd remember where she'd left it. A minute with closed eyes yielded no clue.

Perhaps she'd carried it to the coffee room, unlikely as that seemed. She hurried off to check the kitchen. Two engineers were making coffee when she arrived, and one turned to congratulate her on her pregnancy. His wife had delivered twins two weeks earlier. He was bubbling over with the thrill of it, intent on letting Jeanne know what she had to look forward to. She thanked him for his warm wishes, although he looked impossibly young to be a father. Was he thinking the opposite of her?

A quick glance around the room told her she hadn't left the notebook there, so she turned to leave. "Didn't you want to use the coffee machine?" the young man asked. Flustered, she placed a cup on the brewer plate, selected a decaf pod to insert, and hit "brew." When the coffee was ready, she pressed a lid onto her cup with fumbling fingers that failed to secure it and splashed her hand with hot coffee.

"Shit," she muttered under her breath. Hair-on-fire was an unaccustomed state for her. If Maggie were there, she would counsel Jeanne to meditate. Not going to happen, Jeanne thought, but took several deep breaths anyway.

On her way back to her office, Jeanne stopped in reception to ask Eduardo if anyone had turned in a notebook. "I have three pairs of sunglasses, a Mont Blanc pen, and a single pearl earring, but no notebook. "Was it very important?"

"No," she replied breezily, "just some information for a friend, but I'd like to get it back." Eduardo promised to keep an eye out and asked if she'd checked the women's restroom, which she made her useless next stop.

She was busy berating herself for bringing the notebook to work when Mariana caught up with her. "Would you sign this requisition, Jeanne?" Handing off her coffee, Jeanne flattened the paper against a wall so she could sign it. "Thanks. Oh, and I just saw Parker by your office. I think he was looking for you."

Jeanne wasn't about to seek him out. She shrugged. "He'll

be back." Mariana disappeared down the hall, and Jeanne plunked herself down at her desk and chewed her lip. Gingerly, she opened each drawer as though she expected a rodent to jump out. When she reached the right bottom, she spotted the notebook nestled between her purse and a box of business cards. *What the fuck!*

She had Maggie's number on speed dial. "I'm losing it," Jeanne whispered into the phone. She related the story of the missing notebook.

"Alzheimer's doesn't come on that fast. Sounds to me like a touch of pregnancy brain fog. Take a few deep breaths, and if you can't compose yourself, leave the building for a quick walk."

"Alzheimer's has to start somehow. Maybe this is the first episode. What if I misplace the baby? Don't laugh. Remember the guy who drove off with his baby in an infant seat on the roof of his car?"

"Jeanne, I hate to cut you short, but I'm in the middle of mediating a dispute between two residents with high blood pressure. I'll call you back in a few minutes . . . promise." Jeanne grabbed her coat and left the building, heading for a residential area behind Salientific's office park.

The houses were modest split-level homes with lawns that looked raked clear of all leaves save the ones falling as Jeanne walked. The day was gray and chilly, the streets empty. Where backyard swing sets were visible, no children were playing, presumably all at school. A nanny, or perhaps a grandmother, came toward her with a sleeping toddler in a stroller. Jeanne moved onto the berm to let her pass. *I could sooner envision myself walking on the moon than pushing a stroller down a suburban sidewalk.* Her ringing cell displayed Maggie's name. "Whatever this is supposed to do, Mag, it's not working. I feel more stressed out than when I left the office."

"How far have you walked, half a block?"

"I'm telling you, I never put my notebook into my desk. If I walk from here to Canada, that won't change. Either I'm hallucinating, or I have Alzheimer's, or both."

"Or you've passed Canada, and you did indeed stick that notebook into your desk. It's the drawer where you keep your purse. What could be more natural? Keep walking. What happened when you met with Luke? Did he make you think you were on the verge?"

Jeanne recounted the conversation on Lincoln Street. "He seemed to think having the genetic testing was pointless because of the rarity of the predictive genes and because I have no other family members with early-onset Alzheimer's. Since my father's not alive, there's no way to test his DNA. Luke suggested maybe finding out my APOE status. It may be moot, though, if today is the first of many memory lapses."

"If you called me for medical advice, here it is: walk around the block again, and when you get back to your office, put Alzheimer's out of your mind. Oh yeah, tomorrow morning, leave your notebook at home." By the time Jeanne completed her second circuit of the block, her high heels were squeezing her feet into their pointy toes. Maggie's therapy had just replaced one kind of pain with another. Some nurse!

A series of marketing meetings left Jeanne with no time for worries about memory loss the rest of the day. Feeling more washed out than usual, she packed up her laptop at five and made her way slowly to the parking lot, where she was brought up short by her empty space.

Her heart rate ratcheted up as she turned the corner to the side lot, where the sight of her black car allowed her to release the breath she hadn't known she was holding. *I will remain calm,* she told herself, as though *become calm* weren't the more appropriate instruction. Yes, the lot had been crowded in the morning, and she'd turned the corner to park. At least, she was pretty sure she had. Maybe she'd been lost in thought and just forgot to note where she was leaving her car.

Maggie's right. I'm just stressed. She listed the reasons for herself, imagining them on a pie chart: pregnancy, paternity, family secrets, Bricklin's cancer, Jake's PTSD, Parker's mutiny, Vince's anger. If she could assign each of them a percentage, a slice of the pie, she could own and manage them. But wait. Her heart lurched. She'd forgotten to put on the pie chart her own symptoms of Alzheimer's.

Although Jeanne didn't feel like talking to anyone but Bricklin that evening, she took Maggie's call. "Could you come to Dawning Day tomorrow?" Maggie asked. Dawning Day was the last place in the world Jeanne felt like going, but Maggie had a Saturday shift again, so that was the only option.

"We won't eat in the office or back in the Alzheimer's wing. I'll bring lunch for us, and we'll sit in the dining room. It'll be empty by one." Jeanne agreed and prepared herself to be further admonished to reduce her stress level.

When Jeanne arrived at Dawning Day and asked for Maggie, the receptionist, who looked as heavily made up as a cosmetics salesperson, drew her penciled eyebrows together. "Are you sure she's working today? I haven't seen her come in."

Jeanne hesitated. Since they'd set up their lunch date just last night, she couldn't have the date confused . . . or could she? Yesterday had been a tricky day for her memory. "Yes, I'm sure," Jeanne declared. "We have a lunch appointment."

The receptionist adjusted her reading glasses, picked up the phone, and punched in an extension. From the audible half of the conversation, Jeanne gathered Maggie's whereabouts were a mystery. She should have been in over an hour ago. "Why don't you have a seat?" The receptionist gestured toward the lobby chairs. "Someone's checking."

Jeanne parked herself gingerly on an upholstered armchair next to a middle-aged man with skinny crossed legs the length of Ichabod Crane's. "You have a parent here?" he asked her. She shook her head. "It's a great place, but back there . . ." He pointed at the door to the Alzheimer's wing. "My mother was upstairs, but they insisted on moving her. Alzheimer's is a one-way downhill street."

When Jeanne saw him tearing up, she turned her head away. Someday, maybe soon, she could be a resident of that land beyond the door. Would anyone be sitting here waiting to see her? No one she could think of would shed a tear over her diminishing memory and mental acuity. Someone at work would step up in a heartbeat to take her place. The hand that wasn't gripping the arm of her chair covered her abdomen. Her child might be the one sitting out here, holding the hand of whom? A foster parent? No way. She withdrew her hand.

An aide poked her head out from behind the door of the locked wing and sang out, "She's ready," to the man beside Jeanne. He covered the distance between them in a few strides. No matter how bad off she is, Jeanne thought, he's eager to see her. Jeanne had had friends, most recently Mimi from the gym, Sasha who'd worked for Jeanne's last company, Amanda from . . . where had she met Amanda? No matter. One by one, they'd stopped calling. Or had she?

"What?" The receptionist's phone was against her ear. She looked directly at Jeanne. "Yes, yes, I understand." She wrote something on her notepad and replaced the phone in its cradle. "Young lady." Jeanne jumped up. "I'm afraid Maggie's been in an accident. They say she's all right, but she's been taken to Metro West Hospital."

"If she's okay, why is she at the hospital?" The receptionist shrugged.

Jeanne ran to her car. Maggie had been a friend, listening to her dilemma, offering advice, dedicating her precious time to helping, yet Jeanne hadn't reciprocated. She wasn't aware of a single problem that worried Maggie besides the digital scale's readout at Weight Watchers.

Jeanne accelerated down Route 27 and rushed into the emergency room lobby. She talked her way past the triage nurse by claiming to be Maggie's half sister and found her in the third examining room from the entrance.

Her owl-patterned smock was streaked with blood from what appeared to be a newly sutured cut on her forehead. Abrasions covered her arms, and a large hematoma swelled her shin. "Jeanne, what are you doing here? Oh, lunch. I'm so sorry."

Jeanne covered Maggie's hand with her own. "I came to make sure you were okay, not to check out the hospital cafeteria. What happened? Are you up to talking?"

A young nurse popped her head around the divider. "Maggie, you need to take it easy."

"I can go." Jeanne reached for her bag.

"No, stay." She smiled weakly at the nurse, who withdrew.

"I'm impressed at their attentiveness," Jeanne observed.

"Professional courtesy. They know I'm a nurse." She tried to shift into a more upright position.

"Let me help." Jeanne fumbled with the mechanism to raise the head of the bed, so Maggie coached her.

"I can see you haven't spent any time in a medical setting. Lucky you."

"Just wait till my Alzheimer's advances and nurses have to change my diapers. Then we'll see how dependable my luck is."

Maggie laughed. "Spoken like a true risk assessment professional. Mine certainly wasn't dependable today. I stopped at the dry cleaners on my way into work and when I got out of my car, noticed my vision was blurry. I must have stepped out too far into the street, because a car clipped me."

"You were hit. Oh my God."

"It was only a Mini Cooper." Maggie managed a weak smile. "Could have been worse. That's a bus route."

Jeanne had no chance to respond before a petite Japanese doctor appeared in the doorway to discuss the results of Maggie's blood test. Jeanne was about to search out the waiting room, but Maggie urged her to leave the hospital and salvage her Saturday afternoon. "Not a chance. I'll leave when you leave."

On her way out of the emergency area, Jeanne asked a nurse where she could get a soda. After dawdling at the vending machine, she stopped at a restroom on her way back to give the doctor enough time to brief Maggie and arrange for her discharge.

The doctor was just leaving the examining room, and Jeanne was surprised to find Maggie blowing her nose, red-rimmed eyes visible above the tissue. "Do you want me to go back out to the waiting room?" Maggie shook her head, so Jeanne pulled a chair in close.

After two minutes of silence, Maggie began. "I'm diabetic." Once again, her tears flowed. "That's what happens to us fatties," she spat out.

Jeanne leaned out of her chair and embraced her. "It's not your fault." Maggie's tears wet the front of Jeanne's blouse.

"You don't understand. That's the biggest risk factor for type 2 diabetes." She banged her fist on her thigh. "I should have had more willpower. I knew the risk from my parents." Jeanne jumped up to retrieve the tissue box from a metal table in the corner. “They were both very overweight. My mother gained so much weight when she was pregnant with me, she developed gestational diabetes. That put her at greater risk after I was born, and, sure enough, she got type 2 diabetes just like my father.”

Jeanne’s first reaction was a could-be-worse, but she stopped herself. No one wants to hear her feelings delegitimized because others in the world suffer greater misfortunes. She searched for the right words. “It’s a manageable condition, isn’t it? Once you get over the initial shock and settle into a routine with medication or whatever, it may not be so bad. Maybe it will even improve.”

“Thank you for saying that. I know you mean well, but, in my family . . . well, you don’t need to hear the gruesome details.”

Jeanne felt guilty, because Maggie was right. She didn’t want to hear those details, further proof of how messy life could be. She remembered the moment in Jake’s office when he had told her what he’d experienced in Afghanistan. She wanted to flee now as much as she had then. Jake hadn’t given her a choice, but Maggie would let her go. In fact, Maggie didn’t want to burden Jeanne. Had she always abandoned her friends without realizing it, she who met head-on any quantifiable problem? “I can handle gruesome.”

“Should I start with the amputations or the stroke?”

Jeanne shuddered, but she stayed put.

CHAPTER 9

By the time Jeanne arrived at Newford Wellman Hospital on Monday morning, her nerves were fried. Traffic down Route 30 was worse than usual, as though the commuting hordes were conspiring against her. She was coming down with a cold which forced her to keep one hand plumbing her purse for tissues. Blowing her nose was a delicate operation that normally required both hands. She held the wheel in place with her knee. "Move," she growled at the SUV that first blocked the entrance to hospital parking and then crawled around each turn in the garage all the way to the top, where there were finally spaces.

She got out of the car and smoothed her jacket before adjusting her bag on her shoulder. After a deep breath, she started toward the elevator. Appearing calm was important. Weird that only a few months ago, losing her cool was the last thing she worried about.

Sharon Basko's office was on the third floor. Jeanne's directions took her past the gift shop, where fuzzy stuffed bunnies and kittens crowded the window, observing Jeanne with their glassy, noncommittal eyes. A few minutes later, she sat in the small, spare waiting area outside Sharon Basko's office.

An administrative assistant tapped her keyboard at a rate that matched Jeanne's quickening pulse. A copy of *Genetics* on the coffee table caught her eye, and she flipped through it, scanning fruitlessly for the word "Alzheimer's."

The diminutive Ms. Basko appeared before her in a flowing tunic and trousers. Her silk scarf was wound loosely around her neck, and her dangling beaded earrings reminded Jeanne of a photo she'd seen of a sixties folk singer, although the genetics counselor was too young for the Woodstock generation.

Jeanne's pregnancy was sending her on a journey away from her natural habitat. She was suddenly self-conscious about her corporate appearance. Ms. Basko, completely at ease, showed Jeanne into her tiny office. Her metal desk and bookcase took up most of the space, but there were two guest chairs opposite for prospective parents. Jeanne took the one closest to the wall, feeling as though the emptiness in the second chair was itself a presence.

Ms. Basko's smile was warm as she urged Jeanne to call her "Sharon," but she wasted no time in laying out the issues. "I see you're forty-eight years of age, so I'll come right to the point. The odds are your baby is normal, but I don't want to deceive you. There are significant risks at your age. I usually go through them with the baby's father at the same time, since he'll need to be tested too."

"Uh, last-minute emergency business trip. Sorry."

Sharon asked questions about her ethnic background and Vince's, since ethnicity figured into some inherited diseases. African Americans were at greater risk for sickle cell anemia, Caucasians for cystic fibrosis, and Jews for Tay-Sachs. Jeanne, unfortunately, had no information about her father's biological parents.

Sharon also went through the statistical risk for Down syndrome and two other trisomy mutations. While amniocentesis would answer several important questions, she recommended Jeanne not wait, since a relatively new test was available to rule out Down syndrome. It was noninvasive and required only a blood test so the lab could analyze the small amount of the baby's DNA in her bloodstream.

Jeanne fidgeted in her seat. Sharon offered her a glass of water. "I know this can be nerve-racking. We'll try to get you the results as soon as we can, but the sample has to be sent out. You may not hear for two to three weeks."

"I know I should be focused on these big risks, especially with such a geriatric pregnancy." Sharon said nothing, waiting. "But I recently discovered my father exhibited serious early dementia before he died in his fifties." Sharon's eyebrow rose at the word "dementia." "The news of his condition really staggered me." Sharon nodded and murmured words of encouragement as Jeanne described her father's symptoms and what she'd learned about early-onset Alzheimer's from Luke.

"I understand completely. Of course you're frightened by the implications for both you and your baby." Jeanne hated being in this position of profound neediness. She'd never been the one requiring comfort and expressing fears. It was she who mentored and reassured others.

Jeanne straightened up as though better posture could help her shake off her discomfort. "I need to know with absolute certainty if I carry the PS1, PS2 or APP genetic mutations that will give me early-onset Alzheimer's. I'm running out of time to end my pregnancy."

"So, if you knew you had one of those genes, you could nail down 'with certainty' your own risk of developing Alzheimer's? Your child would have a 50 percent probability of inheriting, assuming the baby's father passed on a normal gene."

"At least, my course of action would be clear."

Sharon leaned back in her chair and looked up at the ceiling before answering. "It is a comfort to know the odds. After all, that's what we've been discussing with regard to Down syndrome. Unfortunately, you're not likely to have that clarity with Alzheimer's.

"The chance that you have one of those genes is tiny. They're rare. Your father more likely had two copies of APOE-e4, or else something entirely different may have been behind his condition, like vascular or Parkinsonian dementia. Even armed with your APOE status, you won't know the future for sure. Most scientists think that APOE-e4 is a factor in 20 to 25 percent of the cases. Over 90 percent of Alzheimer's is late onset, after sixty-five."

"If the deterministic genes cause so few cases, and the predisposing ones don't account for all the rest, then what does?"

"Probably interactions between genes and other risk factors like heart health. Remember, too, there may be genes and environmental influences involved that scientists haven't uncovered yet." Sharon's information matched what Luke had told her.

Jeanne's fingers curled into a fist. She was so frustrated that she wanted to punch a wall. She chafed at the knowledge that no matter how thorough she was in capturing the data she needed to support a risk-free choice, only the future could provide proof of her prescience or impose the consequences of her error. She gripped the arms of her chair. It just wasn't fair. "Are you saying there's no point in testing me?"

Sharon's gaze was steady. "You'll need to decide that for yourself, but we don't do that kind of testing here." She rose from her chair. "Now, let's set you up for the Down test I mentioned earlier and rule out what we can."

Jeanne emailed Luke after seeing Sharon Basko. He responded at the end of the day with the message that he would try to arrange an appointment for her to see a geneticist who could clarify what Sharon had said.

A week later, Jeanne was shaking hands with Dr. Cross, a towering redhead in an impossibly long white coat. Jeanne listened intently while he explained. "I don't know how much detail you've been given, but there are hundreds of mutations in APP, PS-1 and PS-2, the three genes that are known to cause familial early-onset Alzheimer's. We can do targeted gene sequencing now, but unless we find one of the known gene mutations, the results can be ambiguous. A person could have a mutation not known to be disease causing."

Dr. Cross leaned across his desk. Even with the unlikely discovery of one of the rare predictive genes, the age of Alzheimer's onset might be affected by the presence of other predisposing genes. Dr. Cross was uncertain of the lead time if Jeanne insisted on all possible tests. Careful interpretation of the results was required. It seemed to Jeanne that the more information she recorded in her notebook, the less she knew.

He advised against the testing, but if Jeanne insisted, he suggested she have her blood drawn at Newford Wellman. They would ship over the sample. The calendar was not her friend. Once she passed the twenty-fourth week of her pregnancy, she could no longer have an abortion. Pro-lifers were trying to get legislation passed that would remove that choice at twenty weeks or sooner.

Dr. Cross wasn't finished raising issues. "I don't know if cost is a consideration for you, but insurance doesn't cover testing for predictive purposes, sometimes not even for diagnostic, when a person is already exhibiting clinical symptoms of dementia. Anyway, you wouldn't want your insurer to know, would you? They're not, in theory, allowed to boot you based on genetic information, but who knows? Our system of coverage in this country is a political football." His tone softened. "Did you say you are or aren't experiencing memory problems?"

After responding with an emphatic no, Jeanne bit her lip, remembering her panic over the missing notebook that had turned up in her desk. How sure of her memory could she be when she'd needed to search the parking lot for her elusive car? "Uh . . . do people ever imagine symptoms?"

"Not imagine so much as read too much into episodes of forgetting. You can have a neuropsychological evaluation if you're concerned. Takes about three hours—an interview and a battery of tests." Jeanne would have to wait another two weeks for a neuropsych eval, but she wanted to do it.

Alberta was not in her office that afternoon, although several people stood outside it peering at the now extensive display of childhood photographs. Jeanne had been debating the wisdom of consulting Alberta on the insurance issue raised by Dr. Cross. While all such conversations were supposed to be confidential, and Alberta took her job seriously, Jeanne found it hard to compartmentalize her appalling romance with Bart.

Sal Finiello and Mary Coolidge from engineering were laughing at a picture of a wispy boy with large ears, blond hair that stood up like a Hare Krishna's, and suspenders. "Has to be," said Sal.

"Bert Caldor from shipping, for sure," Mary replied.

Jeanne looked over their shoulders. "I don't know. True, Bert has a dirty blond Mohawk and looks like he isn't exactly a foodie, but those ears . . . Unless Bert's had his pinned back through cosmetic surgery, I'm thinking Bill Kane from support."

Sal nodded. "You might be right, Jeanne." Mary looked unconvinced. Jeanne's eyes wandered to the gymnastics team photo she'd seen on her last trip to HR. She still didn't recognize the child the red arrow designated, but that coach in the back row—if only she could place him. Sal and Mary had moved on to the next picture. "Think this girl could be Laurie Cronin from accounting?"

"No way," Mary spoke with certainty. "That's Lisa Sculley." Sal agreed, and they each wrote down their guess. Mary turned to Jeanne. "We're sharing answers, because if one of us wins, we're splitting the turkey."

"Clever strategy," Jeanne said. "Save me a drumstick."

Alberta appeared at her side. "No drumsticks for senior management, even if you win." Her pink lipstick contrasted with dark pink lip liner surrounding it, which matched her snug sweater. "Can I help you with anything?"

Jeanne lost her courage. She would not discuss with Alberta whether there was insurance coverage for genetic testing—not that day, not any day. "Some of these are priceless," Jeanne said, forcing a smile before she turned away.

Perhaps a sanity check was in order. She detoured through the lobby before returning to her office. No sign of the crash remained. The new windows were pristine and allowed the sun to pour in unfiltered.

"Hi, Jeanne." Eduardo smiled and nodded.

Suddenly she knew. "Oh my God, Eduardo, you need to see this." She grabbed his arm and pulled him away from the reception desk.

"Where are we going?"

"To HR." Once they stood in front of the photo display,

Jeanne jabbed her finger at the kid under the red arrow. "I don't know who that is, but tell me if you recognize the man in the back row."

Eduardo squinted, moving his face closer to the board. "The kid is Lisa Sculley, at least I think it is, and that guy in the back? Could that be the guy who crashed his car into the lobby? His name was in the news stories, Milton . . . Milton Cox."

"Yes!" Jeanne said triumphantly. "Or his doppelganger."

"His what?"

"He's a dead ringer."

"But this is a much younger man. Don't you think it's a coincidence?"

"I don't know—maybe—but it's been bugging me. Thanks."

"Wait a minute." Eduardo cocked his head and squinted at the picture again. "See this other kid?" He put his finger on a different face topped with a mop of hair. "Do you think that could be Parker Neal?"

Jeanne peered at the spot where Eduardo had left a fingerprint. "Could be—not sure." Parker had been in the lobby the day of the crash and even commented to Jeanne on Jake's couch leap. He would have said something if he'd recognized the driver.

Maggie looked wretched when she appeared that evening at the entrance to Starbucks. The pouches under her eyes were as purple as the area around the bandage on her forehead. Her bloodshot eyes met Jeanne's, but her attempt to smile was feeble. "Jesus, Maggie, sit down. I'll get you a hot drink." The wooden chair opposite Jeanne creaked as Maggie collapsed into it.

"I'm fine."

"Bullshit, you are." Jeanne walked up to the register to order. While the barista poured two cups of decaf, Jeanne turned to check on her friend, who remained immobile, her jacket still buttoned, eyes downcast. Maggie's bag had slid off her shoulder and lay on the floor. Jeanne placed one of the cups in front of her and slipped back into her chair. "Is this about your diabetes?"

"Did you ever feel like you were getting sucked back into your childhood, like everything you'd put behind you was pulling you back?"

"You're not your parents. I know you're having a hard time with your diagnosis, but, Maggie, you look like you need professional help . . . and maybe a prescription for antidepressants." Jeanne inspected Maggie's face more carefully. In spite of its roundness, there were hollows Jeanne hadn't seen before. "You're losing weight, aren't you? Fast?"

Maggie's mouth tightened at the corners. "We're in Weight Watchers. That's what I'm supposed to be doing."

Jeanne was pretty sure diabetics weren't supposed to cut way back on what they were eating, especially diabetics like Maggie, who'd just started on insulin. Maggie was a nurse, though. She'd know better than to abuse herself that way.

"I'm just a little down. I'll bounce back." Maggie's eyes were wet, and she swiped them with the back of her hand. "The blurry vision that caused the accident—I'm worried about its effect on my work. What if I give someone the wrong medication?" She gave an angry pinch to a roll of fat on her stomach. "I've got to get this weight off. No more farting around." She extricated her arms from her sleeves and let the jacket fall against the seat back.

"But you haven't been—"

"I need the restroom." Maggie leaned down and clutched her bag before rising from the chair. She swayed for a moment and crumpled to the floor.

Jeanne scrambled to her side. "Maggie!" The store manager rushed from behind the counter, his cell phone already to his ear. He untied his green apron and fashioned a cushion for Maggie's head.

By the time the ambulance arrived, Maggie's eyes were open. "She's diabetic," Jeanne told the EMT, who nodded and spoke reassuringly to Maggie. He checked her pulse and blood pressure before attaching electrodes to her chest. To Jeanne's relief, the portable EKG machine showed a normal heart rhythm.

When the EMT pricked Maggie's finger and checked her blood sugar, he frowned. "When did you last eat?"

"Um, this morning?"

"And you're on insulin?"

Clearly embarrassed, Maggie nodded and looked away. He urged her to let him take her to the emergency room, but, in the end, she signed a release form stating that against medical advice, she had refused. "I'm going to stay here and eat something, okay? My friend is going to buy me a sandwich."

Jeanne fought down the urge to scold and brought a turkey sandwich back to the table. The EMTs packed up and left as soon as they'd finished their paperwork. A few patrons were still standing and staring, but Jeanne's glare ended their rubbernecking. When the barista brought a fresh cup of decaf to the table, Maggie unwrapped her food. "I'm sorry," she mumbled. "I'm sure you think skipping a meal was dumb, but—"

"Don't talk. Eat." After calling Lionel Chambers to arrange for Bricklin to be fed and let out, Jeanne turned off her cell and waited for Maggie to finish. She could understand having the desire to fix a problem all at once. If Maggie could get her excess weight off, perhaps the diabetes would go away. Jeanne had no idea if rapid weight loss was an antidote for diabetes once someone was symptomatic. She suspected Maggie was treating a different condition altogether: self-hatred.

Managing people for two decades had given Jeanne experience with the neuroses of her subordinates. Anxiety, depression, or obsession was manifest in people's behavior, even when they didn't realize it. Jeanne was always sympathetic, sending them to HR for a referral, but she lumped these conditions together as productivity issues—just something to factor into her project plan. Never had she felt personally weighed down by their issues the way she did at that moment. Maggie's pain was her own, and she felt unusually helpless. "Why aren't you giving yourself credit for all the weight you've lost already?"

"I had no business getting this heavy in the first place. I knew the risk. When two people with diabetes have a baby, the odds are 50 percent their child will develop diabetes."

"But that makes it your parents' fault." *Fault?* Maggie's parents had only done what Jeanne herself was doing. Continuing her pregnancy put her child at serious risk of developing Alzheimer's disease. Forty years ago, Maggie's parents may not have known they were placing their unborn daughter at risk, but if they had, would they have been wrong to have her? What a child they'd had, a terrific person and a nurse to boot. She'd helped so many people. Surely Maggie didn't regret being born.

Whom had Jeanne helped? In her head, she knew the companies she'd worked for provided value in the form of the products they sold. She'd contributed to generating the revenue that paid people's salaries so they could support themselves and their families. Yes, she'd helped herself and many others make money, some of them serious money. Her work ultimately benefited many lives. But Maggie helped people one-on-one. Jeanne wondered why she couldn't figure out how to do that for Maggie. She shut her eyes to keep out the questions.

Perhaps she could relate, after all. She remembered the box from her mother's attic with its revelations lying beneath the stuffed animals. She, too, had experienced an unexpected tug from the past. She wouldn't allow tonight to be about her, though. Any hope she'd had of Maggie's being a sounding board on genetic testing was quashed. She reached out and rubbed her friend's arm. "Tell me why you're getting sucked back into your childhood. Reminds me of how I felt when I would come home from college for the holidays, full of womanly independence. My mother treated me in the same old way—told me to eat my vegetables."

Starbucks closed at nine. The two of them were the last to leave.

Jeanne was a heavy sleeper, but that night she hovered between wakefulness and fitful dozing.

Two o'clock in the morning: lying on her back and staring at the ceiling, she considered her pregnancy issues, weighed alternative consequences, and debated with herself. She was a fierce defender of women's reproductive rights, but she'd always thought of the women she defended in the aggregate. Now she was that woman. Was she supposed to consider morality alone, and if so, whose? Maybe her biggest problem was the "alone" part.

Three o'clock in the morning: she'd decided to have her baby because she wanted him, not because she opposed abortion. Someday, she imagined, fertilized eggs would be implanted in a robot's uterus to satisfy both those who wanted to adopt and those who didn't want to be pregnant. Abortion would just move the fetus to a different zip code, pregnancy would be optional, and both sides of the abortion debate would be served.

Of course, there would be moral objections to that too, and some people wouldn't want to know they had a child out in the world who might be suffering.

Four o'clock in the morning: lying on her stomach, hugging her pillow, she felt oppressed by the choices science was giving her. If there were no genetic testing, she'd have no way to know if she carried or had passed on an Alzheimer's gene. Maggie's parents didn't know that by having a child, they were putting her at risk. Jeanne envied them. What if Jeanne found out she carried the gene, but the baby didn't. Should she abort her pregnancy so her child wouldn't be motherless? Give her baby up for adoption?

Rolling onto her side, she felt Bricklin's warmth beside her. She had to help him onto the bed each night, but it's where he wanted to be. He was still alive because she'd given him a chance, and he'd shown his will to live. Didn't her baby deserve at least as much as she'd given her beloved pet? But who would raise her child if she couldn't?

Five o'clock in the morning: on her back again, she tormented herself with her choice—find out for sure, and maybe not even for sure, if she carried the deterministic gene for Alzheimer's, but possibly too late to have an abortion; settle for data on the predisposing gene alone. In either case, she would never have the clarity she craved.

Jeanne arrived at work late, exhausted, and in no mood to talk to anyone, but she had to call Sharon Basko with her decision. "I know you think this is a mistake, but I just have to know—all the genes they can test for: PS-1, PS-2, APP, APOE-e4. I can't walk away from the chance to acquire more supporting data, no matter what the expense. I can afford to pay."

"You don't need to please me in this, Jeanne. It's your call. I'll let Dr. Cross know. I'd also like to set up a time to meet the baby's father so I can learn his family health history and test him."

Jeanne swiveled her chair and stared out the window at a sky that had no business being such a crystalline blue when life below was so complicated. "I should have explained when we first met that I'm pretty sure, but not entirely sure, which of two men . . ."

"I understand, Jeanne. Your situation is not as unusual as you may think. I'll get back to you on the genetic testing. Okay? Good luck."

Jeanne tilted her head back and let her arms hang down on either side of her chair. She hadn't realized how tight her shoulders were till they dropped what felt like several inches. Tension drained from her muscles for only a few moments, though, before guilt pulled her erect.

For the first time in her life, Jeanne's work was suffering. She forced herself to shift attention to her screen, where a report from Mariana on plans for January's sales kickoff had languished in Jeanne's inbox. The event seemed trivial.

As soon as she arrived home, Jeanne peeled off her work clothes. Only four months pregnant and already they were too tight. Could she be carrying an extra-large child? The maternity outfits she'd purchased with Maggie hung in the back of her closet. She thought she'd feel self-conscious wearing them so early in her pregnancy. If she ended up having an abortion, the change would appear more radical if she were already in tent-sized blouses.

She looked at herself in the full-length mirror on the inside of her closet door and made a face. If only she had nothing more serious to worry about than the size of her belly. She pulled the elastic-paneled maternity jeans off their shelf and stepped into them.

Thanksgiving was less than a week away, and she had no plans for the holiday, her first since her mother had died.

She felt a pang of longing for the house in Newford—not the cold hollow shell it had become since her mother's death but the Thanksgiving home of her youth, its windows reflecting the incandescence within, its air warmly scented by the oven's savory promises.

A while back, Vince had hinted he might want Jeanne to come with him to New Jersey, where most of his large, noisy family lived. Thanksgiving was a big deal for them, with each household contributing its Italian specialty to his parents' feast. That trip was off the table now, as Vince hadn't called her since the conflagration over her attributing paternity to a sperm donor.

Somehow, she would manage to fill the day. Perhaps she and Bricklin would find a new conservation area and take a longer walk than usual. She always had work or industry news to catch up on that could fill a couple of hours. By then she'd be ready to prepare something special for herself, not turkey—the leftovers would last forever—but maybe stuffed Cornish hen.

Jeanne's shoulders slumped. Who was she kidding? The day would be cheerless. She plucked her cell from its case and pulled up Maggie's number. After six rings—Jeanne didn't expect her to pick up—she left a voice mail. Silly, she supposed, but maybe, just maybe, Maggie would be her guest for Thanksgiving.

It was Saturday morning before Maggie called, leading with profuse apologies for her delay in responding to Jeanne's message. "Don't worry," Jeanne urged. "I'm the one who's usually apologizing to people. You can only return just so many calls during the workday. The important thing is you sound better than you did on Thursday."

After Maggie assured her she was trying to be more sensible in coping with her diabetes, Jeanne extended her invitation, hoping she didn't sound desperate.

"Here's my problem, Jeanne. I agreed to work that evening

so I could free up one of our caregivers for the holiday. Hey, you could come to Dawning Day. I'm serious. We always need volunteers, especially at this time of year. We wouldn't be in the Alzheimer's wing at all, if that upsets you, and you could bring Bricklin."

Jeanne looked out her large living room windows. She'd loved how much sunlight filled these rooms when she'd decided to buy this condo, but at moments like this, with a sky the color of an old aluminum pot, gloom invaded. Dawning Day Assisted Living was an unappealing holiday destination, but solitude on Thanksgiving, this particular Thanksgiving . . . She'd see her neighbors' windows lit up and the cars of their guests parked everywhere, even outside her front door. "Okay, I'll do it. Thank you—I think."

Maggie laughed. "I think you think too much. We'll have fun. You'll see."

Under the Dawning Day portico, Jeanne snapped her umbrella open and closed, spraying water from its surface onto the grass. Bricklin's leash was looped over her wrist, and he strained against it to avoid the shower. The previous day had been gorgeous, which Jeanne supposed was a blessing for all those traveling on the busiest travel day of the year. The fastest speed her windshield wipers could whip back and forth had been barely adequate to the downpour as she'd driven toward Dawning Day. Such dreary weather would have made for a depressing afternoon to be trapped at home alone.

Even Bricklin had been reluctant to go out, but his tail began wagging as soon as they entered the lobby, and the receptionist's eyes lit up. When she saw Bricklin was an amputee, she scowled. "Poor baby. That's just wrong." Bricklin bobbed his way around her desk and began nuzzling her lap as though it were his job to reassure her. As she petted his wet fur gingerly, she complimented Jeanne on her courage taking to the road in such wretched weather. "Aren't you the woman who was here the day of Maggie's accident? Should I call her for you?"

By the time Maggie appeared, Bricklin was surrounded by admirers, and Jeanne began feeling like a local celebrity. The residents wanted to know why he had only three legs and for how long he'd been an amputee. Could he still run? Was he happy? Jeanne had wondered what she'd talk about with the elderly denizens of Dawning Day, but Bricklin was leading the way.

"I don't know why I invited you," Maggie said. "Bricklin's fine on his own and far more entertaining."

"I can be entertaining," Jeanne protested. Maggie's eyebrow rose. "Okay, I used to be. It's been a while."

Maggie shepherded everyone into the lounge, where a flutist was getting ready to perform. Beside her sat a paunchy man with sparse white hair, tuning a violin and adjusting a handkerchief between his double chin and his instrument. "She's famous," Maggie whispered. "That's her father."

The flutist introduced herself and her father: "Although, of course, he needs no introduction to you. What you may not know, however, is that he is accomplished on several stringed instruments and used to be the conductor of the Buffalo Symphony." He bowed slightly in his chair and smiled at his daughter. "Ready, Dad?"

They began the promised Fauré *Pavane*, and, as they played, Jeanne noted the effect on the gathered residents. Faint smiles, dreamy looks, and expressions of outright pleasure appeared on every face. They actually look younger, she thought. Bricklin, who lay on the floor beside her, radiated canine contentedness.

Father and daughter performing together—how lucky

they'd been to share their love of music over the years. Imagine the bond. It would have sustained them even through the rocky years of adolescence. The *Pavane* enveloped Jeanne in its poignant strains. She missed her father, a man who hadn't lived long enough for her to love. How sad that her child would grow up with the same hole in his or her life.

Several minutes into the piece, the violinist faltered, and after a couple of restarts the flutist stopped playing. "Dad, that was wonderful, but I think we've played enough. Let's not wear out our welcome." Jeanne winced at the painful scene, the father's embarrassment at failing to perform what he'd known by heart, his humiliation at his daughter's caring but patronizing tone. Only the swelling applause diminished his look of consternation. A staffer yelled out, "Bravo!" and others followed.

When did they make the switch, Jeanne wondered, to daughter parenting father? Did something happen—a fall, an illness—or did his faculties diminish bit by bit? The daughter probably wondered if it were her imagination that her dad was slipping. The father lied to himself about his lapses, then covered them up until he lost track of how frequent they were.

She turned to Maggie. "Is he courageous or just too foolish to know he can no longer perform?"

"We want them to do everything they can, even if they can't do it as well as in the past. It helps that the other residents are supportive."

Jeanne thought about Jake and his PTSD. "Maybe it's less than helpful to remember the past."

"Part of aging is learning to live with all kinds of loss. Resilience and a sense of humor help them survive."

How lucky Fay Bridgeton had been. At the same age as some of these Dawning Day residents, she'd been able to prepare a Thanksgiving feast in her own home. As methodical and accomplished in the kitchen as she'd been as an accountant, she charted the meal ahead of time: ingredients, cooking time, pots, serving pieces. Each dish was ready to come to the table at the correct moment, and it didn't matter if she were cooking for friends or just Jeanne. The preparation and precision were the same, culinary debits and credits in balance.

Although Fay had shown no signs of cognitive decline, Jeanne wanted to believe she would have been supportive. Who'd be there for Jeanne? Her child? Would her child resent her for knowing she'd fall ill and sticking him or her with the problem?

"Since I won't be able to sit down, would you mind if I put you at a table with three residents?" Maggie was standing, and Jeanne could see the parade of wheelchairs and metal walkers with their incongruous tennis ball feet that had started toward the dining room. Maggie lowered her voice. "The fourth person at the table died yesterday, and I hate to have that empty seat staring at the other three on Thanksgiving. We often switch seating around, what with people moving to the Alzheimer's wing and new residents arriving, but this death was so sudden, we haven't had time to regroup. You'd be a stabilizing influence."

Jeanne did mind, but she couldn't say no. She hoped she wouldn't have to carry the conversation and regarded with trepidation her three tablemates as Maggie introduced her. Two were women. Marta, to Jeanne's left, looked sixtyish and was in a wheelchair. Rose, sitting cattycorner, was surely ninety. Her expression was lively in spite of her watery blue eyes, half-eclipsed by sagging lids. The bald gentleman to Jeanne's right rose stiffly. "Max Keystone," he identified himself before Maggie had the chance, and he insisted on pulling out Jeanne's chair.

"Be careful," said Rose. "He's a terrible flirt."

"That's okay. It's a little late in the game," Jeanne responded wryly, resting her hand on her belly.

Maggie laughed. "Looks like you'll fit in here. Please excuse me. I don't get my turkey till later, so don't eat it all!"

Marta asked Jeanne how she knew Maggie. As reluctant as Jeanne was to discuss Weight Watchers, no subject was a more natural icebreaker for women, even of disparate ages. Max conformed to Rose's description of him, complimenting them on their hourglass shapes. "Well," he looked at Jeanne. "Maybe not yours. May I be so bold as to inquire when you're expecting?"

They clucked over Jeanne and extolled the joys of parenthood and the even greater rewards of grandparenthood. Jeanne saw Marta looking at her ringless left hand. "The father's missing in action?" she asked.

"Marta, shush," Rose chided. "That's how they do it now. Girls are very independent." Marta pushed away the fruit cup appetizer that had been placed in front of each of them. "I wasn't judging her. Better to be rid of him now than to believe you can depend on him. My husband waited till my MS was bad enough to cramp his style before he took off." Marta looked away, and Rose squeezed her shoulder.

They must have heard this story before, probably many times. Marta was still a striking woman, with green eyes and a complexion fair enough for her auburn hair color to have once been natural. Jeanne could taste her bitterness. A degenerative illness had reduced her options, and a disloyal partner had robbed her of the rest. Dawning Day might be in Jeanne's future too. Would she be at a table like this until her memory lapses, cognitive changes, and odd behavior caused another Rose, Marta, and Max to shun her? Who would decide when it was time to join the residents who lived beyond the secure door?

"What type of work do you do, Jeanne?" Max asked.

Jeanne became animated describing her work at Salientific but stopped when she noticed Rose's vague expression. "I hope I'm not boring you."

"Not at all," Max insisted. "Never realized marketing folks could be so quantitative." He seemed enthralled with the concept that risk management was integral to marketing strategy. "Thought all of you were creative types—ads, brochures, and the like."

He'd been an actuary, he told her proudly, and had outlived the predictions on all his charts. "You ladies have a distinct advantage, you know, when it comes to longevity." Max informed them he had a master's in probability and statistics, a credential that impressed Jeanne and took them further down the road of statistical analysis in business decisions.

Jeanne almost forgot Marta and Rose until she noticed they were focused on the lobby. Bricklin had moved from his spot and sat in the archway to the dining room, staring at the plate of turkey just deposited on Jeanne's placemat. "Is he going to join us?" Rose asked.

"He's too well trained to beg, but he's not above gazing longingly at my food." Jeanne put half a dozen small pieces of turkey on her bread-and-butter plate and carried it out to the lobby, where she deposited it beside the water bowl the receptionist had provided.

After the instant it took Bricklin to inhale Jeanne's treat, she hugged him and planted a noisy kiss on top of his head. "Got to obey the public health laws, boy. You stay out here." Though ignorant of health regulations, Bricklin knew "stay" and, with a mournful glance at Jeanne, lay down beside the desk.

When Jeanne returned to the table, Rose was nodding. "I can see from how much you love that dog you're sure to be a good mother."

Jeanne was about to reply that her boyfriend had made the same observation but stopped herself when she realized she could refer to Vince as nothing more than the baby's probable father. "Most people wouldn't describe me as the mothering type, and my love didn't do Bricklin any good when he got sick. I couldn't protect him from cancer."

"Unfortunately, love doesn't protect anyone. If it did, all our children would be safe." She looked down and rubbed her fingers back and forth on the edge of the table. "Nothing to be done about that but not to have them, and then where would the world be?"

Maybe the world would be better off, Jeanne thought. She could protect her child by not having him.

Marta tossed her hair. "Forget protection—most you can hope for in this world is a little support—if you're lucky."

Max seemed lost in thought, chewing his green bean casserole with his mouth open. Jeanne looked away.

"Listen to me, young lady." He touched her arm. "Guarantees you get in heaven. I know data. I used to swear by risk analysis, but after you fill in the numbers and draw your conclusions, how do you use the information? No—such—thing—as—objectivity." He jabbed his forefinger to emphasize each word. "You give more weight to some numbers than others and make them support whatever conclusions you want. Hell, most of us just come to the conclusions first and find the numbers we like to support them after. Just watch the politicians—masters at it." He sat back, triumphant.

Rose rolled her eyes. "Max," Marta chided, "leave her alone and finish your turkey. You're the one who should have been the politician—always making speeches."

"More important," Rose said, "Max is holding up the pumpkin pie."

No such thing as objectivity. Jeanne smiled politely at the old man, finding his conclusion as unpalatable as the dry stuffing in her mouth. She pushed her plate back, and a smiling server whisked away their dishes.

If the pumpkin pie was *homemade*, the *home* was some catering company's institutional kitchen. No one seemed to mind but Max, who took one bite and laid down his fork. "No comparison to my wife's. She used fresh pumpkin." Decaf coffee and tea arrived, prompting Max to circulate his teabag once, scoop it onto a teaspoon, and wrap the string around it to squeeze out the remaining moisture. "Ever hear the expression 'reading the tea leaves'?"

Marta sighed audibly, but Max was undeterred. "Same with 'seeing the handwriting on the wall' or 'sniffing out the truth.' Just because you have the data doesn't mean you'll let yourself see it, much less draw the right conclusion. People use their gut to take them the rest of the way. Human nature."

Why did people say to trust your gut, heart, or any other body part, when it made a lot more sense to trust your brain? No benefit in arguing the point. Jeanne waved her white napkin at Max. "I surrender."

"Now, Max, you stop it," Rose scolded. "Don't mind him, dear. He does that to all of us."

Jeanne looked around for Maggie, who was nowhere in sight, but she could see Bricklin, still curled up by the receptionist's desk, and felt a sudden urge to lie down beside him and bury her face in his lush coat. It wasn't that Max had disturbed her so much as that everything happening in her life seemed to have unmoored her from her perennially stable footings. Bricklin was her refuge and, yes, the focus of her maternal feelings. She might as well admit Vince and Rose were right about that.

When the meal was finished, Rose urged Jeanne to accept

an extra slice of pie to take home. Jeanne accepted the soggy, napkin-wrapped dessert so graciously proffered, because Rose subscribed to the "eating for two" theory of pregnancy and insisted. Gently placing the pie in the top of her open bag, Jeanne joined the exodus from the dining room.

Bricklin had anointed himself a one-man receiving line and was enjoying the procession of stroking hands, his tail thumping with enthusiasm. When Jeanne reached him, the line stalled, as two women tried simultaneously to tell her about their childhood pets. Not until Jeanne felt a tug on her arm did she realize Bricklin had his muzzle in her purse like a horse at a feed bag. At her "leave it," he withdrew his head, although the shredded napkin hanging from his mouth was all that remained of the pie.

Maggie, who had just emerged from the Alzheimer's wing, came up behind Jeanne, laughing. "Uh-oh, Bricklin, I have a feeling your Mom is about to take you home."

Marta wheeled her chair alongside. "I thought you said he didn't beg."

"Technically, he didn't," Jeanne said. "He helped himself—and just when I was beginning to think he should be a regular here."

"He should—and so should you. Look around. Everyone's enjoying the show." Maggie hugged her and retrieved Jeanne's coat from the closet. "You both made quite an impression."

"I got a lecture from Max on the dubious value of risk analysis. Didn't realize I'd be taking pointers from a former actuary."

Maggie's voice dropped to a whisper. "He's a brilliant man, Jeanne, but he was never an actuary. He taught philosophy at Wellesley. When he makes stuff up, he's confabulating, although some people refer to it as 'honest lying' or 'false memories.' It's an Alzheimer's symptom. Eventually, we'll have to move him to the other wing."

Jeanne was stunned. "So convincing. . . ." They hugged once more before she stepped out into a fierce northwest wind. The temperature must have dropped fifteen degrees since she'd arrived. No longer wet with rain, the shiny asphalt was slippery beneath her feet. She walked gingerly to her car, holding tight to Bricklin's leash and mulling over Max's words.

No such thing as objectivity. She'd studied perception in college—Plato? Berkeley? Kant? Who could remember that stuff? Shivering, she pulled her coat more tightly about her. *Everything subject to interpretation.* Crazy, confabulating old coot.

CHAPTER 10

Dreading her neuropsychological test made no sense, but Jeanne couldn't control her racing heart as she entered the Fenway Medical Center. Her intestines shifted in a way that foretold gas. *Not on the elevator, please.* Her innards shifted again as she joined the others turning to face the closing elevator doors.

Oh God, it's a kick. While her eyes were fixed on the changing floor numbers, she felt another internal bump and looked around, half expecting other faces to register these alerts from within. Her fellow passengers were oblivious as she placed her hand on her stomach, which seemed necessary to acknowledge her baby's communication.

Her first impulse was to call Vince, but that was not an option. After her evaluation, she would try to reach Maggie. *Restless baby, please don't kick me during this test.* She took three deep breaths in an effort to calm herself.

In high school and college, she'd approached most tests of her cognitive abilities with confidence. To be over the hill in her forties scared her. That anxiety blocks memory was one of

Jeanne's newly acquired bits of information. It wouldn't do to flunk her test for no other reason than nerves, and what about pregnancy brain? Was that real?

The waiting room was spare, but Jeanne had barely perched herself on an unforgiving vinyl loveseat before the neuropsychologist came out to get her. The conference room where she was to spend the next few hours had upholstered swivel chairs around a blond wood table, and between the comfortable seating and the doctor's warm smile, she felt blood begin to circulate again in her clammy hands.

She could see why she'd been required to provide ahead of time her medical records and family information, sparse though that was. She was asked to elaborate on her father's condition, though Jeanne knew only what her mother's safe deposit box had revealed, and the doctor probed the symptoms that had worried her about her own mental state.

Somehow her missing and mysteriously reappearing notebook and her misplaced parked car sounded trivial in that setting, where she knew people had been interviewed who couldn't find their way home or recognize their friends. At least she was able to respond.

After a lengthy interview, the neuropsychologist introduced Jeanne to the medical student who would administer the tests. She was a serious young woman, Indian perhaps, with dark hair pulled back in a low ponytail. Nara Shah's nametag sat at an angle, as though she had clipped it hurriedly to her white jacket. She wasted no time arranging her papers and forms and setting up her stop watch, giving Jeanne the impression she needed to run off as soon as possible to do something more interesting, like viewing brain slices under a microscope.

The first test required Jeanne to listen to a brief, detailed story and repeat back as much of it as she could. Nara would come back to the story two more times during the battery of tests, and Jeanne was pretty sure, whatever the details she might have failed to recite the first time, her rendition of the story remained the same. Nara was impassive, so Jeanne could take neither heart nor despair from her performance. She wondered if she had acted the same way with her subordinates when they'd presented to her, and vowed to provide more positive body language in the future, if only to reduce their anxiety.

Some of the tests were fun, completing drawings or creating new ones, listing all the farm animals she could think of or words beginning with the letter "F" and connecting numbered dots. After easily remembering groups of numbers Nara read aloud, Jeanne's self-confidence grew.

Gradually, the strings of numbers grew long. Some needed to be repeated back in reverse sequence. Responses were timed, and Jeanne found herself flashing back to college, to her panic in her first art history exam when the professor changed slides so fast that Jeanne couldn't identify the paintings. The more she missed, the more she missed, like interest compounding on credit card debt. When the evaluation was over, Nara allowed herself a small smile as Jeanne shook her hand, thanked her, and wondered if she dared regard that change in expression as a positive sign.

After texting Maggie about the baby's first kicks, Jeanne checked her email. She wasn't the only one invoking exclamation points, since a message from Jake asked her and the rest of the executive team to join him in his meeting with Lou ASAP. If Lou had been summoned, there had to be a product problem. She put her car in gear and drove as fast as the garage's switchbacks allowed, but the exit line moved in fits and starts through the card insertion device.

Bart and Lou were already in Jake's office when Jeanne arrived. Bart stood at Jake's whiteboard, dry marker in hand, enumerating the requirements of the Stellarstore Retail request for proposal just received by one of Bart's sales reps. Jake, seated at his conference table, leaned on his elbows, while Lou sat with pursed lips, arms crossed above his belly. "It's an awesome opportunity," Bart concluded.

"Would be," Lou said, pointing at the board, "if we could do all that."

"But isn't most of it in our product plan already?"

"*Most* is not *all*, Bart. Sales reps exaggerate. VPs shouldn't."

"One of our competitors will do it all. It's too big an opportunity to pass up." Bart was right, and Jeanne was pretty sure she knew which competitor had the engineering bandwidth to pull it off.

Lou shook his head. "This is where companies go off the rails. They deviate from their strategic plan to chase a single piece of business, and then they don't have the resources to do the really important stuff."

"Maybe we partner with another company to cover all the bases," Jeanne suggested.

Jake leaped out of his seat, eyes burning with blue flame, and pounded the table. "I want this deal, all of it. I'm not giving a piece of it to a partner, you hear me, Jeanne? Lou will find a way to get the engineering done so Bart can close it! Lou, is that clear?"

Lou jerked upright in his chair, propelling it from the table. Even Bart backed away, hardened though he was by years of angry customer abuse. Jeanne felt the table vibrating beneath her hands as Jake struck it. Lou's fists were clenched, and, for a moment, Jeanne thought the argument would turn into a brawl. She felt vulnerable in a way she never had before. Pregnant women didn't break up fist fights.

"Guys, guys," Bart pleaded. "Let me go back to my rep and have her test the waters with the customer. He may be flexible on the timing of some of these product features. Maybe we don't need everything ready on day one. Let's find out his implementation schedule." Jeanne let out her breath and silently forgave Bart for all previous transgressions.

A silent Lou got up from his chair and walked out, leaving Jake to watch his exit and collapse back into his chair. "I'll get right on this," Bart said, gathering his papers. He glanced at Jeanne as he pulled the door closed behind him. Neither Jake nor Jeanne spoke, but as the wall clock's second hand measured the quiet in audible increments, Jeanne pondered how to avoid provoking his anger while suggesting he take time off. This wasn't the best timing, but she had to do something.

"Jake—"

"Don't! I'm the CEO of this company, and I have the ultimate say. Just because Lou pissed me off doesn't mean I'm the one with the problem." He rose and began pacing his office. "Franklin Burrows called to ask how I was doing. He wanted to know if I'd recovered from the shock of the car crash. 'I'm fine,' I told him." He stopped inches from Jeanne. "Who said I wasn't, Jeanne? You? Because you were the only one who knew." He leaned over and grabbed the arms of her chair, trapping her in her seat. "And you're the one in line for my job."

Jeanne felt electricity coursing through her body, but she tried to speak in measured tones. "Franklin was in our office the day of the crash. He must have seen how upset you were, justifiably upset. I wouldn't read anything into the honest concern he expressed on the phone." *It was Parker*, she wanted to yell, not her—Parker plotting a coup d'état and marshaling his forces. She couldn't say the words, not when Jake was making Parker's mutiny seem rational.

As soon as Jake released her chair, Jeanne bolted for the door—late for a marketing meeting—had to go. She could hear the ping of text messages arriving on her phone but ignored them as she raced to Lou's office. His door was closed, but she could see through the narrow glass panel beside the door he was conferring with Bart.

Lou spotted her and beckoned. "Still not ready to make a decision about Jake?" he asked.

"I'm still kind of—" She was going to say "numb," but Bart interrupted.

"Weren't you in the same meeting as us? Jake's ready for a padded cell."

Lou sighed and swiveled back and forth in his chair. When he finally spoke to Jeanne, his voice had softened. "I understand why you're resistant. You want to be fair to Jake while he's going through a rough patch."

"Rough patch?" Bart snorted. "Parker's right. We need to go to the board—unless something's still holding you back, Jeanne. Jake got something on you?" His eyes wandered down to Jeanne's abdomen.

"Alberta got something on you?" she shot back.

"Hey!" Lou intervened. "Jeanne, not helpful. Bart, way out of line." Only Jeanne's lingering gratitude for Bart's role in pacifying Jake kept her from further attack. She was going to have to sign on with Parker's effort to move Jake aside, but Bart was making it harder for her to relinquish her holdout position.

She wanted to do what was best for Salientific, but there would be an opportunity cost to deposing Jake. He was popular with company employees, especially the engineers who appreciated the synergy between Jake, the technical visionary, and

Lou, the capable engineering executive. It felt so wrong, taking Jake's job away because of a relapse of PTSD. Companies readily bundled off their alcoholic executives to detox and welcomed them back to their jobs. Why should Jake's sacrifice for his country be punished?

"I agree with both of you," Jeanne said. "Jake was over the top today. We can't go on like this. Give me one more shot at getting him to take time off and get help. Bart, you said you wanted Jake here through the kickoff. It's only a month away. If any other crazy stuff happens or I'm unsuccessful, I'll join you so we can present a united front to the board—he goes or we go."

Bart was shaking his head before she finished. "The guy practically goes postal on us, and she wants to give him more time. Unbelievable."

Lou chimed in, "I get it, Jeanne, but we only have a few days to decide what we're doing with the Stellarstore RFP. This week—get him out of here this week or I'm going to kill him myself. Bart, talk to your rep about the customer's implementation schedule before we tear the management team apart over this."

Jeanne devoted her evening to researching PTSD. The depression, withdrawal, irritability, and anger she read about were all observable in Jake's recent behavior. Recklessness, however, including drug and alcohol abuse, was not. Cold comfort, but at least Jake's situation seemed salvageable.

She sat back and chewed her pen. Could she be sure he wasn't a substance abuser? All she really knew was that he was divorced. The websites she looked at emphasized the importance of a support system. If Jake didn't have one . . . Of course, when Luke had asked her if she had one, she'd lied. No way could she chastise Jake for being a loner, even if their reasons were different.

On the US Veteran's Administration website, Jeanne found information on a variety of therapeutic approaches and medications currently in use for the treatment of PTSD. She wondered if her relationship with Jake was strong enough for him to tolerate her offering advice. He might think her presumptuous. If, after yesterday, their relationship was broken . . . She dreaded a replay of that conversation.

The next morning, Bart copied Jeanne and Lou on the email exchange with his sales rep for Stellarstore. She was pretty sure it would be okay if engineering provided enhancements to Salientific's product in phases. She would set up a meeting ASAP to verify that the phase-in would still meet her customer's schedule. Bart asked her to set up an executive-level meeting, promising he would fly out for it. If Bart could get high-level buy-in, it would defuse the tension between Jake and Lou over the engineering schedule.

Jake replied immediately to Jeanne's email querying his availability. She had until two to gird herself. She was glad she'd get one more crack at getting Jake to deal with his problem but couldn't shake her discomfort with her own motives. Was she doing the right thing for the wrong reason, or maybe even the wrong thing? How difficult it had become to separate her ethics from her emotions.

She couldn't forget Jake's sweet, sheepish smile the morning they'd woken up in the same bed. She couldn't forget he might be the father of her child. If this new menacing Jake couldn't fulfill his duties as CEO, though, she had a responsibility to report that fact to the board. That's what Lou would say. Don't get philosophical and worry about motives, yours or anyone else's. When she and Lou had first taken their walk together, he'd been untroubled by Parker's motives.

Jake's door was open at two o'clock when Jeanne approached, fingers twitching with trepidation. He looked up from his laptop when she rapped the doorframe. He wasn't smiling but appeared calm as she took a seat across the desk from him. Beginning with her respect and admiration for him and going on to express her genuine concern for his health and well-being, she suggested he treat himself to a week's vacation.

Jake seemed willing to hear her out, so she pointed out that Salientific had no deadlines from that point till Christmas. Bart's revenue numbers were over target, Stellarstore was open to a looser schedule from engineering, and people in the company were focused on the approaching holidays. Not only could Jake be spared, but he was owed a respite.

Jeanne saved for last the suggestion she feared would get her thrown out of his office. "Perhaps a vacation would give you some space to touch base with a therapist at the VA hospital. Bet you haven't had time for that in a while."

Jake sighed and leaned back in his chair. "Sorry if I came on a little strong yesterday. You're right. I have been on edge lately, and I appreciate your concern. Tell you what, let me think about it, check my calendar—see what commitments can be moved out a week. I'll let you know, okay?"

Jeanne exhaled with relief. She was tempted to continue the conversation, so armed was she with arguments for him to seek help, but she knew the sales maxim: when you get the order, stop selling and get out. The problem was she hadn't quite closed the deal.

Jake was leaving her no choice but to thank him and retreat. "I'm so glad you're going to take some time away. Just let us know when." The presumptive close was worth a shot—pretend he had actually committed.

When Jeanne returned to her office, she was tempted to burn incense and pray to the gods of reason—anything rather than wait for Jake to let her know his decision. The gods smiled, and half an hour later, Jake's email on his weeklong vacation, beginning Monday, appeared in her inbox.

The message had gone out company-wide, and Jeanne referenced it in her follow-on message to Bart and Lou. Bart responded with a simple "thx" from his cell phone, but Lou praised her effort and expressed hope they'd see a change in Jake's behavior on his return. While Jeanne knew any real progress depended on whether Jake saw a therapist, she had no way to ensure he would.

At Weight Watchers, Maggie had her purse on the chair she always saved for Jeanne. Lucy had already begun the session and was soliciting good-news stories about the week's weight loss successes. The first thing Jeanne noticed when she slipped in beside Maggie was how thin and drawn her face seemed, even though Jeanne had seen her at Dawning Day a week ago. "Have you eaten anything since the holiday?" she whispered in Maggie's ear.

"Yes, Mom," she whispered back, straightening up when Lucy glanced their way. Most of the good news reported by others in the meeting related to coping successfully with Thanksgiving dinner, and Lucy invited applause after each testimonial.

As the discussion turned to strategies for healthy eating on Christmas, Jeanne felt the companionable warmth of Maggie's arm against hers. She wanted to buy Maggie something special for Christmas but wasn't sure what she might want. Jeanne and her mother had always exchanged lists before birthdays and holidays to avoid unwanted or impractical gifts. There were no surprises in the Bridgeton household.

At the end of the meeting, Maggie asked how she did. Jeanne grimaced. "Up two pounds."

"You're allowed."

"If I keep gaining at this rate, I won't fit behind the wheel of my car."

"Walking's better for you anyway."

"Good old Nurse Maggie, always telling me to take a walk." Jeanne was about to ask Maggie how well the scale had treated her this week when Lucy approached them and asked Maggie if they could have a word. Jeanne left them and went over to the cookbook display, which reminded her she was hungry. She wanted to buy a package of brownies but felt guilty about having a sweet before dinner. Maggie's ribbing notwithstanding, a better purchase might be a Fitbit.

Maggie's voice was soft, but Lucy's had a shrill edge, and a few of her words carried to Jeanne, who admittedly had one ear cocked. Lucy expressed concern over the rapidity of Maggie's weight loss. The words "slow but steady" drifted over, but Jeanne couldn't hear Maggie's response. She imagined Maggie had put Lucy off with some equivalent platitude.

If Maggie was screwing around with partial fasting, she might have another fainting episode like the one at Starbucks, or worse yet, behind the wheel. Maggie looked annoyed and seemed eager to get away from Lucy, so Jeanne didn't want to pile on and admonish her too. "I've got to get home to Bricklin, but let's go to dinner, maybe this weekend, if you're off? A new restaurant just opened at the Natick Mall, and it was well reviewed."

Jeanne's quickly conceived plan was to talk with Maggie about her diet in a relaxed, neutral setting. After that, they could stroll around the mall, perhaps allowing Jeanne to divine Maggie's heart's desire in clothes for a Christmas gift. Maggie was always admiring Jeanne's outfits, and her own clothes were doubtless getting too big as fast as Jeanne's were getting too small.

Emerald House, contrary to its name, was not green and sparkly in its decor. The Emerald was the chef's signature dish, a quail with parsnip puree and haricots verts. Other dishes had jewel names too.

Jeanne had never seen Maggie dressed up. With a blue V-necked dress that matched her eyes, set off her flowing blond hair, and revealed serious cleavage, Maggie might still be big, but she was positively alluring. Shedding more weight was needed only to enhance, not achieve, the effect. "Oh my God, look at you! You're a fox. What a shame you're only having dinner with a model for Omar, the tentmaker." Jeanne smoothed her maternity top over her belly.

"Can't think of anyone I'd rather spend Saturday night with."

"Sweet, Mag, but a bald-faced lie. A dry martini will fix that. Works better than sodium pentothal." The restaurant was crowded, and Jeanne was glad she'd made a reservation. While it was a bit high-end for the average mall shopper, patrons of Neiman Marcus and the designer shops probably helped fill seats.

The maître d' ushered them to a table by the window, where other tables for two were clustered. To her horror, Jeanne recognized Vince two tables away. He was clinking his glass of

Chivas with the champagne flute of a striking brunette, twenty years his junior. When he saw Jeanne, his eyes widened. He took in her face and baby bump, while Jeanne took in the red knit dress pulled tight across his dinner companion's thighs, her endless legs, and her open-toed red suede platform heels.

Jeanne handed the menus back to the maître d' before he could finish saying their server would be with them in a moment. "It's drafty by the window." She crossed her arms and rubbed them for warmth. "Would you mind seating us elsewhere in the interior of the restaurant?"

Moments later, they were offered a table twenty feet from Vince with noisy diners in between. Jeanne would have preferred having Vince out of her line of sight, but out of earshot was acceptable. She wished she could order a double tequila to help her regain the sense of festive anticipation Vince had quashed. Maggie didn't wait for her sauvignon blanc and Jeanne's ginger ale to arrive before insisting on knowing what was going on.

"Don't turn your head, but that guy with the hot brunette, over by the window, is Vince."

"Aren't you—?"

"I didn't want to tell you, because I haven't done the paternity test yet. Remember our lunch at the Cheesecake Parlor? You beat me up because I was worried about the career implications of letting everyone know who the father was. Vince came over later. We spent the loveliest evening cozied up together until I told him my sperm donor cover story at work. He was insulted, to say the least, that I hadn't acknowledged him. Thought my career concerns were bogus and stormed out."

"I'm so sorry; not surprised, but sorry."

Jeanne lowered her eyes. "I never thought I was more driven or calculating than anyone else in my business. Do you think there's something wrong with me?"

"I'm guessing you haven't had many occasions to question yourself. You're so accomplished, Jeanne. You obviously make smart professional decisions. Only you can answer the question you're asking me. Are your priorities working for you?"

"Am I supposed to go on some kind of retreat and meditate on that question?"

Maggie laughed. "I can see you in a long robe sitting cross-legged in front of a cave in India—actually, I can't envision that at all. Introspection doesn't require a trip, except inside your head."

Jeanne raised her glass. "Here's to the inside of my head, whatever I may find lurking there."

She glanced sideways at Vince's date. *She's in a slinky dress and fuck-me stilettos, and I've got a protruding belly and sensible shoes.* When Jeanne saw Vince's eyes on her, she turned back to Maggie. "Let's order."

The meal was excellent. Jeanne ate with embarrassing gusto, but Maggie buried some of her veal under the garlic mashed potatoes she hardly touched. It seemed like the right moment to initiate a conversation about Maggie's freefall weight loss, but before she could begin, Vince appeared beside her. His companion wasn't with him or at their table, so he must have waited till she went to the ladies' room.

"Jeanne, you're looking well." So formal, and he wore his business face, pleasant and hard to read. When Jeanne introduced Maggie, he found his smile.

She looked at him with interest. "I'm told you're the person I call when I need venture capital to start my own business."

"Happy to help, Maggie." He handed her his card, which she stowed in her purse. Turning to Jeanne, he was all business again. "I have something I need to discuss with you. Will you be in tomorrow night around eight?"

Jeanne nodded, and Vince moved out of the path of a busboy with a tray. His mouth opened as though he had more to say, but he turned instead and walked out. "So," Maggie asked, "what do you make of that?" Jeanne shrugged and rubbed her forehead. When their server appeared, dessert menus in hand, Maggie shook her head and requested the check.

As soon as they left the restaurant through the exit leading to the mall, Maggie put her arms around Jeanne and gave her a quick hug. "Don't let him get to you. You're strong enough to go through this without him." With wet eyes, Jeanne fished out a tissue and tried to smile. "Let's walk around and burn off some calories," Maggie urged.

Jeanne had intended to talk to Maggie about her intense dieting, but the right moment had passed. Maggie seemed buoyed by the lights in the store windows dramatizing the posed mannequins in their sophisticated garments. "I can't remember the last time I was here. It was certainly before they added this wing."

Jeanne seized the opportunity to steer Maggie to a couple of her favorites, where the displays were particularly luscious. Most of the clothing stores were showing cocktail outfits for holiday parties amid Christmas greenery and tinsel. "Wow! Geez!" Maggie had an exclamation for each window they passed.

When they reached the Ferragamo store, Maggie came to an abrupt halt. An elegantly tailored red leather handbag sat under a spotlight behind the glass. The leather looked butter-soft, the hardware tasteful. "Would you look at that. Hundreds of dollars for sure," she added wistfully.

Jeanne felt a swell of affection for her friend. She wondered if sisters had that kind of bond, a warmth from within, and if Maggie felt the same way. An idea leaped into Jeanne's mind. Crazy, but maybe . . .

"Maggie, let's sit down for a minute. I want to ask you something." When they were seated on one of the wooden benches under a cluster of artificial birch trees, Jeanne turned to her. "I know this is going to kind of come out of left field, but would you be willing—do you think you could consider—"

"Jeanne, just ask already."

"You're younger than I am. If something happens to me, Alzheimer's, I mean, would you be willing to take care of my child?" The smile faded from Maggie's lips. She turned her face away and fell silent.

"I'm sorry. I shouldn't have sprung that on you. If you want to think about it, I completely understand."

When she returned Jeanne's gaze, a deep crease had formed between her brows, and her mouth was taut. "I thought we were friends—friends who wanted happiness for each other. Instead you're still focused on yourself. Do you think poor Maggie is so fat, she could never find a man to love her? Do you think I don't want children of my own?" Her voice rose. "Do you think Nurse Maggie lives only to help others?"

"That's not at all what I . . ." Maggie gathered her coat and bag and vanished around a corner, leaving Jeanne shocked and staring after her. She curled forward, face buried in her hands. All she could do was fervently wish the last ten minutes would roll themselves back. She'd struck a nerve with Maggie. *No wonder I have no friends. Don't have the gene for it. Hopeless.*

As the mall emptied out, she remained on the bench, bereft, wondering why she'd always thought the worst loss one could experience in life was financial—a bankruptcy, a failed company. She hadn't allowed herself to consider the more painful feelings that accompanied personal loss. Even her mother's death had left her strangely cut off from grief. She groped for tissues from her bag to sop up the tears. She had no mother, no friend, and no father for her child. She was a sister to the mannequins around her, perfectly posed and poised, well-dressed and pretending to be human.

When Jeanne opened her door at eight the next evening, Vince hesitated at the threshold. How different this entrance was from his past confident strides through her doorway. He grasped a manila folder in front of him with both gloved hands. He didn't smile, nor did Jeanne. "I've brought some paperwork I'd like to review with you."

She gestured toward the living room, but Vince had trouble moving from the foyer with Bricklin blocking his path. The dog insisted on Vince's usual affectionate greeting before retreating. "I understand, boy," Vince said, ruffling Bricklin's fur. "It's been a while." Jeanne didn't offer to take Vince's coat, a signal she hoped he'd pick up on and keep his visit brief. He made no move to remove it. She'd spent the day tied up in knots over her rift with Maggie, replaying the sickening scene in her mind.

Vince sat on the edge of the couch. Jeanne took one of the facing club chairs, while Bricklin sat on the floor close to Vince and placed his one front paw on his knee. "Off," Jeanne ordered, and Bricklin complied. He lay down beside Vince but kept his eyes on Vince's face.

"I've had legal papers drawn up that provide for a monthly contribution toward child support. The payment will come directly from my bank. I'm relinquishing, however, all my parental rights, now and in the future."

He laid the folder on the coffee table. "I think when you go through these, you'll see I've been more than fair. The contract prohibits us from revealing to the child or anyone else that I'm the biological father. That should fit nicely with your sperm donor story."

Jeanne stared at the folder with dull eyes. In her lifetime, she would see no end to the secrets. Her child would grow up knowing even less about his father than she had about hers, wondering, always wondering, why so little could be told. Imagining what her father was like, Jeanne had come up with an entire history for him. Never had it crossed her mind to include early-onset Alzheimer's.

Vince rose. She'd be alone in a minute. Surely, she could hold herself together for that long. She put hands over her face but could stop neither the tears leaking through her fingers nor the wrenching sobs that shook her body. A minute went by with Vince immobilized, although Bricklin was instantly at Jeanne's side, pushing his nose between her cheek and fingers.

"I don't understand. I thought you'd be happy with this arrangement—my anonymity, the money. What's wrong?"

"Alzheimer's" was her muffled reply.

"What?"

Jeanne dropped her hands, compelled to share her fear and feeling a perverse desire to make Vince as miserable as she was. "Alzheimer's disease—I may have the early-onset gene. Even the baby might have it."

"But . . . I don't understand. Early-onset? You mean, like, now?" She nodded. "You're already—what—forty-seven or eight? How old are people who get early-onset Alzheimer's?

"By sixty or sixty-five."

"So, if you got it in the next few years, that baby"—he pointed at her belly—"might have no mother." He looked at the ceiling, then shook his head. "That settles it. You have to get an abortion. Anything else would be nuts. You know that, don't you?"

No one wanted to be responsible for her child, not Maggie, not Vince. Regardless of her level of risk for Alzheimer's, the consequences of being on the wrong side of that calculation were dire, especially for her. She was alone. Not just alone but rejected.

She watched Vince walk to the door but didn't rise from her chair. "You can toss those papers," he said and closed the door behind him.

CHAPTER 11

The Salientific lobby was strung with plastic evergreen garlands. An artificial tree, adorned with tinsel and colored balls, stood in the corner, illuminated by less-than-celestial fluorescent lights. Christmas aroused no sense of anticipation in Jeanne, who could scarcely muster a smile in response to Eduardo's cheerful greeting. At least she wouldn't have to deal with Jake this week.

When she reached her office and checked email, she found an elated message from Bart to the management team reporting that his sales force would end the year beating its quota. Bart's quota was an aggregate of his reps', and though two reps were still struggling to hit their number before the fiscal year ended on December 31, a few had blown theirs away.

The holidays were a tough time to get customers focused on buying software. Hungry reps found a way, though, occasionally by booking orders they knew might be canceled after year end. If orders had to be taken down, Parker would be all over Bart, but successful sales VPs were pretty much a protected species.

January's sales meeting would be as much a celebration of the year just ended as a kickoff for the new fiscal year. Feeling guilty about her lack of involvement, Jeanne emailed Mariana, requesting an update on the status of sales meeting plans. Mariana appeared on the dot of ten. After settling herself at Jeanne's table, she laid her pen parallel to the top of her folder and handed Jeanne an agenda before commencing her update. Every detail of the sales meeting logistics had been worked out. "Are there any remaining obstacles, Mariana? Seems to me you've thought of everything."

"Getting responses from Jake has been a challenge for me." She bit her lip. "I mean—he's probably very busy."

"Yes," Jeanne said wryly, "very. I think you'll find him more focused when he returns from his vacation. You seem to be working well with Bart."

"He's demanding, like all the sales people. They expect marketing to be waiting by the phone in case they need help. Bart has good ideas, though, and he's never late with anything he promises me."

Jeanne rose from the table. "Excellent. Don't hesitate to ask for my help."

Mariana didn't get up. "There is one thing." She blushed, and Jeanne lowered herself into her chair. "Bart's a really . . . friendly guy, and like friendly people do, he touches kind of a lot. At first it was just his hand on my elbow or shoulder. Now when he compliments me on some task I've handled, he puts his hand over mine. When I leave his office, he walks me out with his arm around me. I mean, it's probably nothing, right? He's a vice president."

Jeanne rubbed her forehead thoughtfully. She was sure the undeniably hot Mariana knew the difference between Bart's being friendly versus coming on to her. She was being deferential.

"Maybe I shouldn't have, but I mentioned it to HR, just so someone could coach him a little. I thought you should know. Doesn't management get training on harassment?"

Jeanne's eyes grew wide. "You told Alberta Bart was hitting on you?" Jeanne didn't know how many people in the company knew about Alberta's relationship with Bart, but clearly Mariana was unaware of it.

"I didn't lodge a formal complaint or anything. I can't afford to hurt our working relationship."

"I'm sure Alberta will be . . . discreet." Jeanne wasn't sure at all, but why worry Mariana ahead of time. "I think you should lodge a formal complaint, but I won't force you. There isn't anything about his *friendly guy* behavior that's appropriate. Please let me know if he gets *friendly* again." Mariana agreed, and once she had left the office, Jeanne sat back, contemplating what form Alberta's wrath would take. She almost felt sorry for Bart.

Alberta was a known car nut who drove a vintage Mustang. She'd once told Jeanne her father had taught her and her brothers how to take engines apart and put them back together. A car bomb wasn't out of the question. Bart adored his slick black BMW. Maybe Alberta would choose a stealth approach, maybe keying the side of it after dark. Interesting to speculate. Mariana, however, was Jeanne's responsibility. She'd have to get involved—somehow.

She returned to her desk and sent a note to Alberta requesting a meeting on a personnel matter. As she checked her inbox, she saw Parker had copied the management team on his congratulations to Bart for hitting his revenue number. Bart was dedicated to the company's success—no denying it. She remembered his earnestness when he'd proposed his military theme and his desire to turn the company into a quick response force to chase high-value targets. Yes, Alberta's blowing up Bart's BMW, however entertaining to Jeanne, would not be good for Salientific.

If Alberta's ears were burning, Jeanne couldn't tell from her next message. The subject of Alberta's email was not Bart's roving hands but the Christmas turkey promised to the winner of the photo contest. Alberta was urging everyone to get their entries in by the deadline.

Jeanne accompanied Clara Nordell on three analyst briefings the following day and didn't pick up Sharon Basko's call till five o'clock, too late to catch her before she left for the day. All Sharon said in her message was that the results from Jeanne's initial blood work were back. She didn't say anything about the outcome or indicate by her tone of voice whether she had good news or not.

Jeanne felt trapped in "pause" by some cosmic DVR, awaiting test results she wasn't sure she wanted. While her life was on hold, the creature inside her was growing exponentially and kicking so she wouldn't forget it was there.

Her best shot at reaching Sharon was likely to be first thing in the morning. Jeanne made the call from her car to ensure privacy and was relieved to hear Sharon's live voice.

"I have some great news for you, Jeanne. Your results are back from the fetal cell-free DNA in your blood. Your baby doesn't have Down syndrome. I'm so relieved for you. I mean, given your age . . . I also have your APOE results."

Jeanne pulled over to the side of the road and put on her flashers. As Sharon continued, she extracted her notebook and pen from the floor of the back seat. Sharon reminded her that the e4 allele of APOE could increase the risk of late-onset Alzheimer's but was not deterministic. "You inherit one copy of APOE from your father and one from your mother. Two copies of the e4 allele increase your chance of getting the disease and lower the age when Alzheimer's symptoms are likely to appear. Jeanne, you have one copy of e4, but only one, which puts you in the same category as a great many others. You may or may not develop late-onset Alzheimer's. No need to worry."

Jeanne allowed herself momentary relief. For someone who made it her business to stand out from others, being like "a great many other people" provided a reassuring kind of anonymity. Sharon went on to remind her that they would not know for weeks the results of tests for the genes guaranteeing early-onset Alzheimer's. "I know how worried you are about the remaining results, but honestly, Jeanne, you've had considerable good news so far. Your neuropsych evaluation was normal, and you have only one e4."

"But my father—I still don't understand the cause for his condition. He had early-onset Alzheimer's."

"There's no way to know for sure what he had. In spite of the prevalence of Alzheimer's disease, there are other causes for dementia. Look, this waiting is hard, but try to be patient and keep things in perspective."

Jeanne saw an inkblot from her ballpoint on her notebook page. She hadn't realized how heavily she was bearing down after writing, "1 copy of APOE-e4." She remembered reading that the anomalies in one's genetic code were like bugs in software. Software engineers liked to joke that bugs in their programs were just features. When the anomaly was in your own genetic code, though, the joke was on you.

That night, Jeanne delved into the upper file drawer in her desk and widened the space between two Pendaflex folders to provide easier access to the one labeled "Thomas Bridgeton." The contents were skimpy, but just the few manila folders within testified to her father's existence and gave Jeanne a comforting sense of his corporeality. She removed the one holding the newspaper story "Senile Man Killed on Highway." "Ruth MacGregor," read the byline.

Probably dead. It was worth a shot, though. Google didn't disappoint. Ruth MacGregor had had a long career in journalism, much of it in the Boston area. She'd spent years at the *Boston Globe* covering everything from the statehouse to national disasters. Jeanne saw no entries indicating an obituary or memorial, so she tried the online white pages. Perhaps Ruth still lived in the area.

Whether or not she was local, she had several namesakes, and Jeanne didn't have time to call them all. Even contacting the *Globe* would result, best case, in getting handed off from one department to another. After the *New York Times* acquired them, the *Globe* had laid people off. She'd have to find someone old enough to remember Ruth. *Ironic*, she thought. In spite of everyone's paranoia about electronic fingerprints, the past can be obscure. With no digital trail, Jeanne's father was unknowable.

Bricklin was losing patience with Jeanne's reverie. His nose burrowed beneath the folder on Jeanne's lap, sending its contents sliding to the floor. "Sorry, boy, forgot about you." She surveyed the papers fanned out on the rug and rubbed Bricklin's forehead. A rueful smile tugged at one corner of her mouth.

"This is what I do, isn't it? Bury myself in data from the past and analyze the hell out of it so I can better predict the future. Makes me not so good at noticing what's going on or who's around me. People leave me, and half the time I don't even notice. Only you stay, Bricklin, and, really, what choice do you have?" She leaned over and kissed his muzzle.

The nurse checked Jeanne's weight a second time. "It's correct," she declared. "You're up seven pounds this month." Jeanne groaned. At this rate, she'd look like a giant helium balloon by the end of nine months. She reminded herself her pregnancy might end well before that, but the mere thought left her deflated.

Lying on the table in Dr. O'Rourke's examining room, she tried without success to turn her eyes away. "Looks like a boy," the doctor said, smiling broadly.

"A boy? You can tell already?"

"Depends on the position of the baby, but your son is obliging us. Eager to show off his manhood."

Jeanne's elation dissipated. *A man she might not recognize twenty years hence, might not even live to see grow up.* "I can't . . ."

O'Rourke frowned. "Can't what, Jeanne? Still can't decide about an abortion? In a month, you'll be at twenty-four weeks, the latest you can go. Just the fact that you've waited this long—it says something, don't you think? Get dressed, and we'll talk in my office."

Sitting opposite him, there was no avoiding his stern eyes. "I'm being as patient as I can, Jeanne. I know how difficult this decision is, but you have your amniocentesis appointment coming up. It's pointless to go on with these procedures—cell-free DNA, amnio, Alzheimer's genetic testing—if you're either going to terminate the pregnancy or not terminate *regardless* of the results."

"I'm sorry. It's not that I don't want my baby. I'm just not sure having him is the right thing to do, and I keep second-guessing myself . . . and third-guessing. The baby's father—"

He looked down at his notes. "Vincent Cavello?"

"He may not be the father. I know I should talk with him, or both of them, but I can't. There are professional implications that I don't expect you to understand. I do need . . . want . . . to know, though, now—not after the baby's born." *If I let it be born*. "I'm going to send away for a kit." She wished she could blame the doctor for her embarrassment, but the words coming out of her mouth the last couple of months were all unlike her. She felt possessed by an evil twin who was not so much evil as weak, needy, and indecisive.

"Do you have DNA from either of these men?"

"A toothbrush and a hairbrush—surely a lab can get his DNA from one of those and compare it to the baby's." After she and Vince had argued, he'd taken home his favorite tomato sauce pot but left his toiletries. If he'd taken only the latter, she would have had more confidence in his return.

With trepidation, Jeanne crossed the threshold of the Weight Watchers meeting room. Lucy was already at her flip chart stand illustrating the perils of Christmas eggnog. There were a number of scattered seats open, but the one next to Maggie was taken by one of the regulars. Lucy's eyes flickered from Jeanne to Maggie, but her animated delivery never faltered while Jeanne made her way to a seat on the opposite side of the room.

Jeanne's resolve to eat less and exercise more had flagged, but the distressing data supplied by Dr. O'Rourke's scale had made her eager for the booster shot of Lucy's cheerleading. In spite of Jeanne's good intentions, her eyes kept wandering from Lucy's face to the back of Maggie's head, which surely, Jeanne thought, would turn in her direction. At a quarter of the hour, before Lucy's wrap-up, Maggie gathered her coat and bag and hurried up the aisle, never glancing Jeanne's way.

When Lucy finished, Jeanne couldn't get up. A weight greater than seven additional pounds kept her in her chair staring blankly at the "Healthy Rules for Eating" posted at the front of the room. Lucy's acolytes dispersed after several minutes, and she sat down in the seat next to Jeanne. "She knew you were here." Jeanne nodded. "Can I help?"

"I appreciate the offer, but this problem is pretty far from your area of expertise."

"I'll tell you what isn't. Maggie is still dropping weight too fast, but when I tell her that, she just says she's a nurse and has it under control."

"That sounds familiar."

"I know you overheard me warning Maggie about her dramatic weight loss. I hope that's not what caused your falling out." Jeanne assured her it wasn't and thanked her again for her concern.

The mall parking lot was so jammed that even the illegal corners were occupied with Mini Coopers—whose owners thought no one would mind—and Ford Expeditions parked in crosswalks. Who'd call the cops on *them*? they figured, two weeks before Christmas. Jeanne drove around in circles, wondering why she'd chosen Saturday for what was surely a fool's errand. She ended up in a spot behind Macy's at the opposite end of the mall from her destination.

Though no lover of mall shopping, Jeanne was happy to escape the dank weather and step into the decorative wonderland of retail Christmas. As a marketing professional, she had to admire a creation that so raised the spirits without arriving in a shot glass. The aisles of Macy's were crowded, and myriad strollers increased the degree of difficulty of getting from ladies' shoes through jewelry, junior fashions, cosmetics, and out into the mall itself.

She bypassed the freestanding stations where merchants hawked everything from wireless services to teddy bears that at second glance were bedroom slippers. The crowd thinned as Jeanne turned onto the wing leading to Neiman Marcus. The Emerald was open for lunch, but the memory of her evening there with Maggie stirred a queasiness that she knew was unrelated to her pregnancy.

When she stopped before the window of Ferragamo, the display had changed. The bags were beautiful, but she didn't see the one Maggie had so admired. The rich scent of leather greeted her as she entered. Before Jeanne could peruse the shelves, a smartly dressed young woman offered her assistance. After listening to Jeanne's description, she guided her to a collection of red bags.

So impractical, Jeanne thought, especially for someone who spends long hours in an assisted living residence. Maggie's pocketbook probably lived in her desk drawer, but maybe that was the attraction. Jeanne tried to remember when she'd last made a frivolous purchase—a bandana for Bricklin's neck—nothing for herself. "I don't see it," she said. "It was in the front window last week." While the salesperson went to check in the back, Jeanne shifted her weight from one foot to the other.

Smiling and holding the bag in the air, the sales clerk emerged through a curtained door in the rear. It was even more expensive than Jeanne had anticipated, but she had her credit card on the counter before the clerk touched her register. "Christmas wrap, please."

Her purchase complete, Jeanne joined the line at a juice

bar. She wondered what she was going to do with the bag she'd just purchased if Maggie rejected the gift. Jeanne had been imagining their reconciliation—even dreaming about it—creating in her mind a grateful Maggie willing to overlook Jeanne's faux pas. *Faux pas!* She bit her lip at the thought of her self-serving minimization.

"Can I help you?" the teenager behind the counter asked her with an attitude that implied it was the second time she'd had to ask. Jeanne apologized and ordered her orange-and-cranberry juice. She carried it over to one of the tables in the center of the food hall and settled into a wire mesh chair, her package balanced on her lap.

Two women with strollers at the next table observed Jeanne with curiosity. *Too old to be pregnant—that's what they're thinking. If I have the baby, people will ask if it's my grandchild.* A Salvation Army bell ringer set up his pot across the hall, and the jangling created an unpleasant discordance with the Christmas music emanating from a shop close by.

When Jeanne turned to see where it was coming from, she spotted a face she recognized in the doorway of the athletic shoe store. "Milton," she called out, leaping to her feet. He recognized her—she was sure of it. Maggie's bag had slipped to the floor, though, and in the moment it took her to lean down and grasp it, Cox disappeared.

Jeanne tried to speed through the mall, hoping to catch a glimpse of him in one of the stores to her left or right. Her head rotated back and forth as she glanced into each store, and she almost missed him hunched over behind a display of canisters in the tea shop.

A young Japanese woman partially blocked the entrance, where she was offering samples of the day's green tea to all who slowed their pace. She held out a plastic cup to Jeanne, who dodged her so she could reach Cox. "You're the driver, aren't you? You crashed into my company's lobby in October."

"Unintended acceleration. Not my fault." He replaced the canister he held on the shelf, knocking off another in the process.

"I hope you weren't hurt."

"Just shocked, I guess." He picked up the container.

"Is your name Milton Cox?"

His eyes narrowed. "Yeah, why?" Jeanne was about to ask if he had been Lisa Sculley's and Parker Neal's coach when he interrupted. "Excuse me. I'm late for an appointment." He bumped into the display and knocked several canisters onto the floor. "Sorry, sorry," he mumbled to the woman at the door as he rushed out into the mall.

"How rude," observed an elderly customer, shaking her head.

"Rude or odd," Jeanne said, wondering if he were eccentric, although, she had to admit, he had every reason to think she was the odd one for chasing him down. Maybe she was. Weren't behavioral changes part of Alzheimer's? Jeanne was no longer certain her memory was reliable, and she had never realized how heavily her self-confidence depended on it. If her memory eroded and she couldn't retain information, would she still be smart?

Jake's return to the office was uneventful, just as Jeanne had hoped. Better yet, his first staff meeting was calm, and other than Parker's expression, a frown that deepened from a hint of displeasure to full-blown frustration, an atmosphere of comity prevailed. Jeanne hoped fervently Jake had seen a counselor at the VA but didn't want to ask.

When she checked her phone, she found an unexpected text from Vince. Businesslike, even curt, it requested a half-hour meeting at a nearby Starbucks. The subject line read "Salientific's strategic plan," a subject that would take more than a half hour to discuss. His lack of specificity was both annoying and out of character, and he didn't say why he wanted to meet off-site. Still, he was a Salientific investor. Jeanne could hardly blow him off.

Vince's distant, professional manner lasted only as long as it took them to buy their coffee. After leading Jeanne to a table in the back near the restrooms and depositing his jacket on the back of his chair, he told her Parker had been to see him. Mystery solved, she thought, as he sat down opposite her. Vince got right to the point. "Why didn't you tell me Jake was losing it?"

"Because the episodes were intermittent, and I had every reason to give him the benefit of the doubt. His PTSD isn't because he's a flake. He served in Afghanistan. Anyway, he's taken a week off, and since Monday he's been much better."

Vince rolled his shirtsleeves and leaned his arms on the table. Hands that had once caressed her were tense. "Parker claims you're the only member of the executive team who's defending Jake. He claims you're not objective. Why wouldn't you be objective, Jeanne?"

Had Parker implied she and Jake had an improper relationship, or was Vince inferring it from his words? She didn't think Parker could know about her indiscretion last summer, but Vince's question, so close to the truth, made her catch her breath.

Making no particular effort to keep the ice out of her voice, she replied, "Jake is brilliant. He's been a fine leader for Salientific and deserves a chance to get past this difficult period. If he can't, or if it becomes manifest he isn't capable of taking the company to the next level, I'll support removing him. I believe the board should give him more time to—"

"How much time? Till July or August, after you have *your* baby and return from maternity leave? Is that the strategy? You figure you're already the apple of Jake's eye, and if he were forced to step down, he'd surely reward your loyalty. He'd retain his position on the board and press the other members to make you CEO." He sat back and took a sip of his coffee, finally lowering eyes that had been locked on hers.

He wanted to see her reaction. In no way was this angry blast about the company. She'd never seen him so worked up over a business issue, even when large sums of money were at stake. "So, Vince, you think we need to embark on a CEO search? You're an investor—go for it." There was nothing left to say. Let Vince think what he wanted. She picked up her cup and was about to push back her seat.

"Parker would be a good choice," he said quietly. "I think it shows professionalism and grace that he's been able to work for Jake, when Jake's competing technology was the reason Parker's last company went under. He deserves a shot at the CEO job."

She planted her cup and ignored the coffee splashed on the table. "What a crock! Parker has never been a CEO because he's not good enough. He's always been too in love with himself to do what he needs to do to get there, and he knows that soon he'll be perceived as too old. Why aren't you questioning *his* agenda?

"It's Jake's vision," she rushed to add, "that has set the company on the correct course, so, of course, Parker feels safe now making his move. Salientific is Parker's last chance at the brass ring, and you think *I'm* the grasping one?" She was shaking.

Vince struggled to speak in a measured tone. "If you were reasonable, Jeanne, you'd see that even at Parker's age, he may have more of a shot at longevity in the job than you."

"How much shit are you going to throw against the wall, Vince? You think my favored status with Jake is because he's screwing me in the supply room? You're implying my hidden agenda is to save him until just the right moment to take his place?

Or is it my risk of Alzheimer's? Is that where you're going? You're no longer privy to any personal agenda of mine. I don't owe you anything but marketing's business plan." She withdrew a copy from her bag and dropped it in front of him on her way out.

Lou was in the parking lot when Jeanne alighted from her car. "You okay? You don't look so good." Jeanne assured him she was fine, which she absolutely was not.

She would have preferred to talk with no one, but he fell into step beside her as she walked toward the entrance. "Just wanted to let you know I met with Jake this morning. Very much on an even keel and reasonable. Don't know if it will last, but, so far, your strategy of getting him to take a week off to collect himself is working. I have to tell you, though, I'm pessimistic about its lasting."

"Just talked with . . . one of our investors. Parker is still muckraking."

"I'll have a talk with him. Don't worry. I think Bart's right about making no management change before the kickoff. Parker needs to keep his powder dry." He laughed at his unintended reference to the kickoff theme, and Jeanne forced a smile.

The ugly scene with Vince replayed itself in her head. At that moment, she hated him, yet she couldn't make herself cease caring that he hated her. It was hopelessly complicated. If he were the father of her child, how could they go on this way?

Her amniocentesis appointment was in two days. She was considered twenty-one weeks into her pregnancy, although nobody knew for sure. If she were going to have an abortion, she'd have three weeks to get it done, unless the social conservatives in Congress succeeded in changing the law.

Friday morning ushered in a cold front. The thermometer outside Jeanne's kitchen window read ten degrees. Just opening her back door for Bricklin deprived her of any lingering warmth from her bed.

Although she had tied her chenille robe snuggly beneath her breasts, it fell open below her stomach. Bricklin was unperturbed by the frigid air, so Jeanne closed the door behind him, barely clearing his tail, and retreated to a heating vent across the kitchen. After she let him back in, she noted a poop a few feet from the deck. "I'll have to get that later. Wish I could wait to get it till spring, or, better yet, wish you could scoop it yourself, Bricklin. Aside from not having an opposable thumb, you are a perfect pooch."

When she leaned down to kiss the top of his head, she noticed his panting sounded a bit hoarse. Even Bricklin was affected by the punishing cold. After sipping her coffee, which was almost too hot to drink, Jeanne felt sufficiently fortified to collect the newspaper from the porch. She was most of the way through the front page when she realized she had no idea what she was reading. She was about to have a long hollow needle penetrate her baby's inner world, and nothing from the outside world was of equal importance or interest.

The amniotic fluid withdrawn would tell her more than she already knew about the presence of genetic anomalies. But paternity, that "Who's your daddy?" question, was data she'd been ambivalent about learning. Either Jake or Vince would be problematic as the father.

She pushed aside her coffee along with the newspaper and crossed the kitchen to the drawer opposite her sink. Two large Ziploc bags were all she'd need. She carried them into her bathroom and gingerly withdrew Vince's toothbrush from her toothbrush holder. She dropped it into the first bag with the utmost care, as though she were the one responsible for the lab's sterility. The hairbrush from the middle drawer went into the second bag. She'd put off the paternity test for too long, but this exercise felt like pursuing a forensic investigation of a crime.

A bottle of aftershave sat on the counter, and, on impulse, she opened it and held it to her nose. She could almost see Vince there, a genie freed from the bottle, towel wrapped around his waist, slapping lotion on his freshly shaved cheeks and chin. She closed the bottle and dropped it into her bathroom trash. Before leaving the house, Jeanne made certain she drank a large glass of water, as instructed, so she would arrive at the hospital with a full bladder.

When the procedure was over, she was told to go home and rest. There might be cramping or other side effects. The nurse asked if someone was there to drive her. Jeanne lied and assured her a cousin was in the cafeteria waiting for her.

On her way through the waiting room, Jeanne heard someone call her name. Fran Margolis rose from her seat. Jeanne recognized her immediately, although it had been several years since they'd worked together at LMN Corporation, where Fran had been the HR director. A young pregnant woman seated beside Fran rose too and smiled as Fran introduced her daughter, Liz. Liz glanced at Jeanne's belly, her eyes registering momentary confusion.

"Wow, Jeanne," Fran said. "Didn't realize how out of touch we'd been." She gave Jeanne a quick hug. "Belated congratulations on your marriage and . . . and . . ." Liz, who'd checked Jeanne's ring finger, was discreetly nudging her elbow into her mother's side. "Oh, sorry. Since I retired from human resources, I seem to have lost certain . . . uh . . . sensitivities."

"Liz is observant. Don't worry about it. You know me—always trying to be a step ahead. Too busy to take time for marriage."

"Do you know what you're having yet?"

"A son." Why had she said that instead of just "a boy"? She needed to keep her distance. She had to remember her vow that no child of hers would one day wish he'd never been born. Abortion now would be the lesser pain. "I really have to get going. Liz, good luck."

"Jeanne," Fran called after her. "Let's get together for lunch. I'm listed in Weston."

"Sure." Jeanne wouldn't call. She didn't trust herself to pursue another friendship, as much as she liked Fran. After the blowup with Maggie, it was clearer than ever; there was no point. Maybe, instead of worrying about Alzheimer's, she should be worried her child would inherit her impaired relationship gene. Too bad there was no amnio test for that.

Someday there would be a test for everything. By then, scientists would have figured out the genetics behind every human characteristic. In spite of the ponderous debates over what ethical restrictions should apply to prevent designer babies, people would create them anyway, if not in this country, then somewhere. The probability something that *can* be done *will* be done is always greater than zero. There will be babies destined to become killing machines, sex kittens, geniuses, Olympians . . .

Jeanne unlocked her car and slid into the driver's seat with difficulty. Again, she'd have to adjust it farther back. It was becoming more difficult to find a comfortable position anywhere.

CHAPTER 12

"This is Ruth MacGregor. Please leave a message and I'll get back to you as soon as I'm able." The quavering voice sounded elderly, yet there was a clarity to it that said, *I'm still going strong.* At least, that's how Jeanne interpreted it. She very much wanted Ruth MacGregor to be in full possession of her faculties.

Jeanne left a message explaining only that she was eager to talk with Ruth about an article she'd written a number of years ago. "Desperate" would have been more accurate than "eager," but she didn't want to sound as though she were as off-kilter as she felt.

It had taken Jeanne a number of phone calls to track Ruth down, and every day that went by brought Jeanne closer to her go or no-go abortion date. She craved information, anything at all, that might shed so much as a lumen of light on her father's life and illness.

Jeanne sat on her couch holding her phone, even after she'd ended the call. Bricklin lay at her feet, and she automatically patted his head. What if Ruth didn't return the call? What if she visited family for a month at Christmas?

Bricklin, who was not satisfied with less than her full attention, laid his head on Jeanne's feet. He was panting hoarsely again. She checked her contact list for the vet's number. She really should have called Dr. Chu before this, but she'd told herself the rasping was caused by the greater exertion required with only three legs.

After leaving a message that she needed an appointment as soon as possible, she slid down off the couch and lifted Bricklin's muzzle into her hands. She kissed him on his forehead, a gesture of affection he returned with a few well-placed licks on her nose.

The following afternoon, while Jeanne sat nervously in the corner of Dr. Chu's examining room, Bricklin trembled. Dr. Chu checked Bricklin's temperature, inspected his mouth, and ran his hands over the dog's body. When he'd finished his examination, his voice was gentle but his message harsh.

He couldn't be sure, but he suspected a tumor in Bricklin's lungs. Jeanne started shaking her head before he finished. "That wasn't supposed to happen," she protested. "They said they got the whole tumor. The margins were clean."

"With this type of tumor, the shoulder isn't usually the point of origin. It's the lungs, and, unfortunately, it may have been too small to be picked up on an X-ray when Bricklin had his amputation. I'll contact your veterinary oncologist at Angell and let him know Bricklin will need to be seen."

Since he had to be sedated for his X-ray at Angell, Bricklin spent the next day at the animal hospital, while Jeanne tried not to think about what she was going to hear at the end of the day. As soon as the automatic doors opened, her heart beat faster. Stepping up to the reception desk, her fight-or-flight response took hold.

Please, please, please, she repeated to herself during her wait on the hard bench of the waiting room. Whom was she entreating, Vince's big guy in the sky? She would have burned incense on any altar and petitioned any god if it would have brought good news.

The oncologist confirmed Dr. Chu's suspicions. Bricklin's lung tumor was unusually aggressive. When an assistant brought Bricklin into the office, Jeanne began to cry. "Can you treat it?"

"It's inoperable, I'm afraid."

"How much time?" she managed to get out.

"That's hard to say. Honestly, not long, but you'll have to be the judge of that yourself. With a euthanasia decision, the issue is quality of life." While Jeanne struggled to get control of herself, he waited with long-practiced patience. "I'm so sorry. He's a sweet dog."

Jeanne gave Bricklin a boost into the back seat of her car and started the engine. She only managed to get a quarter of a mile down the VFW Parkway before she was sobbing and had to pull over. Sweet dog? More like her best friend, the only one she could count on, the only one she hadn't pissed off.

Jeanne sat brooding at her kitchen table, trying to find the energy and appetite to prepare her dinner. It took a return call from Ruth MacGregor to rouse her. Jeanne thanked her effusively for calling and described the article she'd referenced in her message. "You wrote it more than forty-five years ago. I was hoping you might perhaps have some memory of it." She held her breath.

"Fay Bridgeton is your mother? I do indeed remember her. Does she still live in the Boston area?" Jeanne explained her mother had died the previous summer. Ruth sighed. "I'm getting used to that. All of us dinosaurs are gone or going."

"I'd like to meet with you, if it wouldn't be an imposition. I know it's close to Christmas, but . . ."

"Oh, that's no problem, but I can't meet you. I'm pretty much housebound now. You'll have to come here. Do you know where Stockbridge is?" Jeanne hadn't been to the Berkshires in years, since an old boyfriend who played the cello insisted they drive out to Tanglewood to hear Yo-Yo Ma. Jeanne would have driven to Eskimo country to meet with Ruth MacGregor and readily agreed to an appointment Saturday afternoon.

Jeanne's next call was to Scott. She left a message on his voice mail that she needed his help on Saturday. "I know that night is Christmas Eve, but if there's any way you can swing it . . . Call me when you have a minute to talk. Bricklin is sick again."

Hearing his name, he looked up at her. "C'mon boy. We're going for a long walk. I've finished throwing myself a pity party. From now on, you're going to be living the high life."

Alberta's email invited everyone to the lobby at eleven thirty for the awarding of a fresh turkey to the winner of the photo contest. Jake traditionally dismissed his employees at three o'clock the Friday before Christmas weekend, but many cubicles seemed to empty out after lunch. Alberta's timing guaranteed a good turnout to admire the formidable turkey sitting on the reception area's coffee table.

In spite of Eduardo's hawking his punch, the bowl attracted few takers until Bart moved to his side and produced a bottle in a paper bag. "Secret sauce," Bart announced, and before Eduardo had time to react, dumped the contents into the punch bowl. After that, Eduardo could scarcely keep up with the demand.

Alberta shushed everyone so she could announce the winner. "Where are the pictures?" a Rastafarian-haired systems engineer yelled out.

"No way to bring all those to the lobby," she said, "or fit all of you in the hallway in front of my office, but the names are posted on the board now, so you can see how all those beautiful children turned out." Alberta shot Bart a dirty look. "Okay, drum roll, please. The winners—with a joint submission—are Sal Finiello and Mary Coolidge!"

After the cheering subsided, Louis asked his two engineers how they intended to share their prize. "Just like you taught us—by collaboration." A couple of groans accompanied by "brownnose" and "suck-up" emerged from the group, but Sal just grinned. "Mary likes the white meat, and I like the dark."

Jeanne spotted Lisa Sculley, punch cup in hand, leaning against a doorway. She was a slender woman with shoulder-length gray hair and a lined face unadorned by makeup. Comfortable with her age, Jeanne thought, in contrast to Parker Neal, who had appeared the same age as Lisa in their childhood photo. Jeanne made her way over and wished her a happy holiday. "I've been meaning to ask you, was the coach in your picture Milton Cox, the fellow who crashed his car into our lobby?"

"I wasn't in the building that day, but when I saw his name in the paper, I realized he was the guy Parker Neal and I took gymnastics with. Milton would be much older now, so maybe he got confused. Probably shouldn't still be driving. Weird, huh?"

"What was Parker like back then?"

Lisa shrugged. "Oh, you know . . . the same." She lifted her cup and sloshed the meager remaining punch. "Think I'll refill."

After Jake wished everyone a merry Christmas, the party broke up. By the time Jeanne returned to her office and packed up her laptop, it seemed everyone had fled the building to begin the holiday. It was family time.

Jeanne carried her family within: her mother in her memories, her father in her imagination, her child . . . Her child was no more than a transient, a reverse silhouette on a sonogram. Thank God she had Bricklin, even if she only had him for this Christmas. He was her family.

Route 128 southbound was as congested as on Friday afternoons in the summer, when it seemed the entire population of metropolitan Boston was endeavoring to reach Cape Cod. Christmas week, too, was popular with vacationers. Ski racks and Thule packs rode atop their SUVs, dwarfing Jeanne's businesslike sedan. Make way for families and fun, they seemed to say.

She wished she could stop at her mother's house in Newton, but, of course, no one was there. A sense of desolation settled like a weight on her chest. All that stood between Jeanne and a cheerless Christmas weekend was Ruth MacGregor. She prayed Ruth would give her a shred of the family history she craved.

The overnight snow obligingly finished while Jeanne was still enjoying her morning coffee. By ten o'clock, the wind had pushed out the clouds before them, leaving an intense wintry blue framed by Jeanne's sunroof. She had counted on a two-hour trip west on the Mass Pike, but traffic was heavy until she reached Sturbridge. Most everyone took the exit for Route 84 to Connecticut, New York, and points south, so the reduction from three lanes to two actually opened up the highway.

Just after the Westfield exit, the road began to climb. Jeanne couldn't decide if the Berkshires were giant hills or small mountains, but either way, her ascent up the highway inspired her the way a glimpse of an unexpected view made her catch her breath. Stalactites hung suspended from the rock formations the Pike had created as it sliced across Massachusetts. Jeanne felt the pressure of the climb on her eardrums, a not unwelcome muffling that matched her sense of entering a quieter world.

The main street of Stockbridge was dominated by the Red Lion Inn and its generous veranda. Perhaps she shouldn't arrive at Ruth's empty-handed. It might be her lunchtime, and even if it weren't, she would surely offer Jeanne refreshments. The charming lobby of the inn was a Victorian delight with a large tree and a roomful of seasonal trimmings. Jeanne couldn't see the piano but heard the Christmas music as soon as she stepped inside. She passed it, tucked into a parlor, on her way to the gift shop.

All the merchandise in the shop basked in the warm light of well-placed spots and floods. Jeanne had a vague idea about a gift, perhaps a jar of homemade preserves, but stopped before an arresting display of children's gifts. A diminutive onesie on a hanger had a sleigh embroidered on the front and a matching Santa hat. In front of it sat a wicker basket filled with small stuffed animals. She picked up a sweet bunny with a red bow tie around its neck. So soft, it reminded her of the silky fur on Bricklin's head, and she couldn't resist holding it to her cheek.

In the next room, Jeanne spotted a jar of apricot preserves with a calico wrap and straw ribbon. She handed it to the cashier. "You want that too?" asked the rotund matron behind the counter. She pointed to the rabbit in Jeanne's other hand.

Jeanne's face flushed. *Don't do this to yourself*, she thought. "I . . . uh . . . yes, I want it." She laid the bunny gently on the counter and took out her wallet.

Ruth MacGregor lived in a cottage on Main Street a short distance beyond the shops of town. Jeanne didn't need to see the date plaque mounted on the gray shingles to know the house was of an early vintage. She wouldn't have been surprised to see it in a Norman Rockwell painting, since the famous illustrator had lived and worked in Stockbridge.

A young woman with the elongated features of a Modigliani answered the door. "Ms. Bridgeton, come in, come in out of the cold." She shivered and pulled at the sleeves of her white turtleneck. "I'm Ms. MacGregor's aide, Hannah. She's eager to see you. There aren't many visitors anymore, especially since her husband died."

Was it possible the house actually smelled like gingerbread? Jeanne took in the pine walls, braided rugs, and wicker chairs, all of it so authentically country without the preciousness Jeanne saw on the covers of country life magazines in the supermarket.

A frail woman, as yellowed and brittle as the clipping Jeanne had brought, sat in an upholstered fireside rocker. Her bright eyes and broad smile kept Jeanne from immediately noticing the plastic tube leading to her nose from the oxygen tank on the floor. A walker was parked close at hand. "Jeanne, please excuse me if I don't get up to greet you."

Jeanne grasped the shaky extended hand. "No need. I'm just so happy you were willing to see me—that you even remember the article you wrote about my parents." Hannah brought Jeanne a chair and placed it close to Ruth before disappearing into the kitchen.

"My memory is great. Unfortunately, the rest of me isn't doing so well." She called out to Hannah, "Jeanne will be joining us for lunch." Her raised palm held off any protest. "Hannah's chicken soup is irresistible, and there's gingerbread for dessert." It was settled.

Jeanne didn't want to tire her out. Perhaps Ruth napped after lunch. She looked as though the sum total of her energies lay in her eyes and her smile, as though she might disappear like the Cheshire cat, leaving those to fade last along with any knowledge of Jeanne's father. Jeanne pulled out the yellowed article from her mother's safe deposit box and laid it on Ruth's lap.

The elderly woman rubbed her fingers across it. "Newsprint—someday it will be in a museum, probably where I belong. Your world is all digital. I'm glad I won't be here to see that. You know, I've traveled all over the world covering stories, and in my day, I couldn't be scooped by someone posting breaking news on the Internet." She looked into the fire. "I was just doing human interest stories when I met your mother. We actually became friends."

Jeanne didn't think of her mother as a person who made friends readily, but then her mother had been young and probably traumatized by the accident. "I'm sorry I never heard her mention you. What was she like back then?"

"She loved your father very much, in spite of the nightmare she was living, caring for a man with dementia and an infant at the same time. We stayed in contact for a while, but when I became a foreign correspondent, we lost touch. No Facebook, you know." She laughed.

"Did she talk about him? I . . . I don't know much. My mother was a very private person."

"Sorry to interrupt," Hannah said, "but lunch is ready." Jeanne wanted to help in some way, but Hannah deftly swept up the walker and raised Ruth out of her chair so she could grasp it. "You can bring the oxygen. That would help."

"Thanks for offering, Jeanne. Hannah makes sure I get my exercise, even if it's just from that chair to the table." Once Jeanne and Ruth were settled in the dining room, Hannah brought out two steaming bowls of chicken soup, really more like a stew with chunks of chicken, potatoes, and vegetables fighting for space in the fragrant broth. "Nothing compares to Hannah's soup for chasing away the winter chill, unless it's brandy." She winked at Jeanne. "They won't let me have it anymore, since it fights with my medicine."

The soup both warmed and soothed Jeanne from the inside out. She couldn't remember when she'd last felt cocooned like this. A vision of Vince flashed into her mind, Vince with an apron and wooden spoon, Vince leaning over the stove and saying, "You're gonna love this soup, babe. Isn't she, Bricklin?"

"Your mother had her reasons, Jeanne, for sharing so little with you about your father. She'd endured the pain of watching his mind decline, the exhaustion of being his caregiver when she had you to care for too, and the terror of not knowing what was wrong with him. She watched you like a hawk to make sure you were a normal baby with no sign you might have inherited a disease from him."

"But I thought his doctor diagnosed him as having Alzheimer's."

"That was his best guess, but no one knew for sure. The disease was less well understood back then." Jeanne's crestfallen look elicited a quick reach across the table from Ruth, who covered Jeanne's hand with her gnarled fingers. "You were hoping I knew what was wrong with him, weren't you?" Jeanne nodded. "This is about your future—yours and your baby's. How far along are you?"

"Twenty-three weeks. A week from now, I might not be pregnant anymore." How strange those words sounded, especially with the bitter note she couldn't keep out of her voice.

"Ah, punishing yourself." Jeanne searched Ruth's eyes for her meaning. "Punishing yourself for conceiving a child when your mother meant for the risk to end with you. She owed it to you to make sure you never went through the hand-wringing she did over the future of a child."

Hand-wringing over the future, Jeanne thought, a dubious talent she'd inherited. "Her plan didn't work out so well. She just delayed my conceiving until, at the last possible moment, nature decided to play a trick on me."

"Nature, God, the randomness of the universe . . . who knows? I had a similar experience earlier this year, when I was in hospice care—palliative treatment only. Insurance covers a maximum of six months, but most people die much sooner. I 'graduated.' Who knows why? You really want this baby, don't you? Here you are only a week away from the legal limit, and you haven't had an abortion yet." Jeanne nodded and blinked her moist eyes. Ruth's forehead creased into a hash of wrinkles.

"I'm so sorry for bringing my problems to you and ruining your Christmas Eve. Let's not talk about the baby. The story you related in the paper was touching and beautifully written. I'm not surprised you became a success. If you and my mother were friends for a time, did she tell you about my father?"

Hannah took away the bowls and put china dessert plates and coffee cups in their place. Out from the kitchen came a platter of gingerbread men with red and green frosting faces and borders. Jeanne was transported to her childhood, to Fay Bridgeton's holiday baking, and to a lost memory of hugging an aproned waist and being enveloped in her mother's arms. Maybe it was her mother Jeanne didn't know enough about or didn't remember—or maybe had chosen not to remember.

"She showed me your father's picture. You look like him, Jeanne. In spite of his being orphaned, he was lucky in his adoptive parents, who were warm and loving. Your parents complemented each other, she the disciplined and orderly type, and he the physical and more effusive of the two. She said he gestured with his hands when he talked. I'm afraid the depression and moodiness of his illness made her miss him even before he died."

At that moment, Jeanne felt her mother's loss in a visceral way. She had blamed Fay for the secrets, but oh, how hard his death must have been for her. Hannah poured the coffee and urged another gingerbread man. "Perhaps one for the road."

Jeanne looked at her watch, mindful of Bricklin awaiting her return. "Is there anything else my mother told you about him? Did she mention interests? Hobbies?"

Ruth smiled. "He loved football, was a star offensive lineman in college, or something like that, a very physical person. Seemed like she named other sports too, said he played something in every season. Even after college, there was no end to his athletic injuries." She put her hand to her forehead. "I'm afraid the details are a bit hazy." Jeanne marveled at her memory, not in the least hazy—no Alzheimer's there.

Hannah appeared and moved to Ruth's side. "Let's get you back into your comfortable chair." Her meaningful glance at Jeanne was unnecessary, as she was already rising to leave.

"I hope my visit hasn't been too taxing. This afternoon has been wonderful—magical." After Hannah had helped Ruth back to her chair by the fire and thrown another log on the flames, Jeanne leaned over and took both Ruth's hands in her own. "Thank you. Thank you so very much."

"I'm glad you came to see me. Have a wonderful Christmas." Hannah brought Jeanne's coat and slipped a bag of gingerbread men into her hands at the door. Jeanne turned to wave, but Ruth's eyes were already closed.

Christmas morning was overcast. Jeanne turned on every lamp in her condo trying to dispel the gloom with incandescence. She turned on her gas fireplace and sank to the floor to give

Bricklin special hugs. There was no reproducing the coziness of Ruth MacGregor's home, for its source was not simply the charm of her vintage home and antiques but the warmth of the woman herself.

As she contemplated the empty hours of the holiday, with the office closed Monday as well, she wondered what kind of Christmas Ruth MacGregor had planned. Were any of her friends still alive? Surely, she must have family—someone besides Hannah.

Jeanne remembered Thanksgiving at Dawning Day and how many residents had no place to go or were too infirm to travel. "Think you're up to the role of therapy dog today?" Bricklin's head tilted quizzically as he tried to divine her meaning.

Two hours later, when Jeanne pulled into the Dawning Day parking lot, she felt snug inside a red maternity sweater, and Bricklin sported a green ribbon and bow around his neck. She eyed the large holiday box beside her in its shopping bag and decided to take it in with her. What she would say to Maggie, she wasn't sure, but she prayed the right words would come to her.

The volunteer manning the reception desk remembered Jeanne and assured her that, unexpected or not, her assistance would be welcome. "Do you know if Maggie is here?" Jeanne asked.

"Someone else just asked me that," she replied, stretching her neck to locate the source of the query. "Roberta," she called out to an aide, "are you sure Maggie's supposed to be here today?"

"Positive," the woman replied, turning momentarily from the wheelchair she was pushing toward the elevator. Not wanting to cause any more commotion, Jeanne asked the receptionist if there was somewhere she could stow Maggie's gift. She was just leading Bricklin out of the program director's office, where she'd left the box with a note, when she heard her name.

Max Keystone's bald head looked especially polished for Christmas, and his red-and-green bow tie gave him a jaunty aspect. "Max, you're looking well." She peeked past him into the empty dining room set for Christmas dinner. "Still spending your meals arguing with Rose and Marta?"

Max's bow tie seemed to droop along with his smile. "Rose is gone, I'm afraid. She had a stroke right in front of us in the dining room." Max's eyes were wet.

Just like that—how fast life could change. "Remember Bricklin?" Jeanne asked, pulling the dog forward. Max bent over to pat his head, and others who either remembered Bricklin from Thanksgiving or were simply drawn to the handicapped canine filtered in from the lounge, where a group of teenagers was singing carols to the assembled.

When it was time for Christmas dinner to be served, Jeanne hung back till everyone was in place. Two new tablemates filled in where Max and Marta had been seated, so Jeanne offered to help serve the meal. Bricklin took up his post outside the dining room and waited for leftovers.

Jeanne couldn't shake the empty feeling she'd had at home, in spite of Dawning Day's festive rooms. She remembered her first visit and the magical moment that had moved her to her core, the infant that had enabled a great-grandmother to emerge from her dementia and reengage with life. *Why are you back here—for another epiphany?* She glanced over at Max's table. *Well, there it is—life can go south in a heartbeat.*

A flushed resident at a corner table pressed his hand to his breastbone. "Heartburn again, Joseph?" an aide asked him. "Isn't Maggie here?" she called to a coworker, who shrugged. Someone on staff would call the EMTs for Joseph, but Jeanne was worried about Maggie, whom she couldn't imagine pulling a Christmas no-show. A supervisor had joined the aide at Joseph's table. "I'm the most expendable," Jeanne told her. "I'll go check on Maggie."

Bricklin, who'd been the recipient of varied treats from passing staff members, was none too pleased to be pulled out into the cold. Jeanne promised him a speedy return for leftovers and was glad no human occupied the car with her. A passenger might have asked her the question she was trying to ignore: what if Maggie shut the door in her face?

The waning light of the December afternoon reinforced Jeanne's sense of urgency as she tried to make the fifteen-minute drive to Maggie's Framingham apartment building in ten. The last time she had been there was after Maggie's car accident.

Pressing the button to gain entry seemed pointless, since Maggie hadn't answered her phone. The wrought-iron-and-glass door opened, and two young girls balancing gift boxes came through, followed by their parents. The mother smiled benevolently at Jeanne when she noticed her belly, and the father held the door until Bricklin had limped his way in.

Maggie's sixth-floor apartment was at the end of the hall, and though Jeanne could hear laughter from one neighboring apartment and Yule-log music from another, no sound emanated from Maggie's, even when Jeanne put her ear to the door. She rang the bell several times and could hear it ringing inside.

She tried the bell next door and hoped it would be heard over the din of the festivities. A muscular young man with a beer bottle in his hand answered the door. No, he didn't know Maggie more than to say hi, and he didn't have a key to her apartment. He was quick to close the door, leaving Jeanne standing in the hallway feeling like an interloper.

The Yule-log music came from a small television. Its sprightly owner was a white-haired woman who opened the door before Jeanne could ring. She wore a green wool coat with a sprig of artificial holly pinned to the lapel, and she was shocked to see a stranger outside her apartment.

"I'm sorry," Jeanne said. "I didn't mean to startle you." The woman backed into her apartment and started to close the door. "Wait," Jeanne blurted out. "I'm a close friend of Maggie's, and she didn't come to work today. She's a nurse at Dawning Day, and she has health issues of her own, and, and . . . look, I really need to get in there. Do you have a key?"

The woman released her tight grip on the edge of the door and opened it wider. Her eyes dropped to Jeanne's belly and the three-legged dog at her side and seemed reassured Jeanne wasn't likely to be a burglar. "I have a key, but I'm not sure it's appropriate for me to let you in. Why don't you wait in the hall while I go in first?"

Relieved, Jeanne leaned up against the wall until the woman fetched the key and opened the lock. Maggie's inert body was visible from the doorway. Jeanne rushed to her side and dropped awkwardly to the floor. She could hear the neighbor behind her calling 911.

Maggie was alive but unresponsive. While Jeanne patted Maggie's hands and face, agonizing over her own uselessness, Bricklin pushed past her and tried to lick Maggie's face. In his effort, he dislodged a Hershey wrapper from beneath her arm. It was hard to believe Maggie would be eating chocolate when she'd been dieting so rigorously two weeks earlier.

First, just one siren was audible. Then Jeanne heard another, followed by a commotion in the hall. Two EMTs strode into the apartment, a young man with a weight-lifter body and a delicate-looking blonde woman. "She's diabetic," Jeanne said, as they crouched beside her.

The young woman was already checking Maggie's vital signs, so Jeanne backed away into the kitchen. *What if* . . . She opened the cabinet door under the sink to find the trash. There were too many candy bar wrappers in the pail to count. She carried the pail over to the EMTs. "What would these do to a diabetic?"

"Probably cause diabetic coma," the woman answered. They thanked her and tested Maggie's blood. Satisfied with their analysis, they put her on an IV, administering insulin for her high blood sugar and potassium and sodium for her dehydration. Jeanne watched them wheel her out on a gurney and started to follow. Bricklin lay on the floor panting and resisted Jeanne's pull on the leash.

"What hospital are you taking her to?" she called after them. Bricklin would need her attention before she could follow. She took a bowl out of Maggie's cabinet and filled it with water, which Bricklin lapped up from a prone position. She shouldn't have kept him out of the house for so long. He didn't have the stamina for it.

Jeanne dropped down into a recliner in Maggie's living room. Dragging Bricklin off to Dawning Day had been a bad idea, partly an escape for her, partly a way to avoid thinking about how fast he was getting worse. She wondered if she'd always had this talent for self-deception.

Bricklin coughed several times and looked up at her from the floor. Leaving him in a freezing cold car at the hospital wasn't an option. Maggie would be well cared for whether Jeanne followed or not and might even be upset to wake up and find Jeanne at her bedside.

She stooped down and stroked Bricklin's head and neck and ran her hand several times down the length of his back. Her fingers came away with an airy cloud of fur. She rubbed it between her thumb and fingertips. Funny what she did from force of habit. As if it mattered now that he was shedding. "Let's go home, sweet boy."

CHAPTER 13

Bricklin's quality of life was no longer debatable. He wouldn't eat and resisted more than the briefest walk. Jeanne sat on her kitchen floor, legs splayed around her dog while she reached over her belly to hug him. Her own quality of life seemed equally bleak as she faced her twenty-fourth week, her private apocalypse. If only she hadn't allowed herself to contemplate the joy of raising her son. If only she hadn't forgotten who she was, how inevitable it was that she'd push people away. She had no business having a child, no business at all.

Losing Bricklin and her baby in the same week—it was too, too much. Her tears, accompanied by uncontrollable sobs, brought forth a whimper from Bricklin, who tried to rise and offer comfort. "Down, Bricklin." Wiping her eyes on her sleeve, she struggled to steady herself.

The deep blue sky and brilliant sun were an offensive mismatch to Jeanne's mood. Light poured through the kitchen window and skylight, but she didn't have the energy to shut it out. Two days till Wednesday, only forty-eight hours to pull herself together and do what she had to.

"I don't know where you're going, Bricklin. I've never believed in an afterlife, but wherever you are, he'll be there too." Her voice quavered. "Please watch over my son." With soaked sleeve and stiff back, she pulled herself upright. Calm was unattainable. She'd settle for feeling numb.

Jeanne didn't go into the office the next morning till all the arrangements were made. Dr. Chu would expect her at nine Wednesday morning. Bricklin would be given a shot to make him sleepy, and when he was finally euthanized, he would go peacefully in her arms. *How serene they make it sound*, she thought bitterly.

Jeanne's abortion appointment would be at ten thirty the same morning, a scant two days before the legal limit for terminating her pregnancy. The weekend to follow was New Year's. She would go away somewhere—anywhere—and promised herself that would make a difference.

Just before noon, Jeanne's cell phone rang, and she was shocked to see Maggie's name in the caller ID. "I have to take this, guys," she said to Mariana, Clara, and the new marketing communications manager, who gathered their notes and left her office.

"I'm sorry," Maggie said. "I didn't mean to interrupt a meeting. You can call me back."

"We were wrapping up anyway." Jeanne began pacing back and forth across her office.

"I'm calling to thank you for—for saving me. I don't know why you came over, but if you hadn't . . ."

"Honestly, I'm not sure why either. I've never had good intuition about anything but market segment growth." She laughed ruefully.

"Mrs. Eberhardt next door was very impressed. She told me everyone needed a friend like you. Look, Jeanne, can we get together? I don't want to have this conversation on the phone. I have a long shift tomorrow. Maybe Wednesday?"

Jeanne felt herself choking up and struggled for a matter-of-fact tone. "Tied up all day, I'm afraid. Bricklin's cancer has defeated him, and I have to end his suffering."

"I'm so sorry. He's an awesome dog. People at Dawning Day still talk about him."

"Yeah, Wednesday's pretty much a lost cause. I'm having my abortion right after I leave the vet." There was a long silence on the other end. "Maggie?"

"How about if I come to your condo Thursday after work? You may not feel up to dinner out. I'll bring takeout." After agreeing on a time and ending their call, Jeanne leaned back in her chair and stared at the ceiling. Maybe something of this miserable year was salvageable.

After a sleepless Tuesday night, Jeanne got down on the floor and embraced Bricklin. She could feel his heart beating beside her. He'd moved little since the night before. Christmas and its aftermath had left Jeanne emotionally depleted, while Bricklin was physically as weak as the Dawning Day residents they'd visited.

"I need to talk to you, sweet boy. I don't know if I'll be able to at Dr. Chu's office." She stroked his head. "I thought I was so clever naming you after Dan Bricklin, 'Father of the Spreadsheet.' You have nothing in common with the analytical. You're all love, joy, warmth, and loyalty. You've taught me how overrated words are, since we've never needed them for our special kind of intimacy. I'll never ever forget you"—she hesitated—"as long as I can remember anything or anyone." If Bricklin minded the tears spilling into his fur, he didn't show it, so intent was he on licking Jeanne's face.

Dr. Chu let her remain in his examining room after Bricklin died. She hadn't been able to tell when sleep became death. She leaned across his warm body and rested her head on his. "Don't know how I'm going to walk out that door, boy, and leave you behind." She sighed. "At least I know you're off leash forever."

When she heard voices and the sound of dog nails in the hallway, she kissed Bricklin's head and stroked his body one last time. Wiping her eyes, she let herself out and drew the door closed behind her. Bricklin's collar and leash were in her hand, but she couldn't bear to look at them. The receptionist didn't stop her to pay.

Though she was shivering by the time she reached her car, she didn't turn on her engine, allowing the cold to penetrate her limbs and numb her toes as she stared unseeing out the windshield. When she could no longer delay leaving for the hospital, she turned on the ignition and drove slowly down the street.

The hospital's bustling crowd usually annoyed Jeanne, since it obstructed her path as she hurried between work and the medical appointments that pulled her away from her office. For once, it was comforting to be part of the anonymous flow through the halls, not the only pregnant one, nor the oldest, youngest, fattest, thinnest, tallest, or shortest. White coats threaded their way through dark parkas, and a phone was ringing—Jeanne's cell, which she'd forgotten to turn off.

"Jeanne, I've been trying to reach you." There was urgency in Sharon Basko's voice.

"I'm in the hospital for my . . . procedure."

"I know about your appointment. I just don't know why. Your amnio results just came in, and the baby is free of the conditions we were testing for. It's your decision, of course, but I thought you'd be happy. I know you don't have results yet from your DNA sequencing for early-onset familial Alzheimer's, so that can't be your game changer. Something else must be going on. Do you want me to come down so we can talk? There's still time before your appointment."

The elevator doors were about to close, but Jeanne waved off a man who reached out to hold them for her. She turned away from the doors and lowered her voice. "It's convoluted. There are too many reasons not to have this baby, and, honestly, I don't have the strength to wrestle with the issue anymore. I'm all out."

"I hear that in your voice. Still, I'm here if you need me. Okay?"

Jeanne thanked her and went upstairs to check in. She took the clipboard and forms she was offered and sat down to fill them out. When she heard a familiar voice speak her name, she looked up in surprise. "Maggie, why did you come? I appreciate the moral support, but—"

"I'm not here to support you, at least not because of your abortion. I came to tell you I would be delighted and honored to raise your child, though I'm sure you'll never need me to." She took the seat next to Jeanne and removed the clipboard from her hands. "Please don't have an abortion." She took Jeanne's hands in hers. "You want this baby. I just know you do."

Jeanne reached out and hugged her. "That's a kind and selfless offer. I understand you feel responsible for my decision, but you shouldn't. I had no business asking you to make such a sacrifice, and there are other reasons to end my pregnancy. There are risks that have nothing to do with you."

"Which worries you more, the risk of Alzheimer's or the risk of being too much like your mother? Are you even sure you understand who she was? The woman who packed that box in her attic loved you. No matter how much you think of yourself as damaged goods, if she hadn't given you love, you'd probably have ended up in the penitentiary."

Jeanne opened her mouth to speak, but Maggie was intent on finishing what she'd come to say. "I don't want to hurt your feelings. I have to tell you what I think, even if you never speak to me again. You're so good at managing risk in your business, you think you can squeeze the risk out of relationships. You can't, but the risks are so worth it. You would be a great mother, and I believe you're hungry for this child. Please, please, think about why you're doing this."

Jeanne wasn't sure when Sharon came in, but it was sometime during Maggie's entreaties. "I decided not to wait to see if you'd call me, Jeanne. Most of us do better with a friendly face at a time like this. I didn't realize someone was already with you." She introduced herself to Maggie and turned back to Jeanne. "On the phone you sounded like you'd made up your mind. Is Maggie right? Are you sure of your motives? I'm not trying to influence your decision, just help you think it through. You know I'll support you either way."

Jeanne looked from one to the other. Rather than supported, she felt overwhelmed. "I've been thinking, thinking, thinking for months now. I'm so weary." As the little resolve that was propping her up drained from her body, she slumped in her seat. They sat silent, waiting for her to speak. "Maggie, maybe you're right, and a few decades with a shrink would fix me right up, but I'm out of time." Sharon had pulled a chair in close where she could face them both. "Aren't I morally bound to save this fetus from what might be a tragic existence? I admit, I can't exactly quantify the risk, hard as I've tried, but why take the chance?"

Maggie groaned and looked at Sharon. "This is my friend Jeanne, whom I've really come to care for and respect, but help me out here. I feel like she's spent her life wandering through a spreadsheet, and now she's wondering why the columns don't foot."

"Ms. Bridgeton, we're ready for you." A nurse stood in the doorway beside the reception desk.

Jeanne felt as though weights were tied to her limbs. Even breathing was a trial. They were talking about her as though she weren't there, looking at each other in a way that seemed to continue their conversation without the need for words. The nurse in the doorway cleared her throat. Jeanne felt her resolve weakening. "But there are reasons . . ." Her voice trailed off. "The father . . ."

"Ms. Bridgeton, we really do have to start, or you'll have to reschedule." The nurse looked down at the paper in her hand. "Although, I see we're at the deadline, twenty-four weeks."

The deadline, the line of death, the line everyone crosses—her mother, her father, Bricklin, and now her son. Was Maggie's assessment of her correct? Was she trying to do what seemed to be right for the wrong reasons, or were her reasons right but the choice wrong for other, more important reasons? A cost-benefit analysis was never really objective. Emotion was the thumb on the scale, and maybe sometimes it was supposed to be.

She rose and picked up her coat and bag. "Thank you both so very, very much," she said to Maggie and Sharon. The nurse made way for her to enter, but Jeanne mumbled a quick apology and turned into the hospital corridor.

Jeanne's condo was quiet. A trip to the mailbox revealed a condolence card from Scott, enclosing several beautiful poems about the death of a pet. The envelope had no stamp. He'd brought it there in person. She placed the poems on her night table, where she hoped they'd be a comfort this first night without Bricklin. Her mind was a cascade of words and pictures—Maggie's, Sharon's, Dr. Chu's. They slid by like shuffling cards. She'd been trying all day to process them, but too much had happened, and she found herself caught up in second-guessing. "We're ready for you now," the nurse had said, but Jeanne wasn't ready. Was it a failure of courage or an act of courage to walk out the door?

She desperately needed to curl up with her dog and talk out her thoughts to him, but there was an enormous empty space where Bricklin was supposed to be. The space was much larger than the mass of an eighty-pound dog. It was larger than the room or the house and could only be comprehended by one who had loved and lost an animal. She massaged her abdomen and spoke to her child. You'll have a dog. That much I *can* promise you.

After ten minutes of staring at the ceiling, Jeanne got out of bed and retrieved her mother's attic carton. She had to dig to find her tiger and bear. Clutching them to her chest, she returned to bed and closed her eyes.

Jeanne was surprised to see Alberta's eyes looking like her own—red rimmed and puffy. Jeanne, however, had not applied under-eye cover-up and an abundance of eyeliner and mascara in a failed attempt to conceal the effects of a night of crying.

"What's up, Jeanne. Are you sick?" After Jeanne's description of the previous day's trauma with Bricklin, Alberta looked at her curiously. "I didn't figure you for such a softie. Good to know."

Was that how people saw her, as bereft of emotions, or was Alberta just a person who'd never had a pet and was surprised at the depth of her grief? Knowing people might think her tears self-indulgent exacerbated the pain. "And you?" Jeanne asked. "You look like you've had some bad news of your own."

"Just allergies," she replied, not even attempting to put over the lie.

"Yes," Jeanne said dryly. "It's amazing how many allergens one finds in an office." She was sure Alberta's problem was related to Bart, but she wouldn't go there unless Alberta did.

Alberta rose and closed her office door. "Guess I need a Bart-free environment."

"He's a great sales manager," Jeanne said gently. "Maybe it's time to let him be just that. He's got the sales kickoff and beginning of the new fiscal year to worry about. Do you think you can stay away?"

"I know he can't afford any distractions right now. The one he wants to eliminate is me." Alberta balled up her fists. "I would have less of a problem with getting dumped if he weren't pursuing other . . . distractions."

"Mariana? She doesn't welcome his attentions."

"I didn't either, at first. He shouldn't be able to keep doing this to women. I wonder if his wife knows." She slammed a file drawer closed with her foot. "I wonder if I'm the only fool who took him seriously when he said he'd leave her for me. He deserves a—a Lorena Bobbitt kind of punishment."

Jeanne wished she could think of something creative to say, but Alberta's situation was a cliché. She wondered if Alberta realized that. She hoped not. Surely it would magnify her pain to know how unoriginal she was, how many women—millions maybe—had fallen for a line of bullshit like Bart's. Jeanne looked down at her belly. Was Alberta any more of a fool than she?

"I'm sorry, Jeanne. You must have come down here for a reason." Relieved to move on, Jeanne posed her question regarding health insurance for her baby. When she rose to leave, she asked Alberta if she'd be at kickoff.

"Do I have a choice? Jake told me he wants the management team there for the first morning to 'salute the flag' and the closing session to respond to any unanswered questions. I guess you'll be there for the whole conference."

"Look for my presentation the first morning. Given that I'll be appearing in costume with a pregnant belly, I should be good for a few laughs. I'm not sure the reps will pay attention to what I have to say."

"Don't worry about how you look. Everyone respects you." Jeanne was surprised at the compliment. So much had happened to make her reevaluate her self-worth. It wasn't that she didn't measure up; she'd omitted criteria. If only she'd given herself an annual review against the right objectives, the human ones. Could she honestly say that the good things she'd done for her people were motivated by caring rather than pragmatism? Did those deeds still count if it was the latter? She was no saint, but was she a calculating bitch or somewhere in between?

Maggie came over that night and brought takeout as promised. The aroma filled the kitchen and was impossible to resist. The Chinese feast was complete with spring rolls, barbecued spare ribs, beef lo mein, shrimp with lobster sauce, and moo shu pork. "I know it's too much," she said, "but I wasn't sure what your pregnancy appetite was in the mood for. Tonight, we're not counting calories, points, or anything else. It's all healthy, or at least the edamame is. I brought that too."

"Let me pay you back."

"Not a chance. You think someone with a gorgeous pocketbook like this needs help with the bill?" She proudly produced her new purse.

"I'm so glad to see you using it, because I really wanted you to have it. After I left it, I was afraid I'd made a mistake—afraid of insulting you again. I didn't want you to think I was trying to buy back your friendship." Maggie reached out to hug Jeanne with her free arm. "Give me that bag of food before it starts to leak." A small grease stain was spreading across a bottom corner of the paper bag.

While Jeanne set out chopsticks alongside the dishes and glasses, Maggie found a couple of serving spoons and large plates to capture sauce from the dripping cartons. She sipped the glass of merlot Jeanne provided and settled into the chair across from Jeanne, who brought a bone dish for the ribs and a pitcher of ice water to the table. Maggie regarded Jeanne critically and shook her head. "Yesterday must have been brutal for you. I can see it in your face, the exhaustion. I'm happy you made the decision you did, but I'm sorry to have contributed to your pain."

"You were honest, and, yes, it hurt." Jeanne picked up her egg roll with chopsticks and took a tentative bite. After it fell back into her plate, she sat contemplating it as though it represented an engineering problem.

"Was I unfair?"

"I wish." Jeanne picked up her egg roll with her hand and took a large bite.

Maggie took another sip of her wine. "You're the one who needs this. On top of your anxiety over the abortion, you'd put Bricklin down in the morning."

"When I was driving to the hospital from the vet's office, I tried to pull myself together by thinking about the places he loved. Once I had his ashes, I would sprinkle them there. Then I started wondering where my own ashes would end up." Maggie groaned. "The funeral director would ask people where I'd been happiest, and I'd end up in an urn at the center of some conference room table in the office. Pathetic, huh?"

"What on earth made you schedule Bricklin's vet appointment the same day as the abortion? Were you punishing yourself?"

Ruth had asked Jeanne the same thing: was she punishing herself for conceiving a child? Jeanne hesitated. "I'm not sure. I was tired of searching for answers. I wanted all the bad stuff to be over so I could go back to a time when I saw things with clarity, when I was good at imposing order on life."

Maggie smiled. "Your definition of 'life' is pretty narrow. With a lens closed up that much, you can see whatever you want with clarity—a patch of blue in a sky actually covered with clouds. My grandmother used to say, 'One sparrow doesn't make a summer.'"

"It must be nice to have known such a smart grandmother. My child won't have one, but maybe he could have a godmother." Jeanne looked at Maggie with pleading eyes. "It's a symbolic position. You don't need to pay for college or anything."

"Of course I'll be his godmother."

Jeanne patted her stomach. "You're a lucky boy."

Maggie cocked her head. "You know, I'm the one who owes you, not the other way around. You saved my life. I don't know what made you come to my apartment after I was such a bitch to you."

"You weren't a bitch. You reminded me that people are complex and that I shouldn't jump to conclusions. Pretty lame, huh? Needing reminding at my age that there aren't any shortcuts to understanding people or predicting behavior? You can't just click the Maggie icon on your computer's desktop and bring up her profile: name, address, personality—sweet and selfless."

"If you were lame, I was worse. I let my diabetes diagnosis make me crazy, even though I counsel my Dawning Day patients to deal with their diagnoses. I ate the bare minimum, even though I know better, and when Christmas arrived, I felt sorry for myself." Her eyes brimmed with tears.

Jeanne leaned across the table and laid her hand on Maggie's. "I felt sorry for myself too. That's why I went to Dawning Day on Christmas."

"Your self-pity made you look for a way to help others. Mine made me look for chocolate." She smiled and wiped her tears with a napkin.

"I think you're giving me too much credit there, but it doesn't matter. I don't want our friendship to be based on owing a debt to each other. Let's put that behind us." Jeanne raised her water glass. "To a fresh start in the New Year."

Maggie raised her wine glass. "To a sensible diet, but not until we finish the moo shu pork."

On Saturday, they visited Magic Beans to look at furniture. Armed with measurements of Jeanne's guest bedroom, they scouted out infant seats, cribs, changing tables, car seats, and strollers. Jeanne was shocked at the equipment requirements for a person who would enter the world weighing half a dozen pounds. When Maggie pointed out they hadn't even ventured into the part of the store displaying bottles, diapers, pacifiers, and the rest of the paraphernalia needed, Jeanne begged for a break.

"I guess that's enough for now. They'll probably throw you a baby shower at work. But if you think you're tired now, wait till the night feedings start."

"Those are the ones you're coming over for, right?"

Maggie pointed at Jeanne's chest. "What do you think those

things are for? You're on your own. I'm the come-over-and-play type of godmother."

The following morning, Jeanne pulled on her fleece-lined boots and winter coat and crossed Route 30 to the Loker Conservation Area. Without a leash in her hand or Bricklin at her side, she felt incomplete. The biting wind that made her pull her chin farther into her coat would have invigorated him, providing scuttling leaves to chase.

Her obliging muscle memory led her along the trail, leaving her mind free to wander. Where Bricklin had eaten clods of moss, the spring would bring ground cover spreading unimpeded under the shade of the tree. Other dogs would race down the hill that Bricklin, even on three legs, loved to run. Puppies would trot, tired and contented, beside their owners after tearing through the woods, just as he had.

Near the frozen pond, covered with lily pads in summer, she reached the spot she'd been seeking. He had run happy circles in this clearing, played with other dogs, and chased his tennis ball. If no dogs appeared or Jeanne failed to bring a ball, Bricklin would find a stick, sometimes tossing it in the air, sometimes bringing it to her to throw.

Even on a frigid day, the spot was lovely. A mellow wistfulness settled over Jeanne. Her time with Bricklin was over, and much as she wished he weren't gone, she had rich memories. She gained satisfaction from knowing she'd done right by him, saving him when he'd needed saving and letting him go when his pain so obviously exceeded his pleasure in living.

As accustomed as she was to making decisions about other people's careers, she'd had no experience being responsible for their personal lives. God knows her mother had guarded her own independence to the end, giving Jeanne no say in matters of health, lifestyle, or finance. To Fay Bridgeton, this was privacy; to Jeanne, secrecy.

Ironic, she thought, that it was her dog who'd taught her how to love a living creature enough to make its life-and-death decisions. In a way, he'd helped ready her for motherhood. He seemed present at that moment, and Jeanne offered him silent thanks, wiping her moist eyes with her mittens.

CHAPTER 14

The atmosphere around the table was more amicable than it had been for many weeks. Although the sales conference was only days away, Mariana had done a great job of chasing down every detail, which had eased Bart's concerns; Bart had done a great job of bringing in revenue by year end, which had eased Jake's concerns; and Lou was on top of Version Two testing, which had eased everyone's concerns, except perhaps for Parker's, since Jeanne guessed he still sought reasons to complain to the board about Jake.

At the end of the meeting, Jake asked Jeanne to stop by his office. When she arrived, he closed the door behind her. "I wanted to thank you," he said, as he settled into his desk chair, and she sank into the one opposite. "Taking a week off gave me a chance to catch up on my rest. Didn't realize how badly I needed that."

"Were you able to get some help from the VA?"

"Nah." He swiveled his chair back and forth. "Been there, done that. Just needed a break." He smiled broadly and nodded in her direction. "That must be some big baby. You should get plenty of sleep while you still can."

Jake's humor seemed forced. She felt her earlier equanimity evaporating and decided to press him on counseling. If he lashed out, she'd deal with it, but she was unwilling to let him off the hook completely. Though his improved mood was heartening, without help it would be temporary. "I'm glad to hear you feel rested, but don't you still need help with those painful memories? I don't mean to be presumptuous, but I thought there was a lot the VA could do. What do you have to lose?"

Jake's smile faded into a pinched line. "What you don't understand, Jeanne, is that experience and memory aren't the same. Even if some shrink was able to hit the delete key on my wartime memories, I'd still be me. I'd still be the person shaped by those experiences."

His point was valid, and she didn't have the training to respond. Though Jake had turned his eyes to the windows, Jeanne could see they were damp. He was not better. He had merely come back from his vacation determined to soldier on.

Walking back to her office, head lowered, she considered his words. Jake saw his brain as an operating system, irrevocably corrupted. People were as much a product of their choices and experiences as of the programming they arrived with at birth. Those choices and experiences shaped them. For Jake, the past—his past—could never be absent from the present.

What of her own memories? Was the source of Jake's despair a source of hope for her? If Alzheimer's erased her memories, she'd still be the person her choices and life experiences had shaped. The disease could cause behavioral change, but surely she'd hang on to her essence, at least till the late stages. The past would always be with her, for better or worse. She had been ready to urge Jake to live for the present, but that was an oversimplification, another self-help cliché.

Lou grabbed her arm. She hadn't even seen him approaching. "Look where you're going, Mom. You and that baby are going to mow someone down."

As deflated as Jeanne felt, she willed herself to put on a pleasant face. Teasing was inevitable at this point, though Lou took up more room in the hallway than she did. "Sorry, *we* were lost in thought."

"Since a certain someone is back to his old self, I thought I'd see you with a big smile." Jeanne was still processing Jake's words and wasn't ready to share her renewed concerns, so she forced a smile and asked about Lou's holidays. "Too good, I'm afraid," he said, rubbing his belly. "My wife says she's putting me on the grapefruit diet for a month. Hey, I'm actually glad I bumped into you. Was going to stop at your office later to give you a heads-up."

Something in Lou's tone made Jeanne's stomach flip. "Headed there now. Walk with me."

When they reached her office, Lou pulled a chair up close to hers and lowered his voice. "Parker's going back to the board."

"But Jake is better."

"Precisely. He'll claim Jake needed to be packed off for a vacation at a critical time—end of the fiscal year—because he was teetering on the edge. Too much is at stake for Salientific to have an unstable CEO running the show." He took in Jeanne's narrowed eyes and tightened mouth. "Stop and think, Jeanne. He has a point. Loyalty has its limits."

Jeanne was already on her feet. "Thanks for the heads-up, Lou—really—but I have to have it out with Parker. He's wasting senior management's time with these endless mutinous episodes." She left Lou in her office and strode quickly to Parker's.

He was jotting numbers on his whiteboard when Jeanne's knuckles hit his door with a peremptory knock. He looked over his left shoulder at her. "I figured you'd be showing up soon."

"I understand from Lisa Sculley that you know Milton Cox."

He put down his marker and turned to face her. "Knew. He was my gymnastics coach." Jeanne noted he puffed out his chest. Probably wants to remind me how buff he is, she thought. "Haven't seen him in years. Not sure he's still alive."

"Alive enough to crash into Salientific's front window. You must have known that. You were in the reception area right after it happened."

"I didn't recognize him. The guy who drove through the window was an old geezer." Parker looked at his watch. "I have a couple of meetings to prepare for this afternoon, and you interrupted me. Is there a point to these questions?"

Her eyes narrowed. "Just wondering about the accident. That crash made Jake flip out. His PTSD came back. Kind of a coincidence it happened just as you started lobbying to replace him."

"What are you, a conspiracy theorist? Lisa Sculley knows Cox too. Maybe she recruited him. Maybe she wants to be queen of documentation. Makes about as much sense as what you're suggesting. Maybe you're the one with the problem, Jeanne. You really haven't been yourself lately." His face wore an insufferable smirk.

Jeanne stiffened. Parker couldn't know about her Alzheimer's fears. Had her behavior changed enough to make him suspect? "Lisa had no motive. You, on the other hand, want Jake out."

Parker's anger was obvious from his rigid mouth and the rapid tapping of his fingers on the side of his leg. A minute went by before he regained his composure. "Accusing me of excessive ambition? Everyone knows you're the heir apparent in Jake's eyes." His smug look returned. "You should really see someone about this paranoia. That's not a symptom of pregnancy. Maybe you've got something else going on." He paused for effect. "Perhaps I need to expand the subject of my conversation with the board. What I'm seeing is not good for this company, not good at all."

He must be talking about what Maggie calls my "pregnancy brain." He can't mean Alzheimer's. She felt her confidence slipping away. Hadn't the test of her mental acuity and memory been normal—so far? She couldn't let him psych her out.

Jeanne stood and edged toward the door. "You're the one tearing apart the management team, not me or Jake, and you're connected to that crash somehow."

Her declaration and move to the door were intended to prevent Parker's getting in the last word, but he wasted no time in delivering a parting shot. "Why don't you take all your evidence to one of your boyfriends? Is it Vince now, or are you back with Jake?" He laughed and turned his back on her.

Fuck. Jeanne stomped into the hall, then caught herself and looked around warily. He was right. She couldn't prove anything she had said, and, yes, Jake needed to step down. Her hand rested on her belly where a kick-boxing baby seemed as angry as she was.

By the time Jeanne returned to her darkened condo, she was tired, hungry, and in a lousy mood. A glass of wine and a meal of comfort food were what she needed, but the contents of her refrigerator were meager. She and Maggie had polished off all the Chinese takeout except some fried rice and a lonely dumpling. Wine, at least more than a couple of sips, was not allowed on her pregnancy regimen, and no loving dog greeted her at the door.

After entering the kitchen from the garage and flipping on the lights, she continued to her front door, where she peeked through the side glass to check for packages. With so little time to shop, Jeanne used the Internet for her routine purchases. The box she saw had no official-looking FedEx, UPS, or USPS label. She opened the door and picked up the carton. Its top flaps were interleaved, and a handwritten "this side up" appeared on each side.

She set the box on the kitchen table and opened it with trepidation. Since the Unabomber attacks and the anthrax scare, it was hard not to feel more anxiety than anticipation when anonymous packages appeared on one's doorstep.

"What the . . . ?" She lifted the still warm casserole out of the box and tilted the lid. "Ummm." She didn't need to look at the note to know it was from Vince. He was the only one she had told she considered simple mac 'n cheese the ultimate comfort food. Her mother had made the rich pasta whenever anything went wrong in Jeanne's life—it was comfort by proxy.

There had been mac 'n cheese for lunch the day after Jeanne lost the sixth-grade spelling bee and when she lost out on the role of Clara in the dance academy's performance of *The Nutcracker*. The last time her mother made mac 'n cheese, Jeanne's high school varsity softball team had lost the county championship.

In college, the cheesy dish wasn't hard to find, given the average student diet, but the cheese was pasty and the macaroni eons beyond al dente. Jeanne didn't seek it out. As her career progressed, she became accustomed to more sophisticated fare. Why Vince would leave this was beyond her, especially with their last exchange so bitter.

A warm folded sheet lay beneath the casserole. The eight-and-a-half-by-eleven-inch lined page had a few grease spots, but she could see the note was carefully written. Vince must have wanted her to open the dish before she read the note:

Jeanne, I know we've had some major differences of opinion, but I don't want us to leave things as they were at the end of our last meeting. I wish I had heard about Jake's problems from you rather than Parker, but, knowing you, I'm sure loyalty to your CEO and a desire to keep Salientific and our relationship separate were two of the reasons you were silent.

You've continued your pregnancy in spite of your Alzheimer's risk, and I believe that was the wrong decision. I can't help how I feel, but I don't want us to be at war either. We have a business relationship that needs to be professional and cordial at a minimum. I'd like to remain friends. Please accept this peace offering.

Vince

Jeanne sank into a kitchen chair and reread the note. It was an apology of sorts from a distance, delivered not in person but by letter. He hoped for "professional and cordial" relations, yet he wanted friendship. He mentioned her pregnancy but never made reference to the baby that was coming. As a peace offering, it was as distancing as it was personal.

Jeanne had no idea how to respond, but that didn't stop her from turning on her oven to reheat the casserole. She especially needed the comfort food after reading Vince's note. He was a puzzle—always had been—coldly analytical about the businesses he deemed worthy of investment, but warm and charming outside work.

When Vince cooked for her, he was more than skillful, joyfully singing to himself as he measured, poured, and stirred. Although he needed no one to endorse his decisions at work to feel confident, when he cooked, he waited breathlessly for her to signal her approval with a thumbs-up. He'd be waiting the same way for her response to his note.

After such a satisfying meal, Jeanne felt mellow and kindly disposed toward Vince. She missed him. When she thought about their last meeting, though, the feeling evaporated. There was no way she was ready to talk to him. Calling was out. She opened her laptop and composed a short note of thanks. She was impressed and pleased that he remembered her favorite comfort food, and while she'd seen him tackle dishes far more challenging than mac 'n cheese, she couldn't remember enjoying anything more.

Thanking Vince was the easy part. What could she say about how they would deal with each other when he himself was ambivalent? "I look forward to putting our relationship on a normal footing." She clicked "send," not allowing herself time to rethink the message. "Normal" was such a weasel word, but she didn't know her own mind well enough to be more precise. It would have to do.

She moved to her living room couch and lay down. With a throw pillow stuffed behind her head and the remote in hand, she turned the TV on to a light classical music cable station. Chopin filled the room with familiar piano chords while Jeanne stared at the ceiling wondering what to do about Parker.

If she and Vince were still together, she could tell him her suspicions, but she no longer had his full loyalty or confidence, mac 'n cheese notwithstanding. Believing Parker was involved in some way with Milton Cox was one thing, but saying it out loud might convince Vince and the rest of the board she was losing it. Parker would be happy to capitalize on their doubts.

Stepping into the presidency of Salientific or whatever company came next had long been a goal, but with the baby coming, that goal had receded into a future she couldn't visualize. Becoming a mother was an event of such magnitude that she couldn't see around the bend.

If she'd had a child when she was younger, she would have expected it to adjust to her life, and daycare would have been a financial necessity. Her hands massaged her belly. I want my life to revolve around yours, little one, but I don't want to become the opposite of my own mother and smother you with my constant presence.

The box from her mother's attic was still in the corner of the living room, a reminder of how much more complex the relationship between her mother and her had been than she had ever imagined. If only raising a child were as simple as the story of *The Runaway Bunny*. Love was a necessary but insufficient condition for successful childrearing.

Jeanne had disposed of her mother's entire household, yet this one carton had been here for months, its contents revelatory. Would she be even as good a mother as Fay Bridgeton had been? Perhaps it was time to cut her mother some slack.

Boxes and bags filled the marketing conference room. Mariana had made the room sales conference central, and everything would be transferred to the Marriott in the afternoon. There were khaki backpacks for all the reps, and each held a pad, pen, camouflage vest, and flat-topped patrol hat, all with the Salientific logo and QRF for Quick Response Force.

Jeanne and Mariana had collaborated on her costume. Although Jeanne had joked about wearing a tent, she'd settled on a rain poncho, which made ample allowance for her growing silhouette. She'd also chosen a helmet with leaves and twigs affixed to the top, a tongue-in-cheek acknowledgment of her occasional need to hide from Bart. Sales reps had a way of blaming marketing when their pipelines weren't full of leads.

Mariana had obtained combat fatigues for Bart, Parker, Lou, Alberta, and Jake. Jake's jacket was embellished with more stars than any real general would be sporting. Their hats were the same patrol caps as the sales reps'. Mariana was working at the end of the conference room table, stuffing the last of the backpacks, when Jeanne sat down next to her. "Great job on all of this," Jeanne said, her arm sweeping the room. "I'm sure Bart appreciates all your hard work as much as I do. Any more of your previous problems with him?"

"He's been fine. Very sweet, really. Alberta asked me the same thing—two or three times."

Bart, even at his best, was never sweet, so Mariana's response assuaged one concern and raised another. He was a superb sales strategist who was entirely capable of devising more than one approach to close a deal. Alberta knew that too—probably the reason she kept asking Mariana about unwanted advances. Jeanne guessed she was concerned advances might become welcome. Alberta may have said the right words about giving up on Bart, but she wasn't over him. With age, we may grow thick-skinned about life's disappointments, she thought, but our hearts remain poorly insulated against lost love.

Jeanne's mind wandered to Vince and the leggy brunette she'd seen him with at the Emerald House. If he was still seeing her, maybe she was the one who'd advised him to make peace with her. *If I had been in her shoes—six-inch platform heels, as I recall—I'd feel charitable toward a pregnant, middle-aged woman too. No competitive threat there.* The thought was enough to give Jeanne heartburn.

~

The coffee was hot and the pastries fresh at the breakfast buffet. Since many Salientific employees who in some way supported the sales force had been invited for the first half day, the room was crowded and noisy. Jeanne spotted several board members, including Vince talking with Franklin and Jake.

She moved toward the coffee pot, keeping her back to the room in an effort to go unnoticed. The military theme was no longer a secret. As new arrivals registered and received their backpacks, they became part of the homogeneous group, all arrayed in camouflage vests and caps. One of the women had such a small head that her hat came down over her eyes. She entertained her colleagues with a Charlie Chaplin imitation until Lou plucked the cap off her head and placed it on top of his own mammoth skull, where it perched like a billed beanie. A wave of laughter spread through the room.

Jeanne munched a blueberry muffin and sipped decaf. It was heartwarming to see Jake so animated with no hint of moodiness or erratic behavior. He had probably invited the board to come by for breakfast and the opening session, when he would deliver kudos to the sales force. She was glad Vince and Franklin could observe him in command of himself and his company's performance. Was she fantasizing to think Parker's mutiny might just go away?

"Good morning, Jeanne."

She turned, flustered, to face Vince. "Hi, I . . . uh . . . need to return your casserole dish."

"No hurry on the dish, unless you'd like a refill on the mac 'n cheese. Sorry to hear about Bricklin."

"Thank you. It's hard without him." She blinked back the tears that had become a reflex when she thought of Bricklin. She asked about Vince's holidays, which, as she'd expected, had been spent in New Jersey with his mother and family. When he asked about hers, she mentioned volunteer work without identifying Dawning Day. No point in bringing up anything related to Alzheimer's. She looked around the room for someone she could break away to talk to. Conversation with Vince was awkward, with too many landmines to avoid. She excused herself to check in with Mariana.

Inside the ballroom, rows of chairs flanked the center aisle and faced the stage, where a podium stood in the center, skirted with camouflage fabric. A large video screen covered a good-sized chunk of the back wall. When Jeanne climbed the steps to the stage, she heard Mariana's voice in the wings conversing with a sound system specialist about the music and special effects. Jeanne joined them as they moved onto the stage to verify that both the podium and lavalier mikes were functioning so presenters' preferences for speaking from the podium or moving around the stage could be accommodated. "I've double-checked everything, Jeanne. We're good to go."

"When this is over," Jeanne replied, "I'm ordering you to take some well-deserved comp time."

Mariana saluted with a smile. "Kevin and his people have been awesome to work with." The long-haired young man at her side murmured something about giving us their best effort and shoved his hands in his pockets. "Their equipment is at the back of the room, so Kevin and his assistant, Bruno, will be accessible to handle any last-minute adjustments."

Jeanne laughed. "As Mariana can attest, 'last minute' is anathema to me, so I'm hoping we can spare you any of those."

Mariana wrinkled her nose. "Um, there is one wildcard. Bart has something up his sleeve for the opening, and he won't tell me what it is. He wants it to be a surprise and swears it won't be a problem. Just keeps saying, 'No worries.'"

No worries, my ass. Jeanne excused herself and returned

to the reception area to look for Bart, who was nowhere in sight. Jeanne saw Lou heading into the ballroom and looked at her watch. It was almost time to start. Jake must have gone with Bart, because he was no longer at the breakfast buffet. Whatever Bart was up to, she hoped Jake would make sure it wasn't off-the-wall.

Mariana threw open the doors to the ballroom as the bugler began to play jazzy arrangements of Reveille, First Call, and Assembly. Jeanne took her seat next to Lou and Parker in the front row. Alberta stood in the back sharing a laugh with the Kevin-Bruno duo, but as the room quieted, she hurried down the aisle, scooted past Parker, and slid into her seat.

The house lights dimmed, and the bugler departed. The music, soft at first, came up loud and percussive. Jeanne was no fan of hip-hop, but the beat of Aloe Blacc's "I Need a Dollar" was irresistible. She could feel the floor vibrating. Her baby must be a Blacc fan. He gave her a couple of kicks in the ribs that seemed in time with the music, prompting Jeanne to spread her fingers over her moving belly.

"You okay?" Lou asked, cupping his hand to her ear.

Jeanne leaned over. "Baby's twerking." Lou's laugh was subsumed into the sudden roar from the audience. The ballroom's rear doors had been thrown open for what looked like an army jeep. The car, a well-adapted golf cart sporting the Salientific logo, sped down the center aisle with Bart at the wheel and Jake standing and waving.

The sales force cheered and clapped, the music blared, and Jeanne berated herself for doubting Bart. He might have a talent for demoralizing the marketing department, but he was a master at motivating sales. Jeanne felt upbeat, lifted along with the rising applause. When had she last felt so much a part of the company? She became eager for her turn to present.

Bart and Jake strode onto the stage, waving at the reps who were still on their feet clapping. Kevin ran down the aisle, climbed into the cart, and threw it into reverse. Several of the reps began clapping in time to the back-up beeps as the cart retreated toward the doors. Bart looked exceedingly pleased with himself, and Jake seemed to be enjoying the joyful clamor.

As Bart adjusted the lavalier mike, Jake joined the rest of the management team in the front row. The music, which had been steadily diminishing in volume, faded out as Bart began his welcome. He thanked everyone for a great year, hitting the highlights. When he announced the closing revenue numbers, everyone cheered. His next slide was Quick Response Force with the definition he had first told Jeanne. QRF was his acronym to live by for the coming year. "Troops, we're all in this together." He described the responsive, mission-tailored units—from the field as well as from headquarters—that would chase high-value targets.

Bart's message seemed to be going over just as he had hoped. Although Jeanne still had reservations about the military theme, she was pleased to see how well it was received by the sales force. As she looked down the row of her fellow senior managers, she noted the sour expression on Alberta's face. She, alone, was not impressed . . . at least not with Bart.

Jake took the stage next, relaxed and totally in his element. He complimented everyone in the company for superb execution during the fiscal year just ended and waited for the stomping and whistling to die down. Jeanne hoped she was the only one who noticed the nearly imperceptible shaking of Parker's head, especially when Jake spoke of Salientific's futuristic technological opportunities.

As Jake's company strategy overview drew to a close, Lou took the side aisle out of the room. Costume change time,

Jeanne thought. Lou's talk was next. Her own costuming would be a simple matter of throwing on her poncho and helmet and making sure her chin strap was snug. The hardest part would be lacing up her combat boots. Her belly was already something of an obstacle, but Mariana would be available to help.

Since Jeanne's talk was scheduled to follow a coffee break, she and Mariana had plenty of time. After everyone was again settled in the ballroom, Kevin drove up in the golf cart. "I was told to give you special treatment, so hop in." He looked at her girth, exaggerated by the poncho, and came around to her side to help her in.

The theme music started up again, and Kevin accelerated down the aisle while Jeanne waved to the applauding audience. When she climbed the steps to the stage, laughter broke out. She clipped her mike to her poncho and raised a bottle of water from the podium. "Here's to a year pregnant with potential." The audience groaned, and Jeanne grinned. She was back—the old Jeanne—and it felt great.

She was a strong presenter, and with so much positive energy in the room, she knew she was connecting with the reps. They needed to hear that plans for the year—for PR, advertising, product intros, trade shows, and seminars—would raise the company's visibility and bring in leads. She assured them they weren't out there alone. Marketing was their partner. She knew that in spite of her words, there would be conflicts and gripes over the coming year, but, hey, a sales kickoff was all about optimism—optimism and laying out the plan.

She was confident her team could provide the continuity that would be required during her maternity leave. She felt pumped in a way she hadn't since she'd learned she was pregnant. Jake beamed at her from the front row.

Applause followed Jean to her seat. Bart took his place at the podium and opened his mouth to speak. *BOOM!* Out of nowhere came a deafening noise that shook the floor. Gunfire and explosions followed. It took Jeanne a moment to remember they were Bart's special effects, but the volume was intolerable. Bart stumbled back from the podium and clapped his hands to his ears.

Jeanne turned to Jake, who was on his feet. Light glinted off the barrel of the gun in his hand, a gun he was pointing at the audience. At first, she thought it was a prop, but none of this was in Bart's plan—he looked terrified.

Shrieks rose above the gunfire. Jeanne couldn't tell if the shots were coming from the sound system or Jake's gun. Instinctively, Jeanne wrapped her arms around her belly. This couldn't be happening. Wild-eyed, Jake waved his gun toward the corners of the room.

Parker bolted to the aisle and tried to back up the golf cart. Jake winged him, and he went down on the seat. When the gun swung back toward Jeanne, Jake focused on the belly bulge beneath her poncho. "Bomb," he yelled.

"Jake!" Jeanne screamed, searching for recognition in his eyes. "It's not a bomb." She yanked off her poncho. The muzzle of his gun loomed like the mouth of a cannon. "The baby's yours, Jake. *Don't kill your son*," she pleaded.

His eyes drilled into hers, then clouded with confusion. He looked down at the gun in his hand and backed up to the wall. Slowly crumpling to the floor, he lowered his head to his knees. The sound effects had ceased. The room was quiet. No one dared move with Parker bleeding in the cart.

The faint wail of sirens from outside the hotel grew louder. Jake lifted his face as though to speak, pushed the gun into his mouth, and fired.

"No!" Jeanne screamed, falling to her knees, sobbing. She remained, her face hidden, curled over her baby till an EMT gently pulled her to her feet and guided her to a chair. He took her vitals, but his voice sounded distant. Though commotion surrounded her, she was immobilized in a hitch in time when Jake's calculus determined his life had to end so his son's could begin; *or* Jake awakened from his PTSD episode and saw that its consequences had made his suicide necessary; *or* Jake saw a future where, like some Sisyphean warrior, he'd bear the burden of his memories forever; *or* . . . She'd never know why, only that he'd allowed her a scant moment to plead for their son before giving his instantaneous response. She couldn't even say for sure he knew she, Jeanne, was there.

The EMT trailed Jeanne through the reception area, where police officers were interviewing the sales reps who'd been in the front of the room. Alberta, ashen faced, sat in a folding chair twisting her fingers. Everyone fell silent, staring, as Jeanne passed. Lou rushed to her side. "I need to go home, Lou—*please*. Can you find Mariana? She has my bag."

The EMT intervened. "You're in shock, Ms. Bridgeton. You need to come to the hospital, so you and your baby can be checked over."

Lou was firm. "No way you're going home after what you've been through, even if I have to carry you to the ambulance myself."

The triage nurse at the ER directed them to the Maternity and Fetal Medicine Department, where Jeanne was installed in a prenatal room. A nurse, wearing a set of scrubs Jeanne recognized as a staple of Maggie's work wardrobe, checked Jeanne's vital signs again and wrapped a strap and fetal heart monitor around her bare belly. She instructed Jeanne to relax and push a button whenever she felt the baby move. "We've notified Dr. O'Rourke."

"But I want to go home."

"We'll release you as soon as we can. We need to hear from the doctor first." Muriel, as she introduced herself, returned moments later with a copy of *Parenting* magazine and the latest issue of *People*. She placed them on Jeanne's bedside table. "Sorry, best I could do. Here's the TV remote, in case you really get bored." She hesitated. "On second thought, leave the TV off."

She spotted Jeanne's cell phone on top of her purse and turned it off, admonishing Jeanne to rest while she was being monitored. "Let's try to get that heart rate of yours back where it's supposed to be."

Jeanne glanced at the cover of *People*, which showed two kittenish blondes clinging to the arms of an overage, pot-bellied film star. How could such characters have the temerity to exist in the same world where people shoot themselves in the middle of upbeat business meetings?

To enjoy escapist entertainment required a mind capable of escaping. Jeanne's was etched with the picture of Jake blowing his brains out. And Parker—she didn't even know how seriously he'd been hurt. How could the universe be reordered so quickly? Muriel hadn't needed to warn her away from the TV news. The last thing she needed was an endless repetition of the most terrifying and sickening moment of her life. Jake was dead. His son was alive. His baby was inside her, kicking, and she had to record his activity.

It was dark when Jeanne arrived home by taxi. She had been too sapped of energy to fetch her car from the hotel parking lot. Her condo, which she'd thought bereft of comfort after Bricklin's death, felt like a blessed sanctuary. She turned on the lights in the kitchen she'd left a hundred years ago and continued into the living room, where she collapsed onto the couch.

The brass table lamp on the end table beside her cast its sixty watts of incandescence on her face. It was on a timer, more for Bricklin than to deter burglars, and Jeanne thought about the lights in Jake's apartment, switching on and off for no one.

Jeanne turned on her phone and began reading messages. Between texts and downloaded email, there seemed to be more communications than there were people at Salientific. A frenzied voice mail from Maggie begged her for a return call. "It was on the news, Jeanne. What a nightmare! Where are you? Please let me know you and the baby are okay." Okay? Jeanne thought about how uplifted she'd felt that morning when Jake and Bart had rolled down the aisle in their faux jeep, surrounded by laughter and cheers.

She'd never be okay in that same way again, not even close. Jake, pursued by his memories into the barrel of his gun, had left her with an indelible image even Alzheimer's could never erase.

CHAPTER 15

Unable to face reimmersion in the Salientific community, Jeanne spent the morning at home. The sounds of those final moments replayed themselves—the teeth-rattling music and gunfire—no matter whether she pulled the covers over her head or paced from room to room. She kept reaching for her cell phone and putting it away without turning it on.

Her home phone rang over and over, but Jeanne ignored it. Solitude at home was unattainable, but then, who in senior management was at the office? Probably no one but Lou. Maybe she was needed. Guilt and restlessness propelling her, she climbed behind the wheel.

As soon as Eduardo spotted her, he ran out from behind his desk. "Jeanne, you're a hero—heroine. Everyone is talking about you. Reporters have been calling."

"Where's Bart?"

"At the Marriott helping the reps arrange early flights home. He decided the conference couldn't continue with everyone so upset. I heard no one is allowed back in that ballroom, because it's a crime scene. I don't know why anyone would want to—blood and, *Dios mio*, who knows what else."

When Jeanne reached her office, Clara Nordell appeared in her doorway. After Jeanne waved her in, Clara entered and stood behind a guest chair, hands gripping the back. "I'm so glad you weren't hurt, Jeanne. Everyone is just blown away . . . I mean . . ."

"That's okay. I know it's hard to find the right words."

"I felt like curling up in a ball in the corner, but when I talked to Mariana—so close to everything yesterday yet back at the hotel, packing up and helping the sales force deal with what they saw—I knew I needed to step up."

Jeanne's impulse was to say *we'll all get through this together*, but the words seemed trite and hollow given the enormity of what had happened. She patted Clara's arm wordlessly. Who would be the first to mention it, Jeanne wondered—obviously not Clara. Mariana had been there. She must have heard Jeanne tell Jake the baby was his.

"The publicity," Clara said. "It's too late to get ahead of this story, but we need to manage it. The reporters started calling right after, but I sent out a company-wide message saying no one should talk to the press. Someone at WCVB managed to get through to Franklin Burrows. He wouldn't comment until he was sure Jake's family had been notified."

Jeanne sighed. "It is what it is. CEO with PTSD ends his life. Follow it with the usual hearts and prayers going out, etcetera."

"Um . . ." Clara looked away, an uncharacteristic gesture of avoidance. "That's not the part of the story they're asking about. It's what you said to Jake that made him put down his gun, and whether it was a strategy to stop him cold or, or . . ."

"Or whether it was true?"

Clara squirmed.

"Yes, it is Jake's baby, but I don't think we need to put that in a press release, do we?" Jeanne cocked an eyebrow at Clara.

"No, and we're not a public company. You know what I think? What you did was very brave. I could never have faced down Jake, knowing he was about to shoot me and probably everyone else in that room. I think the whole company is behind you." Jeanne thanked Clara for her support. "There's just one more thing. What should I say about Parker?"

Parker—Jeanne hadn't even thought about him. She flushed with shame. Jake had shot him in the shoulder, but Jeanne didn't remember seeing Parker being helped out. "I'll check at his home and see if I can find someone to tell me how he's doing." Clara nodded and hurried out, while Jeanne reached for her phone. She didn't pick up the receiver, though. Instead she allowed her hand to slide back down the buttons and across the desk to her lap. Her last exchange with Parker had been so . . . reptilian, just a pair of snakes hissing and threatening.

She decided to ask Lou before calling Parker's home. He answered on the first ring. "Parker? He needs surgery. Bullet shattered his shoulder. When I talked to his son, it sounded like he was going to be out of commission for several weeks at least."

"I'll send an email to the company. Clara's handling the press."

"Jeanne, can we get together this morning?"

"Can it wait till afternoon? There's so much to sort out since Jake . . ." They agreed on one o'clock, and Jeanne swiveled to face the windows. Lou had seemed reluctant to wait but didn't say why he wanted to talk. She rubbed her temples with the heels of her hands.

"Jeanne?" Franklin Burrows stood in her doorway. "I'd like to talk with you. Would you mind stepping into Jake's office?"

Franklin had a key and, after unlocking Jake's door, gestured toward the conference table and closed the door behind him. He took a chair at the far end. Jeanne's eyes were drawn to

Jake's empty chair. It seemed wrong that someone else should ever occupy it. She sat down with her back to it. "How are you holding up?" Franklin asked.

"A little shaky, to be honest."

"You could probably use some time off."

"Not really. I thought I wanted to be home, but now that I'm here, I feel a little more normal."

"Well, that's good . . . good." Franklin seemed discomfited by her answer. Perhaps she'd been too quick to use the word "normal." "I've been in touch with the rest of the board, and, as you can imagine after this tragedy, we need to move quickly to restore stability to the business."

"Agreed." She was pleased Franklin had taken control.

"We've decided to ask for your resignation, Jeanne." She stared. *Resignation?* She'd been expecting him to ask her opinion on how they should manage going forward, on how to maintain morale after the company's trauma. Instead, it was over. *She* was over. What Jake had spared her, Franklin went on to accomplish. In the vernacular of business, she'd been shot. His eyes momentarily flickered away from her gaze, which surprised her. Surely, he wasn't uncomfortable, not after all the executives he'd fired in the past.

Franklin cleared his throat before continuing. Now that everyone knew Jake was the father of her baby, Salientific couldn't continue to employ her. Without the sales conference and its tragic ending, her relationship with Jake might have remained private. Only a few people had heard her tell Jake the baby was his, but the news had spread fast.

Since the shooting hit the news outlets, questions were coming from all sides, with board members even getting calls at home. "They're asking whether an intimate relationship between an employee and her superior is sanctioned at Salientific. You were courageous, Jeanne, which is what makes this situation so difficult, but we can't ignore a violation of company policy, not to mention standard business ethics. We would look derelict."

The board felt that in the interest of company morale, she should resign rather than be fired. Given what she'd been through and her impending maternity leave, she could easily explain her decision as health related.

Interesting, she thought, an employee couldn't screw around with her superior. Why didn't he say a manager couldn't bang his subordinate? In Franklin's version, she was to blame. He might as well have fired her for getting herself knocked up. Jeanne's mother hadn't been off base after all. A woman's pregnancy changed everything. "I certainly wouldn't want the board to appear derelict," she said dryly.

He ignored the comment and plowed ahead. "Lou will be acting CEO, and Vince will temporarily join Salientific to fill in for Parker as CFO."

Vince—he'd been in the room when she announced Jake was the father of her baby. With all the texts and emails she'd received last night, not one had come from Vince. He was out of her life for good. She remembered the awkward moment at the breakfast reception when he'd tried to talk with her. Maybe it was better this way.

Franklin wanted Jeanne to leave the company immediately. From an ethical perspective, the board needed a clean break with her. Ironic, she thought, venture capitalists as the standard bearer for business ethics. Franklin's definition of a clean break, however, had some rough edges. They wanted her to function as a marketing consultant for the rest of the month at least. She was to manage marketing from offsite, by phone, text, or email. What choice did she have if she wanted to take care of her people? She agreed.

Jeanne detoured around the direct route to her office to avoid being waylaid by anyone in marketing. She stuffed into her briefcase as many personal items as would fit and left the building. Eduardo waved, but she didn't stop.

When Jeanne arrived at Dawning Day, Maggie was checking residents' blood pressure in the Alzheimer's unit. Jeanne told the receptionist she'd come back later, but before she could leave, Maggie emerged from behind the locked door. "You look terrible. What happened?"

"I got canned," Jeanne said with a wry smile. As soon as Maggie's arms enfolded her, Jeanne gave up trying to hold back her angry tears. Thank God she hadn't cried in front of Franklin.

"You can't leave, okay?" Maggie guided her into the empty bistro off the lobby. I have to finish what I'm doing, but I'll be back out here in ten minutes, fifteen tops. Sit down." Jeanne sank into a chair while Maggie stepped behind the counter, unlocked a cabinet, and dispensed a hot chocolate from a beverage machine. "I want you to drink this slowly—it's very hot—and don't think about the calories. If you're not here when I come back out, I'll never speak to you again."

Jeanne felt a wave of relief to have Maggie in charge, since she felt as incapable of moving as a nonambulatory resident of Dawning Day. She took a tentative sip. Whatever the machine-generated hot chocolate lacked in chocolaty richness it provided in heat and caffeine, warming her from the inside out and elevating her mood from desperation to mere misery.

Jeanne offered up no prayers for help from above, but if she had, she could rightly claim they'd been answered, as a draft sweeping into the bistro from the lobby heralded the arrival of four golden retrievers. Jeanne was instantly at the side of the young couple accompanying them, but the dogs wore service vests, so she knew it was wrong to distract them when they were working. She asked permission to pet them and was soon surrounded by cold noses and furry muzzles nudging her to share her affections.

She buried her face in the dense coat of a blond dog named Willow. How she'd missed that scent and the tactile pleasure of hugging a dog. These therapy dogs, one of the handlers explained, were from Golden Years Pet Visits. They'd been trained, both by dog owners and company staff, to remain gentle and unflustered, regardless of noise or intruding distractions, while the elderly petted and cuddled them.

They didn't need to persuade Jeanne of the delight these visits brought to the Dawning Day residents, not to speak of the lowered blood pressure of those who stroked them and the increased responsiveness of Alzheimer's patients. Jeanne was at least thirty years younger than most residents of Dawning Day, and she, too, felt comforted by the encounter. She remembered her Thanksgiving with Bricklin and how the residents had fussed over her three-legged pet.

Jeanne asked as many questions as she could about the origin and training of the goldens and took a business card before the handlers were split up, one ushered to the upstairs lounge, the other to the Alzheimer's wing. When Maggie passed the dogs on their way to the second floor, she found Jeanne staring up at the wagging tails. "Dogs and chocolate—all better now?"

Jeanne sighed. "I wish—but it's a start."

"I know where we can talk." Maggie led the way through the dining room, and for a moment Jeanne thought she was headed into the kitchen. She pointed to the closed French doors at the back of the room. They had white sheers stretched behind their glass and led to a private dining room.

"Elegant. Is this where you hold the weddings?"

"Don't laugh. We've had residents marry. Never too late for love."

"Nice sentiment, but one I can't subscribe to." She sat down across from Maggie and recounted her morning conversation. Although Jeanne had returned Maggie's call the night of Jake's suicide, she'd been too wiped out to relate more than the essential information. "I told Jake the baby was his. People heard. Vince was there. If he didn't hear me say it . . . well, let's just say the word got around." Her mouth twisted. "No job, no more mac 'n cheese, just a lot of free time."

"So, the baby's father is Jake? You didn't tell me. When I saw on TV what you'd said to him, I didn't know if it was true or just your strategy for stopping him."

Jeanne hung her head. "Sorry I didn't call. I put off finding out till my amniocentesis. Then the sales kickoff started, and the world went tilt. Ironic, isn't it?" She put her hand on her belly. "This little boy will be just like me. He'll never know his father." Jeanne put her head down on her folded arms.

Maggie came around the table and rubbed her back. "Your kid is going to have a great life, and so are you. After the trauma you've been through, you're entitled to feel like everything's falling apart. Why don't you stay at my house tonight? Better than being alone. I'll even kick out my boyfriend."

Jeanne's head jerked up. "Boyfriend?"

Maggie laughed. "No boyfriend—at least not yet. I had to say something to keep you from getting mascara on our only twelve-foot tablecloth." Jeanne wiped her tears with her hand and smiled.

"Thanks for the invitation, but I'm going home to cry in my own pillow and do all the important work around my house that I've neglected, like alphabetizing my spices. By now, everyone in the industry must have heard about Jake and me. There'll be no end of gossip and sly jokes. No one will hire me. I'll be radioactive."

"Well, I say *fuck them*!" Maggie's rare profanity startled Jeanne. "The software business doesn't run the world."

"Yeah, Maggie, it kind of does." Jeanne gathered up her coat and bag and pushed open the French doors.

At eight thirty, the phone rang. Clara apologized for calling so early, though to Jeanne the time was of no consequence given how little she'd slept. "Franklin sent out an email yesterday to the whole company about your resignation, and Lou came down to marketing to answer questions and reassure us. He looked awful, which reassured no one. Is it true, Jeanne? Did you really resign?"

Jeanne popped a K-cup in her coffee machine and watched the dark brew stream into her cup while she debated how to respond. "Officially, I've resigned." The last of the coffee hissed into her mug. *Hope my baby forgives me, but I really need the caffeine this morning.*

"Say no more. I get it. You should know, though, I've already fielded calls from reporters, including from industry rags, asking if it's true you were let go because of an affair with the CEO. We'll stick to the official line, but someone's bound to get to you at home."

"Judging from the blinking light on my answering machine, they already have. Thanks for the heads-up."

Jeanne sipped her coffee and listened to her voice mail. She erased the three messages from reporters, though she knew she couldn't duck them indefinitely. She could only hope

Salientific wasn't big enough to hold their interest for long. Their websites were hungry monsters requiring daily replenishment with fresh news.

The *Boston Globe* and local TV networks were more persistent than the trade press. Jake's suicide was big local news, and since she was the one who had stopped his attack, her perspective was the one they wanted. They rang her bell and called her cell. Tracking down her number must have been easier than she thought. Finally, she turned her phone off. For once, she was glad she no longer had a dog and could remain indoors until she ran out of food. If her staff needed guidance, no one called. It was probably too awkward.

The next morning, when Jeanne saw the *Globe* headline, she realized someone had known what to say, accurate or not. "Pregnant Woman Fired After Saving Company from Gunman." She wondered who could have come to her defense and ignored orders not to speak to the press. Jeanne was glad her mother was dead. This would have been no way to demonstrate she had achieved industry-wide recognition.

The article mentioned Parker as the only victim of Jake's breakdown. Parker, whom she'd pushed out of her thoughts, was seriously injured. Though she felt sorry for him, he had been the first to flee the ballroom. He was an officer of the company and might have been able to help defuse the situation. She knew she ought to visit him in the hospital. She definitely would—at some point—maybe when she stopped feeling like a victim herself.

She felt guilty about her self-absorption, but she was the one who'd been fired. Worse yet, a basic tenet of her faith—that given the right data, risk could always be calculated—had been destroyed. The future could never be predicted with certainty.

CHAPTER 16

Parker's family had transferred him to New England Baptist Hospital for his shoulder reconstruction. Jeanne planned her visit for an evening, two days after his surgery, a time, she hoped, when her visit length would be limited by the end of visiting hours. Perhaps Parker's relatives would be in the room chatting, thus diminishing her need to converse.

She stopped at Whole Foods in Newton to buy a box of chocolate chip cookies, Parker's favorite, as evidenced by his scouting conference rooms after meetings to scarf up the leftovers. Her calculation about timing proved incorrect, though, since there were no visitors in his room. He had a roommate, hidden behind the privacy curtain, and Jeanne heard the laugh track of a sitcom emanating from the speaker on that bed.

Parker lay staring at the ceiling, but when he saw her, he lifted his head from his pillow. "I must be on my deathbed if you were moved to visit."

"Not too far gone for sarcasm, I see." She tried to conceal her shock at his appearance, so different without his toupee. The fringe of hair on his bald head was dark brown with a good inch of gray extending from the roots. Other than the two-tone remnant of his dye job, his skull looked better without it.

As she took in the rest of his face, she was struck by how his ordeal had aged him. The skin under his eyes sagged, and his formerly botoxed forehead was deeply lined. She wondered, as she pulled up a guest chair, if she, too, looked like crap. She held out the box of cookies, which he acknowledged with a nod as he took it from her with his good hand. Thirty seconds used up. Now what?

Parker's cologne was notable by its absence. Instead, the room smelled of antiseptic. Jeanne cast about for a banality to help pass the time. "How are you feeling?" If he described the surgery he'd undergone, it might fill up fifteen or twenty minutes of her visit.

"I keep wondering," he said, "if Jake was a good shot or a bad one. Did he mean to wreck my shoulder, or was he unsuccessful at killing me?" Jeanne didn't want to go there, to see in her mind's eye Jake's face, to hear the crack of the gun. The question was rhetorical anyway, wasn't it? She shrugged, but Parker wasn't finished puzzling over Jake's behavior. "Never thought his PTSD would lead to that, or I never would have suggested a military theme to Bart."

Jeanne felt a jolt of anger but tried to suppress it, reminding herself Parker was in a weakened state. Change the subject, she told herself. How-about-those-Red-Sox? Anything. But Parker continued.

"I just wanted Jake out of the CEO slot for the sake of Salientific. Now look what's happened. The company is a mess." Altruism? She didn't believe it. More likely self-pity. "It doesn't help the stability of the company, Jeanne, that you got yourself fired. I guess you only fuck CEOs and VCs? Must be what they mean by managing up."

The vitriol she'd pushed down became a force, a current racing through her body. "It's my fault you're sitting in that bed? You're the one who never considered where Jake's relapse might lead, and you're the asshole who cranked up the music and gunfire at kickoff."

"I didn't do that," he yelled. The patient behind the curtain turned his TV louder. "And Milton Cox, the moron, was supposed to set off his car alarm, not drive through the window." The alarm on Parker's monitor blared a warning, though Jeanne was sure her own racing heart had set off the sensor.

"Don't think you'll get away with this just because people feel sorry for you."

"And who do you think will listen to Jake's baby's mama?"

A nurse entered, looking harried and annoyed. "Heard you both down the hall before the monitor went off. This conversation is over, and so are visiting hours." Jeanne slammed her chair back and rose, leaving the nurse to minister to Parker and his monitoring electronics.

In the hallway, her face hot with rage, she fervently wished Jake had killed Parker. She looked back over her shoulder, as though someone might have divined her thoughts, and jammed her finger into the elevator button several times. If only she could detail Parker's transgressions to the board and the trade press.

Once she was outside the overheated hospital, her pulse slowed. The frigid wind stabbed her cheeks. Huddled over and shivering, she made her way through the parking lot. She was no longer the Salientific hero unfairly excoriated by Parker. She was a powerless nobody, a terminated executive who had slept with her CEO and an investor. If she attempted revenge, she'd be seen as a spiteful ex-employee bereft of credibility. Parker would make sure she was finished in the industry, if her own actions hadn't accomplished that already. Gnashing her teeth in frustration, she maneuvered her belly behind the steering wheel.

~

The next morning, Jeanne tried to come up with a reason to get out of bed. Her fleece blanket provided insulation from the bedroom's cold air but not from the memory of the previous evening's ugliness. It lodged in her brain and gut like acid.

How could Parker continue to see himself as the company's Machiavellian savior? He had denied causing Jake's meltdown at kickoff. If she could believe anything he said, someone besides Parker had been out to get Jake. She swung her feet over the side of her bed.

Wrapping her robe around the belly it scarcely covered, she relied on the generous sash to hold it in place. The living room thermostat read sixty-five degrees. The heat was pumping, as it was set to from six o'clock on, but had not yet reached its daytime warmth. Jeanne wasn't sure if she felt a draft from a poorly fitting window or was chilled from within by the possibility of yet more malice at Salientific.

She opened the kitchen cabinet above her coffee maker and reached for a Salientific mug. With her finger looped through the handle, she paused. She no longer worked for Salientific or the companies whose names and logos adorned every mug in her cabinet. How sad that any visitor would grasp how she defined herself merely by looking inside.

She braced herself against the freezing air of her garage long enough to fetch a carton she'd saved for recycling and the stepladder she kept by the kitchen door. She set the carton on the counter and stepped onto the first rung of the ladder. With one satisfying sweep, she emptied the shelf of mugs, her breath catching at the crash of breaking ceramics.

Just so much trash, she thought, as she carried the carton

out to the garage and set it beside her dumpster. She returned to the stepladder and brought down the Mikasa cups and saucers she'd relegated to the top shelf. After washing one set, she brewed a cup of coffee, which she was certain was her best in memory.

She kept thinking it was Saturday, though it wasn't. Is that what every day would feel like from then on? Even if her employment at Salientific was over, she couldn't just detach herself from the company along a perforated line the way she tore her expense check away from its printed statement.

She sat down at her laptop and looked up the phone number of the production company Mariana had engaged for the sales meeting. Reaching for her cell phone was automatic, and surprised by its absence, she realized it was still on her nightstand. When she returned to her computer, she called Kevin but landed in his voice mail. Feeling slightly guilty, she left a message identifying herself as Salientific's VP of marketing. If he didn't know she'd been fired, he'd be more likely to return the call.

Halfway through Jeanne's shower, her phone rang. She emerged and dried her hands on the towel beside the stall. Pulling it off its hook and clutching it around her, she managed to answer before the fourth ring. Kevin responded to her breathless greeting and inquired how she was doing, but Jeanne had no interest in exchanging pleasantries. She asked if she could stop by his office to talk about the sales meeting, and though he agreed, his voice was wary.

It took Jeanne half an hour to get to Burlington, which left her fifteen minutes before her appointment. She stopped at Starbucks, ordered a decaf and approached a low-slung leather club chair. Would she be able to hoist herself out of it? A nearby table was occupied by men bent over papers spread between them. Their conversation, replete with software industry jargon, was easily audible. She changed direction so she could take a seat farther away and wished she'd brought something to do with her hands.

She remembered the day she thought she'd lost her Alzheimer's notebook. Maggie had insisted she leave the office and walk till she calmed down. On the residential street Jeanne had chosen, with its swing sets and strollers, she'd felt like a tourist. Yet here, she felt the same way. If only she could remember the levels of Dante's hell she'd studied in school. Surely she was stuck in one of them now, somewhere in the middle.

She took the coffee with her. Sitting in Kevin's lobby was preferable to contemplating her misfit status at Starbucks. Lobby was hyperbole, since the entrance was more than filled by an administrator's metal desk and a couple of orange molded plastic guest chairs. Audio equipment was stacked in the corner next to a droopy plant. Fortunately, Kevin spotted Jeanne, sparing her a wait.

His office was full of electronics and what appeared to be contracts piled on his desk. "Business must be good," Jeanne observed as she took a seat on another orange chair. Kevin nodded but didn't respond. "I'd like to know what happened at the sales meeting right before Jake . . . lost control."

Kevin repositioned himself in his chair and didn't meet her gaze. "I've already talked with the police." She guessed his recalcitrance came from fear of legal exposure.

She leaned forward. "What happened when Bart took the stage? The music rose to God knows how many decibels over the soundtrack of guns and bombs. Is that what Bart asked for? Deafening?"

"It was an accident. I don't think Alberta meant it to happen."

"Alberta!"

"She was sitting so close to me, she just kind of knocked into the volume control while I was watching Bart. She'd been curious about our equipment—said her brother wanted to get into the business—so I'd been explaining during the break how we coordinate special effects. Look, I'm sorry your CEO flipped out, but it isn't Alberta's fault. I didn't want to get her in trouble, so I didn't mention it to the police. Just said we had an electronic malfunction. What were the odds someone would freak out?"

"I understand completely." What Jeanne understood, though, was that Alberta's "accident" was likely deliberate. Call it speculation, but Jeanne had no doubt Alberta was capable of sabotaging Bart's presentation in retaliation for his dumping her. Maybe disrupting the perfect orchestration of Bart's kick-off and messing with him at the start of his presentation were part of a more extensive plan to keep him off-balance.

Jeanne wanted to drive straight to the office and confront her, but she was supposed to interact with Salientific remotely. If she showed up at the office, she'd have to answer people's questions. Perhaps she'd even be shunned for her indiscretion with Jake. She ran her hand over her belly. "Indiscretion" was a euphemism. It would hurt to see disapproval replace respect on the faces of her colleagues.

Jeanne's car was already freezing, though her visit with Kevin had been brief. She turned on the ignition and cranked up the heat. Cold air blew from the vents. The seat warmer was on but seemed as reluctant to do its job as the heater. Bart answered on the first ring. "Glad I caught you," Jeanne said. She watched her puffs of breath heading for the windshield as she waited for Bart to figure out how to greet her.

He mumbled a bit before the obligatory, "Sorry about the board's decision to let you go." Was he really? It hardly mattered.

"I need to meet you."

The pause was lengthy. "Jeanne, it's crazy busy here with all the changes. How about next week?"

"No good. Has to be today." He sighed and agreed to a three o'clock coffee at Starbucks in the mall but warned her he could only spare twenty minutes. Jeanne ended the call and slapped the phone down on the passenger seat. Her new suppliant status was humiliating, especially toward Bart. The indignities of her situation were limitless.

Bart arrived at 2:55. In the past, she'd heard him tell his reps if they were less than five minutes early for a sales call, they were late. They took a table in the corner. Bart didn't bother to buy a coffee or even remove his topcoat. There was no sign of his irritating clown smile, even in his greeting. Jeanne set aside her curiosity over what was going on at the office. "Do you know why the kickoff was disrupted?"

"Uh, yeah. The short version is Jake scared everyone shitless before he blew his brains out."

"I'm talking about what set him off—the music, the gunshots."

"You came here to berate me? Okay, I'm guilty. I decided to use the gunshots and explosions at the start of my presentation and not just at the finale. I wanted to be the leader encouraging his troops at the front line. It would have been effective, too, if I'd been able to speak. Happy now?" He started to get up.

"I'm talking about the music that shook the walls." He sat and adjusted his chair, scraping the legs on the tile floor. Jeanne related the conversation she'd had with Kevin about Alberta's "accident."

"No way she'd have done that."

"I realize you may not see me as having the moral high ground here, but Alberta thought you were getting a divorce to marry her." His cheeks flushed. "By the way, Jake and I were not having an affair. We had a one-night stand, which was stupid, and it had unintended consequences. It should have been obvious to you if you wanted to string someone along, it couldn't be another employee. For all I know, Alberta may have it in for Mariana too."

Bart scowled. "Wait till the board hears this. I'm going to get them to fire her ass."

Jeanne laughed. "Oh, really. Based on what proof? And you're going to tell them you were screwing her? Besides, Salientific has no CEO, no VP of marketing, a VP of finance out on medical leave, and you want to get the human resources VP fired? If you don't care about the employees or the company's future, at least protect your stock options."

Bart looked down at his hands, folding and unfolding his fingers, his lips pursed. "Got it." He rose and turned away, then sat down again. "Just curious. Why do you care? You're out. Is this about your own stock?"

She didn't answer, instead taking a long sip of her coffee. Finally, she returned his gaze. "I still care about the company." What else could she say? Bart's eyebrow went up and a corner of his mouth contracted. He was skeptical of altruism as her motive. Who could blame him? She wasn't sure herself of her motive.

Perhaps she was just being as pragmatic as she was urging him to be. Perhaps her rage at Parker needed an outlet. Nor could she discount anger at Bart as the reason she'd called him. His inability to keep his pants zipped had led Alberta to put a match to the tinder Parker had piled beneath Jake.

Weekends had always been so welcome. Why then was home such a hard place to be? Jeanne paced from room to room. She double-checked her home phone's dial tone to see if a broken tone might indicate a message that hadn't gone to her answering machine—nothing. She turned on her cell to see if she'd missed any alerts indicating texts—nothing. Her phone was practically an extension of her hand, and suddenly it was silent. "Even you have abandoned me," she said to the inert metal rectangle. She tossed it on the couch, where it immediately rang.

Jeanne was sure the call was from someone at Salientific and with great relief answered, "Bridgeton."

Maggie responded, "'Bridgeton?' You're a civilian now. How about 'Hello'?"

"Sorry, I'm going nuts. I can't stop thinking about my company and Parker, Alberta, and Bart. Are you going to send me out for another walk?"

"Not a bad idea. It's just an addiction, you know. You can train yourself out of it the way you train yourself to stop eating when you're bored, stressed, or procrastinating. Substitute something else when you feel like reaching for your cell phone."

Jeanne groaned. "You expect me to give up overeating and work at the same time? What's left? And don't say sex. Look where that got me."

"I'm off on Wednesday. I'm going to make it my personal mission to find another focus for you."

Jeanne was used to ending conversations to get back to work or a meeting. Maggie needed to go, and Jeanne stared at her phone. Instead of a red button offering her the option to end the call, it said "call ended." Jeanne sat down on the couch. Abandoned again. Without allowing herself to look, her fingers crept over until she lay on her side with the phone in her grasp. Is this how it feels to relapse into a drug habit? She pushed the thought away and called Lou's number.

She was afraid when he saw her name on his caller ID, he'd duck the call, but he picked up on the first ring. "How are you doing? Maybe that's a dumb question after everything that's happened."

"Probably still in shock, but not letting myself in on it."

"Me too, but without the time to think about it. I've got a full plate, but not the kind that fattens you up."

"I don't mean to burden you further, but there are a couple of things I need to tell you. Can you break away for coffee or lunch this week or even meet me for a drink after work?"

"This is a really bad time."

"Please, Lou," she pleaded.

"Can you come here? I realize it may be awkward, but, honestly, I'm chasing my tail. Just can't get away."

Two days later, when Jeanne rolled into the Salientific parking lot, she wasted five minutes searching for a space before she remembered she could use a visitor's spot. Eduardo's broad smile helped ease Jeanne's discomfort. Signing the guest register felt all wrong. She hesitated at the "Company" column next to her name and considered writing "ex-pat." Instead she filled in the blank "consultant."

Eduardo handed her a visitor badge. "Really?" she asked. He nodded. She peeled the backing and stuck it on her maternity top. "Please don't make someone escort me."

"I have to, Jeanne. You understand, don't you?" He looked miserable. "I'll call Lou."

When she and Lou were settled in his office, she looked at the door he'd left open. He answered her unasked question. "Trying to keep the appearance of cloak-and-dagger stuff to a minimum. Morale is low enough already.

"I'm no fan of the board's decision. They should have put more weight on your value to the company, and, for that matter, your courage at the sales meeting. To me, those matter more than your violation of the rules." He lowered his voice. "It's not like you're the first person to screw around. It's usually a guy, though. They didn't have Jake to blame, so they focused on you. I don't think they knew what to do." He leaned across his desk. "Jeanne, people inside the company are behind you."

"I thought I was a pariah."

"Clara and Mariana even went to the board to persuade them to reinstate you. They were unsuccessful, but that Clara, she's a fighter. Told the trade press you were a hero."

"Talk about courage . . ."

Lou leaned his head back and rubbed his temples. "When Parker comes back, that will help right the ship. Vince is great, but he's distracted by his responsibilities at BTF Ventures."

"Parker! He's the reason for my coming here. Lou, you can't let him come back. He'll lobby the board to revoke your interim CEO status and make him president. He's behind Jake's suicide, maybe not directly, but he wanted Jake to flip out. Once that car crashed into the lobby . . ." She explained Parker's plan to see if a car alarm could make Jake relapse, and how the malleable Bart had embraced Parker's idea for a military theme. It didn't occur to Bart that the sales kickoff might unhinge Jake. Alberta was Parker's unwitting accomplice when she cranked up the gunfire volume to get back at Bart.

Lou listened, wide-eyed. When she finished, he muttered, "Fuck," and leaned his seat back. He was silent for a few minutes, contemplating the ceiling. Before he could respond, Vince appeared in the doorway. Startled to see Jeanne, he asked if the conversation was business or social. "Business," Lou answered, as Jeanne stood to leave.

Lou reached out his hand to detain her. "You need to tell him. I can't stop Parker alone." Vince closed the door behind him, in spite of Lou's open-door policy, and regarded Jeanne with mistrustful, narrowed eyes. Why had she come? Too late to follow Maggie's advice to disengage. Lou broke the silence. "It seems our friend Parker had a hand in Jake's slide." He gestured for Jeanne to continue.

When she was finished, she added, "This is probably a good time to initiate a search for a new CEO. As for Alberta, I have no proof her actions weren't an accident." Vince remained tight-lipped. Avoiding her eyes, he thanked her for the information and asked if she were headed to marketing. Jeanne took that as her cue to leave.

Vince opened the door as she gathered her coat and purse and gave Lou a quick nod goodbye. As she walked out, he added, "Please remember our preference that you finish the month working from home." She walked slowly down the hall, trying without success to replace her misery with indignation. Not till she reached marketing, where her staff crowded around her, did she recover.

What would she do next, they wanted to know. Would she join another technology company? Would she take them with her? Jeanne laughed. "Six months into a pregnancy isn't the most propitious time for a job search, but, if I haven't made it clear before . . ." She looked from face to face. "I value each and every one of you." Clara and Mariana hugged her first, and the others followed. Jeanne choked up and silently vowed to stay away from Salientific, for her own sake, if not the board's.

Maggie refused to tell her where they were going but insisted they leave early in the morning. "It's a long drive, so wear something comfortable."

"Don't worry about me. I can't fit into anything that doesn't have an elastic waistband. I'm not even sure I can fit in your car. How long a drive is long?"

"I'm not telling you. You'll go look at some online map and plot the circumference. Then you'll start calculating the probabilities of different destinations."

Jeanne pretended to be miffed. "When did you become so mean? You're a nurse."

"Yes, but not your nurse." Maggie instructed Jeanne to be ready at eight thirty.

The morning air smelled like snow, and the clouds were a textured gray. Although Jeanne knew the driving might become difficult later, Maggie was in charge. How freeing that was. In fact, Jeanne had begun to appreciate being without responsibilities. She felt lightened by having shared what she knew about Parker and Alberta with Lou and Vince. She'd heard not a word from Salientific and hoped Bart had followed her advice.

She and Maggie were on the Mass Pike and had passed Worcester when Jeanne asked if they were headed for Western Massachusetts.

"You mean what the weather forecasters call Western Mass? Springfield?"

"Where then? The Berkshires?"

Maggie laughed and didn't respond. When they took the Lee exit at ten thirty, Jeanne's hunch was confirmed. They followed local roads traveling north and turned off Route 7 after passing Lenox. The area was sparsely settled, but the views were lovely, and Jeanne felt herself growing drowsy. Suddenly Maggie turned left into what appeared to be a farm and stopped at the main house. Jeanne jerked awake.

She could hear mooing and a dog barking, but the rest of the animals must have been in the fields or the barn. A short, sturdy man with a ruddy complexion emerged from the house, donning a parka and baseball cap as he approached. "Welcome to Pine Tree Kennel. James Murdock." His handshake was vigorous.

Maggie was triumphant. She turned to Jeanne. "You had no idea, did you?"

Jeanne had no chance to answer before James interjected, "I understand you've recently lost a dear canine friend, a golden, and are in need of another." He winked at Maggie. "We're in the business of helping people like you." He gestured for them to follow him and led them through the house and down the basement stairs. Jeanne needed only a glimpse of the low-fenced pen with its eight golden puppies to sigh with pleasure.

Five were playing, two were sleeping intertwined, and one stood by the fence looking at them. The mother sat down beside James, who proceeded to scratch her behind the ears, but she never took her eyes off her offspring. "I'm afraid two of Amber's puppies are gone already, but there wasn't a bad one in this whole litter. Want to know about the father?"

"Not important to me," Jeanne replied with a meaningful glance at Maggie.

"What kind of dog do you like? Real active? Low-key?"

Jeanne knelt beside the pen and looked up at James. "Which one would make a good therapy dog?"

Maggie's eyes widened. "I didn't know you were thinking about that."

James took off his cap and scratched his head. "The parents, Amber and Rudy, neither one of them is aggressive—nice dispositions both. Just pick the puppy you like best. That's always my advice. A dog that's good for therapy is well trained, so you're the one who makes the dog fit the job."

Maggie crouched beside Jeanne. "Don't you just want to take them all home?"

Jeanne nodded and watched. She held her hand out to the puppy eyeing her at the fence, and he came right over. She petted him gently and picked him up. "He has that wonderful puppy smell." She rubbed her cheek on his head before reluctantly placing him back in the pen. One by one, she engaged with each puppy. Maggie cooed to whichever dog seemed to want her attention. The first male trotted around the inside of the fence as Jeanne visited with each of his siblings.

"I'm not sure which one you're going to choose," James said, "but that little boy seems to have chosen you."

"He can tell he's my favorite, and he's just waiting for me to admit it." She laughed and picked up the squirming puppy. She cuddled him while he licked her face with his tiny tongue. "Could he be any sweeter?"

"Good thing we have a two-hour drive home," Maggie said, reaching out to pet him. "Plenty of time to come up with a name."

"Since he's going to be a therapy dog and bring comfort and pleasure to all, his name will be Mac, short for mac 'n cheese."

"That's a new one," said James, scratching his head again, "but I guess Mac is manly enough for when he gets to be a big boy—and he will be big. You have some space for him to run? These dogs need exercise."

Jeanne thought of her last sad walk through the conservation area to spread Bricklin's ashes. Returning with a bounding puppy would be a welcome change. She assured James that Mac would get to run. She couldn't wait to call Scott and tell him he had a new client.

James went to get the necessary papers, and Jeanne placed Mac back in his pen so she could find her checkbook. When she looked up, Maggie was staring at her.

"What?"

"I just can't remember seeing you beaming like that."

"I can't remember either." She threw her arms around Maggie's neck. "In case I forget to tell you, you're the best."

CHAPTER 17

By the end of February, Mac was enjoying Jeanne's undivided attention. She'd completed her obligation to Salientific and forced herself to stay away from her team and former fellow executives. She hadn't even bothered to pick up her usual technology periodicals, renewing instead her acquaintance with the fiction section of the Wellesley Bookstore.

Mac was getting big but still seemed far from growing into his large paws. Jeanne enrolled him in puppy kindergarten and began to research the necessary course of training for therapy dogs. She had frequent conversations with him, as she had had with Bricklin, and though they were one-sided, she had no doubt a dog with such intelligent eyes could understand her every word.

"Your first real test," she said to him one morning, "will be whether you can get along with the baby. Sooner or later, I'm sure, you'll be friends." She leaned over from her kitchen chair, a movement her belly was impeding more each day, and took his muzzle in her hands. "I don't know how you do it, but you seem to absorb the heartache of those around you and provide contentment the way a plant takes in carbon dioxide and gives off oxygen."

At the end of Mac's day, a day that included a class, a run in the woods, errands in the car, and his long-awaited dinner, he stretched out for a nap on the living room rug. Wednesday evening meant Weight Watchers for Jeanne. She buttoned up her maternity coat and wrapped a blue scarf around her neck.

Winter seemed to have taken up permanent residence in New England, and though Mac was unfazed, Jeanne was sick of it. It didn't help that she felt as wide as she was tall. "Ugh," she said, jamming her wool hat down on her head till her ears were covered, "I can't believe I have to weigh in." Mac seemed unsympathetic, merely opening his eyes halfway.

Maggie grabbed Jeanne's arm as soon as she arrived at the weigh-in area. "I thought you'd never get here. Someone asked me out today." Her smile was triumphant.

"I want to know everything."

Maggie glanced into the meeting room where Lucy was beginning her talk. "I'll tell you later."

After a sobering encounter with the scale, reaffirming the bad news delivered by the one in Dr. O'Rourke's office, Jeanne slipped into the meeting and took the seat next to Maggie's. She looked over at Maggie's profile, which appeared to be that of a younger woman than the Maggie Jeanne had first met at Weight Watchers. She was lovely, and though to Jeanne it seemed every pound Maggie had lost had attached itself to her, Jeanne was thrilled to see her friend's diligence paying off.

At the end of the meeting, Maggie pulled Jeanne to the last two seats in the back. Lucy was chatting with several members while the newbies arranged themselves in the front row waiting for her to begin her overview of program basics. "We should be able to grab a few minutes," Maggie whispered.

"Why are you whispering? Is this guy a wanted criminal?"

"He's perfectly lovely, the son of a resident. He's come to

talk with me a couple of times about his mother's meds and potential drug interactions, and we just clicked. Today he asked me if I'd have dinner with him Sunday night."

"To explore potential interactions?"

Maggie tossed her hair. "Maybe. What of it? More important, I have nothing to wear. I can't wear scrubs, and the few nice outfits I own are too big. Do you have any time to shop with me Saturday? You must have some things you need for yourself too. It wouldn't have to be all about me."

Jeanne laughed. "Let's see. In my current state, I can buy, uh, an umbrella, a scarf, and, of course, there's always lipstick. Shoes? No, my feet are swollen."

"Okay, it's all about me."

"Of course, I'll go with you. Didn't you take me shopping for maternity clothes? Just need to keep in mind Mac's walk schedule. He and I pee equally often." Lucy was starting her overview and made shooing motions in their direction, so they made hasty arrangements and bundled up to face the wind. As Jeanne hurried to her car, she smiled to herself at the happy prospect of a love interest for Maggie and forgot to grumble about Bertucci's seductive aroma and infernal proximity to Weight Watchers.

Not until the next morning, as she lay in bed, did it occur to Jeanne that Maggie might well meet someone and marry, if not this new man, then someone else. Maggie's husband and the probable father of her children could be cool at best to the idea of taking on Jeanne's son. No matter how unwavering Maggie's commitment, she'd have to put the needs of her own family first.

Jeanne massaged her belly. No turning back for me, she thought, but I have to let Maggie off the hook. Time and the changes it brought seemed to be on amphetamines this year. Even alone in her own home, with no job and few contacts, she couldn't insulate herself. She reached down to pull Mac onto the bed. He sat as close to her as he could and offered his paw in sympathy.

Mariana's call to Jeanne's cell came in during what was now a waddling trek through the conservation area with Mac. If not for the sight of Mariana's name on her caller ID, Jeanne would not have pulled off a glove to answer. Her curiosity about the company refused to be quashed, so when Mariana asked if she and Clara could meet her for lunch, Jeanne eagerly agreed.

California Pizza Kitchen was busy on Friday, a popular day to lunch out for the office crowd, but Jeanne had arrived early and snagged a table affording a clear view of the door. Clara's towering figure was easy to spot, especially with her high-heeled black boots. Mariana trailed her, but she saw Jeanne first and told the hostess they knew their destination.

As they both tried to embrace Jeanne at once, Mariana pulled away. "Wow, you're a lot tougher to hug now."

"My doctor tells me the baby is the right size for approaching my ninth month, but I'm the one who's extra-large."

"Don't complain to me about extra-large," Clara said with a laugh, pulling out her chair. Jeanne agreed. No more body image discussions. How would the svelte Mariana have joined in anyway? They perused the menu quickly to ensure Clara and Mariana could return to the office for an afternoon meeting. Once they had ordered, they talked about Jeanne's pregnancy, her ultrasounds, and how she felt, and Jeanne was grateful she didn't have to field any at-your-age questions.

While Clara and Mariana shared the latest news in marketing, Jeanne started in on her greens with grilled chicken and wondered how she might elicit the information she really wanted. According to the two women, the company was close to hiring a new VP of marketing, and Clara, Mariana, and other key marketing staffers had been given an opportunity to interview the finalists. Jeanne was pleased the department would have a say in the hire—or, at least, management wanted the staff to feel they did.

Jeanne urged them to eat their lunch and promised not to ask any questions for at least five minutes, though she held herself in check for barely two before asking if Parker had returned from his medical leave. "It's kind of weird," Clara replied. "He's back, but Vince is still there. It's sort of like Parker reports to him, at least that's what people in accounting say."

"Vince?" Jeanne tried to be casual. "I thought Parker might be asked to fill Jake's position. I'm sure Lou is maxed out, at least he was the last time I talked to him."

Mariana leaned across the table and spoke softly. "I know I shouldn't spread rumors, but the board has supposedly initiated a search for a CEO." Jeanne brought her napkin to her mouth to hide her self-satisfied smile. She wondered whether the push for the search came from Lou or Vince.

"I have to confess," Jeanne said, "I haven't paid much attention to the trade press lately, so shoot me an email if someone gets the job, okay?"

They nodded, and Jeanne noticed when the check was paid, Mariana seemed reluctant to leave. "I wanted to say this earlier, Jeanne, but I wasn't sure quite how to say it. I need to apologize to you. As many times as I go over the sales kickoff in my mind, I can't shake the feeling that I'm responsible for what happened to Jake."

"He would have unraveled at some point from his PTSD. I was the head of marketing. I should have forced Bart to abandon the military theme. Clara, help me out here."

"Believe me, we've all been telling her it wasn't her fault."

"Suicides make everyone feel guilty. If you can't shake the guilt, perhaps you should see a therapist for a bit." Mariana nodded. "I bet Alberta can make a recommendation."

"Gone," Clara said, as they pulled on their coats. "Quit."

"To go where?"

"Nowhere, at least no one knows where. I think she's at home. We've got an HR consultant in the job as a temp." Clara led the way out, and Jeanne put her hand on Mariana's shoulder.

"Has Bart backed off?"

Mariana nodded. "All business." For now, Jeanne thought, or perhaps he's learned to be more discreet.

Over the next several days, Jeanne considered what Clara and Mariana had shared with her, and though much of it was welcome news, she couldn't seem to put Salientific out of her mind. Every time she thought about the company, Parker's sneering face surfaced. He excelled at creating the impression his every action was for the benefit of the company. He seemed to believe it himself. He was a negative leader, the worst kind.

When she and Maggie made their way through the Saturday foot traffic to Macy's, Jeanne related her concern. "What's the probability he won't undermine the next CEO? Miniscule." Maggie stopped in her tracks. "Look out," Jeanne said, grabbing her as a stroller plowed into the back of Maggie's legs.

Maggie and the young woman pushing the stroller apologized to each other, and Maggie turned an accusing eye to Jeanne. "That was your fault. I wasn't expecting to hear the word *probability* come out of your mouth again, and what happened to disengaging from Salientific? Any further signs of a relapse, and I'll be forced to confine you to a padded cell."

"No need. Having to watch you try on all the clothes I can't fit into will be punishment enough." Jeanne sighed. "This is going to be a tough month for me—no job, just a lot of long walks with Mac."

"You poor thing. Where did I put my hanky? Now that I think of it, I know something you can do. I've been reading up on an illness that was discovered relatively recently called Chronic Traumatic Encephalopathy."

"Is that the professional football player condition?"

"It's called CTE for short. You're partly right. It is a syndrome seen in professional contact sports like football, hockey, and boxing, in which concussions are frequent, but signs of it have been found in the brains of amateurs too. Some parents are even pulling their kids out of contact sports. CTE causes personality and cognitive changes, depression, and memory loss, among other symptoms, and it's similar to early-onset Alzheimer's. Didn't you say your father was a jock? I mean, not to raise false hopes or anything, but isn't it possible that was what was wrong with him rather than a genetic defect?"

"From your lips to God's ears, Maggie. I'll check it out."

March passed, and Jeanne did her research on CTE. She arranged breakfast with Luke Menton to hear about the latest research, and while she wouldn't go so far as to say she was comfortable with ambiguity, she was growing accustomed to living with indeterminate risk. She had no way of knowing for sure just how much football her father had played or how many concussions he'd had, but maybe, just maybe, CTE was what he had and not Alzheimer's.

Mac, Jeanne's constant companion, passed from puppyhood into doggy adolescence. He was growing large enough that one vigorous wag of his tail could clear a coffee table. He had the sensibilities of a puppy with the stature of an adult golden, yet he showed no signs of reaching his full size.

Jeanne observed him one morning, lying at her feet, as she sipped a cup of decaf. "I'm beginning to think James lied to me. I think your mother had a secret tryst with a Great Dane. I'm going to need a new job after this baby comes, just to keep you in dog food." Mac stood and put his paw on her lap. She was scratching him behind the ears with both hands when she felt her stomach cramp.

She and Maggie had shared a Chinese takeout meal the night before. Perhaps the pork in her moo shu pancake had been past its prime. Ten minutes later she felt another stronger cramp. She texted Maggie. "I don't think Chinese food was a good idea this late in my pregnancy. Do you have cramps too?"

Ten minutes later, after another painful cramp, Maggie replied, "No, I don't, and besides, what do you think Chinese people eat when they're pregnant? You might be having contractions."

"You mean Braxton-Hicks, the false ones? I'm not due for a couple of weeks."

"Could be. Lots of people get them off and on toward the end. Just keep track of how often they come and whether they're getting closer together."

"I'm supposed to come to Dawning Day this afternoon with Mac to introduce him to the setting and work on getting him to sit quietly when people pet him."

"We can reschedule. Just let me know. I was supposed to be off today, but I might see you there. We're short-staffed."

Jeanne felt the contractions all morning, but they never got any closer together, so she did her best to ignore them. Not till she stepped in the door of Dawning Day did she feel a more painful one close on the heels of the previous one. She took a chair in the reception area after asking for Maggie. Was this contraction seven minutes later? Five? Mac sat on the floor beside her, his eyes on her face.

When Maggie showed up a few minutes later, Mac's tail thumped against the floor. She leaned down and gave him a hug. "Aren't you a good boy—you didn't jump on me. He's really—Jeanne, are you okay?"

Hands on her belly, Jeanne shook her head. "Maybe I should go home."

"You're not driving, and I can't leave right now, so just hang out here for a minute till I can arrange coverage." By the time Maggie returned, Jeanne was straining to control her groans.

In between two contractions, Jeanne pointed to her watch. "Five minutes apart—I think. Can we leave now?"

Maggie steered Jeanne to her car, although they had to stop during a contraction in the parking lot. Mac looked up at Jeanne and whimpered. "I'm okay, boy," she said, turning to Maggie. "Do you think he knows I'm lying?"

"Outside my area of expertise." She helped Jeanne into the car and opened the back for Mac. "Give me your cell phone. Is Dr. O'Rourke's number in your contact list?"

"Why? Where are we going?" Jeanne asked, as they turned right out of the parking lot.

"Not to your place, that's for sure. You belong in the hospital." Jeanne was too absorbed in her contractions to object. She was vaguely aware of Maggie's conversation with Dr. O'Rourke's assistant as her contractions came closer together and began rising to an excruciating crescendo. She felt a desperate need to escape them, to somehow flee her body. The car had become a torture chamber.

Mac nuzzled Jeanne's shoulder from the back seat, while Maggie drove white-knuckled down Route 30, accelerating across the double yellow line to pass any driver obstructing her.

She stole looks at Jeanne, who alternated between fierce grimaces and moans. The in-betweens grew shorter. "Hang on, Jeanne."

Maggie's tires screeched as she turned into the circular drive in front of the Newford Wellman Hospital emergency entrance. She pulled Jeanne gently out of the seat she had soaked when her water broke and supported her until an orderly rushed up behind them with a wheelchair. They made it to maternity with little time to spare. The baby's head was crowning. "Maggie, don't leave me," Jeanne gasped.

"No one's leaving you," Dr. O'Rourke said as a nurse brought Jeanne into the delivery room and checked her progress, "except this baby boy. First labors are usually protracted. Guess he hasn't read the book. One last push, Jeanne." She stared in wonder at the tiny wet being the doctor held up to show her, the umbilical cord still a physical connection between them. Severing it would begin her son's journey away from her, but his precious beginning was hers alone.

"Look how beautiful." Maggie's words were barely audible over the baby's wail. Jeanne was dumbstruck. She was a mother, impossible but true. She was Dorothy in *The Wizard of Oz*, opening her front door to a world rich in color. She squeezed Maggie's hand.

CHAPTER 18

Vince's head and chest extended sideways from the hall into the doorway of Jeanne's hospital room. "Permission to enter?"

"Granted." Vince appeared older, weary, the way one looks when a good night's sleep is nowhere near an adequate remedy. He seemed relieved at her smile.

"Maggie called to tell me." He produced a bouquet of yellow roses he'd held behind his back. "Flowers may not be a creative gift, but I wasn't sure of hospital policy about visitors with hot casseroles."

Jeanne buried her nose in the bouquet. "Mmm. These are lovely." She laid them on her nightstand. "I'm going home late this afternoon, and there are no prohibitions against casseroles in my condo."

"I was afraid I wouldn't be welcome. The hospital seemed like neutral territory." He stuffed his hands in his pockets, waiting for a response that didn't come. "Is the baby in the nursery?"

She pointed to the opposite corner. "Sleeping." Vince approached the bassinet with a reverence Jeanne found surprising. After a long moment poised over the swaddled newborn, he turned.

"I'm not good at judging resemblances, but this baby's all you."

"Red and wrinkled?"

"Beautiful." He returned to her bedside, wafting the scent of roses into the air. "I didn't come here to joust with you, Jeanne. I know that was often our way, teasing each other and keeping it light. I can't speak for you, but for me it served to keep my feelings at arm's length." Jeanne stared. His eyes were moist. This was not the Vince she knew.

The advancing second hand of the wall clock filled the silence. "It's weird," he said. "I've had no time to think, yet I always seem to be thinking of you. I can't erase what's been said between us, but I need you to know—"

Jeanne wanted to be kind, but she couldn't stop her tears, angry and sad all at once. She slammed her fist down on the bed. "Damn you, Vince. You always catch me when my hormones are in an uproar." He handed her a tissue from the box on her tray. "You know that baby over there isn't yours, don't you?"

He nodded. "It's Jake's, and I don't care. I'm sure that surprises you. It surprises me. I've let myself in on a secret I was keeping from both of us: I'm in love with you." He perched on the edge of the bed and took her hands. "We had an unspoken arrangement: no commitments. Can't we change that? I want us to be together, married. Please, Jeanne."

She cast about for the right words, but Vince wasn't finished. "I haven't been honest with you, and for that, I'm sorry." He dropped his hands. "I lied to you about never being a father."

"You have a child?" Jeanne's eyes widened. Her bon vivant image of him blurred at the edges.

"Had," he said, looking away. "A car crash—just another crash like you see on the evening news—the accidents you never pay attention to while you're draining your pasta or chopping tomatoes—until it's yours, your story on the news." The media's relentless reporting on Jake's suicide flashed through Jeanne's mind.

"Toby, my daughter, loved riding in my Porsche convertible. What nine-year-old wouldn't? The wind whipping her hair, the speed, they were much more exciting than running errands in her mom's SUV. That kid was everything to me." His voice caught.

"There were no laws then about how old you needed to be to sit in the front seat. We were almost home when a delivery truck pulled out of a blind driveway on my right. I couldn't see it coming from behind the trees until . . . The driver never looked, and I couldn't stop in time. Totaled the car." Vince's voice quavered. "Toby didn't survive. Can't tell you how many times I've replayed that moment in my mind, trying somehow to change the outcome." His finger traced circles on the sheet.

"Devastating," she murmured.

"Dana must have heard the crash from the house, or maybe she heard the ambulance. I don't really remember." He sighed. "Do you know anyone who's lost a child? Marriages seldom survive it. Ours didn't. Dana said it wasn't my fault, but, of course, we both knew it was."

Jeanne shook her head slowly. "I can't imagine ever getting over such a tragedy, but somehow you've managed to come back from it, even marry again—twice."

"Once on the rebound, a short-lived mistake. I waited a long time after that. I don't know that I loved Karen, but we were great together. She didn't want kids—until she did. When we tried, though, I couldn't." His voice was barely a whisper. "I was impotent."

No wonder Vince was like a Sunday driver behind the wheel. Jeanne was horrified remembering how she'd teased him about not having a midlife-crisis sports car in his garage. The complexities he'd faced—no surprise he'd seemed ambivalent about her pregnancy. How unnerving the prospect of fatherhood must have been. She put her hand on his arm, and he covered it with his. They sat in silence. When Vince collected himself, he returned to the bassinet. "What's the baby's name?"

"Thomas, my father's name. I wanted my father to have a namesake, one I can get to know better than I got to know him, but, like me, my little Thomas won't have a relationship with his father."

"Thomas," Vince addressed the cradle. "I'd like the chance to be your father, if your mom will let me." His fingertips touched the tiny bundle.

"Vince, please bring him to me." He lifted the infant tenderly and rocked him. Thomas opened his eyes when Vince placed him in his mother's arms. Jeanne's voice was gentle, her words carefully chosen. "I imagine a great deal of soul searching preceded this visit. I love you for that. I wish I'd known about Toby earlier, but I understand how hard it would have been, and still is, to share that tragedy." Vince turned his head and wiped his eyes.

"Like you, I've learned a lot about myself over the last year. I treasure our relationship." Why had she never told him that before? "I can't marry you, though. I can't marry anyone right now. Having fended off risk my whole life, now is my time to embrace rather than fear the future."

"But we're not so different. I've spent years driving with the brakes on, and not just behind the wheel. I couldn't risk being responsible for another life. Maybe now, together—"

She shook her head. Vince's face fell. She couldn't help thinking, as he ran his forefinger over the tiny arm, he looked every bit the father forced to give up his baby. She reached out and stroked Vince's damp cheek. "I'm truly sorry."

"I understand . . . I guess . . . but it won't change how I feel."

As Jeanne brought the baby to her breast, Vince, downcast, rose to leave. He got as far as the doorway before he turned, his face brightening. "Thomas, sooner or later, you'll crave comfort food. We all do. Ask your mom to call me." He blew a kiss and was gone.

ACKNOWLEDGMENTS

I've been lucky in having family and friends in my corner as I worked on this manuscript. My husband, Bruce, in particular, has been unflagging in his support. I'm grateful to those who took the time to read *Land of Last Chances* and offer helpful observations and suggestions: Virginia Spencer, Maria Black, Victoria Williams, Terry Wise, Heidi Miller, and Susan Golub. I would not have completed this book without the moral support of Maria Black's writing circle (and sanctuary), which, in addition to Victoria and Terry, includes Lydia Littlefield and Julie McCarthy. Thanks are due, as well, to Betty Sudarsky, a great sounding board, who helped educate me about diabetes.

My interest in Alzheimer's disease began with the sad experience of watching my mother's decline. Through my participation on the advisory board of the Boston University School of Medicine's Alzheimer's Disease Center, I learned about the facts and myths associated with Alzheimer's, including its risk factors and the state of current research.

I'd like to think my knowledge will be out of date by the time this book reaches its readers, but in spite of all that research has produced, progress has been slow, and much is still unknown. Alzheimer's is the only top-ten cause of death in the US that can't be prevented, cured, or slowed (according to the Alzheimer's Association). Specifically, I'm grateful to Drs. Lindsay Farrer, Carmela Abraham, and Robert Stern, and to Eric Steinberg, for sharing their insights with me.

I want to thank the editors, designers, and staff at She Writes Press, in particular Brooke Warner and Cait Levin, for their invaluable advice and guidance. Last, I must give credit to my advisors in the MFA in Writing program at Vermont College of Fine Arts. They set me on the right path.

ABOUT THE AUTHOR

Originally from Mount Vernon, New York, Joan Cohen received her BA from Cornell University and her MBA from New York University. She pursued a career in sales and marketing at computer hardware and software companies until she retired to return to school for an MFA in Writing from Vermont College of Fine Arts. She has been a Massachusetts resident for many years, first, living in Newton, where she raised her family, and later, in Wayland. She now resides in Stockbridge, in the Berkshires, with her husband and golden retriever.

SELECTED TITLES FROM SHE WRITES PRESS

She Writes Press is an independent publishing company founded to serve women writers everywhere. Visit us at www.shewritespress.com.

A Drop In The Ocean: A Novel by Jenni Ogden. $16.95, 978-1-63152-026-6. When middle-aged Anna Fergusson's research lab is abruptly closed, she flees Boston to an island on Australia's Great Barrier Reef—where, amongst the seabirds, nesting turtles, and eccentric islanders, she finds a family and learns some bittersweet lessons about love.

Play for Me by Céline Keating. $16.95, 978-1-63152-972-6. Middle-aged Lily impulsively joins a touring folk-rock band, leaving her job and marriage behind in an attempt to find a second chance at life, passion, and art

The Geometry of Love by Jessica Levine. $16.95, 978-1-938314-62-9. Torn between her need for stability and her desire for independence, an aspiring poet grapples with questions of artistic inspiration, erotic love, and infidelity.

The End of Miracles by Monica Starkman. $16.95, 978-1-63152-054-9. When a pregnancy following years of infertility ends in late miscarriage, Margo Kerber sinks into a depression—one that leads her, when she encounters a briefly unattended baby, to commit an unthinkable crime.

Shelter Us by Laura Diamond. $16.95, 978-1-63152-970-2. Lawyer-turned-stay-at-home-mom Sarah Shaw is still struggling to find a steady happiness after the death of her infant daughter when she meets a young homeless mother and toddler she can't get out of her mind—and becomes determined to rescue them.

American Family by Catherine Marshall-Smith. $16.95, 978-1631521638. Partners Richard and Michael, recovering alcoholics, struggle to gain custody of their Richard's biological daughter from her grandparents after her mother's death only to discover they—and she—are fundamentalist Christians.